TRUST HE

TRUST HER

Flynn Berry

VIKING

VIKING
An imprint of Penguin Random House LLC
penguinrandomhouse.com

LIBRARY OF CONGRESS CATALOGING-IN-PUBLICATION DATA
Names: Berry, Flynn, 1986– author.
Title: Trust her / Flynn Berry.
Description: New York : Viking, 2024.
Identifiers: LCCN 2023034999 (print) | LCCN 2023035000 (ebook) |
ISBN 9780593490327 (hardcover) | ISBN 9780593490334 (ebook)
Subjects: LCSH: Sisters—Ireland—Fiction. | Irish Republican
Army—Fiction. | Dublin (Ireland)—Fiction. |
LCGFT: Thrillers (Fiction) | Novels.
Classification: LCC PS3602.E76367 T78 2024 (print) |
LCC PS3602.E76367 (ebook) | DDC 813/.6—dc23/eng/20230731
LC record available at https://lccn.loc.gov/2023034999
LC ebook record available at https://lccn.loc.gov/2023035000

Printed in the United States of America
1st Printing
Designed by Amanda Dewey

For Ronan and Declan

"We must go as quietly as we can," said Mr. Tumnus. "The whole wood is full of *her* spies. Even some of the trees are on her side."

—C. S. Lewis, *The Lion, the Witch and the Wardrobe*

This is a work of fiction,
set in an imagined near-future Ireland.

Part One

TROUBLE

One

THE WHEAT IS almost tall enough to hide inside. Past the road, golden fields ripple toward the horizon, catching the sun.

A heat wave began in Dublin earlier this week. I can see a band of haze in the distance, a storm front coming in from far over the west country. Along the Atlantic coast, the sea will be surging, rain pounding the backs of the waves, fog rising from the water to cloak the headlands, but here the air is hot and close. This morning every single person walking past me in my neighborhood looked sticky, their skin, their clothes.

I'm escaping the city's blistering streets for a swim. Normally I'd swim at the Forty Foot, but during a heat wave, most of Dublin will have the same idea. All of the swimming rocks—the Forty Foot, Howth Head, the Vico Baths—will be jammed, and instead I'm trying a place my sister told me about months ago.

Art's Lough is in the Wicklow countryside, near Ballinaskea. Marian told me the lough is balanced on a hilltop, the water running down through the gorse bushes and boulders at its edge, like an infinity pool. She said you can swim around the boulders, diving between them through the cold, clear water.

I could be spending the free weekend getting ahead on work. I'm a subeditor at the *Irish Observer*, but our work is slower in August, with parliament out of session. Fewer breaking news stories, fewer reporters filing late copy.

I check the pulsing dot on the map, then turn onto a road through more wheat fields. I can see Finn's empty car seat in the rear mirror. It's strange not to have him here with me, staring out the window, asking me questions. Today his father is bringing him to Donegal for a holiday. They must be somewhere near Kells by now. Finn always falls asleep on long drives, and I picture him with his eyes closed, sunshine flooding over his face.

He'll be home on Friday. Five days to go. With Finn away this week, I'll have some spare time for all the things I moan about being too busy to do. An exhibit at the Hugh Lane Gallery, dinner at the Winding Stair, a browse of the bookshelves in Hodges Figgis. The prospect should have me giddy, but instead I only feel restless. Wise up, I tell myself. It's only five days.

I roll the car to a stop at a crossing. With the windows down, I can hear the drilling sound of crickets. I forgot to tell Tom about the bottom strap of Finn's life vest, the one that hooks under his legs. Maybe I should text Tom, I think, and I'm reaching for my phone when something crashes into me. My hands fly back to grip the steering wheel as the car lurches forward, the metal screeching around me. The sound grows louder, then my head whips back against the seat.

The car has come to a stop, shoved halfway into the crossing. I climb out, shaking. Behind me, the driver of a black Range Rover is stepping onto the road and apologizing in a polished south Dublin accent, holding his hands up toward me. "Are you hurt?" he asks.

"What were you thinking?" I say, distantly aware that I haven't

4

actually checked if I am hurt. I tilt my neck, testing it, and feel a deep spasm of pain. My legs haven't stopped shaking. Finn could have been in the car during the collision.

"I'm so sorry," says the driver. "I only looked away from the road for a second."

I stand with my hands on my hips, looking at my car. The back of it is crumpled in like paper, and I hear myself groan. This will take ages to sort out. The driver says, "Here, let me give you my insurance card."

Behind him, heat shimmers above the tarmac, the mirage making the road look wet. He is reaching for his wallet when I catch a movement inside his car. A pale blur of a face, behind the windscreen. Someone else is with him, and fear drops over me. We are alone, I realize, on a road surrounded by wheat fields. Sweat prickles down my back. Around the crossing, the wheat shifts in the wind, dozens of paths across the field appearing and collapsing.

"I'll give you my insurance, too," I say, and turn back toward the car, forcing myself to walk normally. I can't let on that anything's wrong, he can't see. In the hot air, the sound of the crickets rises, ringing like an alarm. My heart thumps, sending out sheets of blood. The driver waits a few paces down the road. Ahead of me, my car door is hanging open, and I'm nearly there when I hear movement at my back.

I run the last few steps and throw myself into the seat, scrabbling for the keys. The man is already alongside the back windows. I shove the key into the ignition and stamp my foot down on the pedal. The engine starts spinning, but the car won't move. Something must be broken from the collision. I push my foot down again and again as a shadow falls over my lap. The man is outside my door, standing over me. I left the car in park, I realize, and shove at the gear stick. The man's hands reach through my open window and his fingers dig into my arms, trying to drag me onto the road. Almost there, the gears are about to release, and then he wrenches me out.

The tarmac scrapes my bare knees. He punches me in the mouth, and pain splits open my bottom lip. Blood sprays onto the road, onto my dress, onto him. I fight him off, panting. If I can break away from him and run into the field, the wheat will close behind me, hiding me from view. I'm already close enough that the stalks are whipping against my bare arms as we fight.

The field is right behind me. I can feel it happening, I can feel the wheat rushing past my face as I run, but then the tarmac is rearing up, and I'm flat on my stomach while he kneels on my back, closing a zip tie around my wrists.

The other man is here, too, now, saying, "Jesus, hurry up," and taking my other side as they drag me toward their car. I can't scream. I keep trying, but no sound comes out. They shove me into the back seat, behind tinted windows. I sit upright, with my wrists bound behind me and blood spilling down my chin, as the driver takes off down the road, veering around my dented car. My heart keeps pounding, fit to burst, like my body hasn't copped on that the fight is over. I force myself to breathe, and cough on the blood in my mouth. Tiny drops spray onto the seat in front of me, too small to see. Good, I think. That will be evidence, that will be one way to prove what happened.

I hear another car behind us. Maybe I can signal the driver, I think, but when I turn around, I only see my own car following us. Someone is driving it away from the scene.

The younger man reaches back from the front seat, twisting me aside and pressing my finger to my phone to unlock it. "What are you doing?" I ask.

Without answering, he drops back into the front seat. I hear him typing, then the swish of a message being sent, and another. He is texting my mother, I think, and my sister, so they won't think anything is wrong, so no one will look for me. He must have snatched the phone from my car.

I could have made it in time. I could have closed the door and hit the automatic locks first, then reached for my keys, I think, playing it through in my mind, like I'll be given another chance.

In the front of the car, the men don't speak, and I stare at the backs of their heads. I am aware of soft places in my ribs and down my legs, but nothing hurts, not yet. Finn, I think, and the need for him roars through me. I cast myself toward my son, some part of me galloping toward him. Finn isn't here. He is with his father, he is safe, he will be safe. That already feels like a triumph.

A mobile rings up front, and the driver answers. "Yeah, five minutes out," he says, and sweat rolls under my hair. His voice has changed from before, he's speaking with a Belfast accent now.

We're driving west, racing across the countryside toward the Wicklow Mountains. I try to work out how far we've driven from Ballyvolan, and where the next village might be. Ahead of us, haze hangs over the mountains. After this much heat, the heather and gorse will be dry as kindling. This entire range is a tinderbox.

"Can you open my photos, please? I want to see my son," I say, and the younger man drops my phone. I don't need a camera reel to see Finn. His face is clear in my mind, every bit of it, but I need these men to understand what they're doing. "I'm Tessa," I say. My dress is plastered to my skin with sweat and I'm shaking, but somehow my voice comes out calm and soft. "You were careful not to hurt me in the crash. Thank you."

Neither of the men answers, but I can tell they're listening.

"You could have killed me, though. My head almost went into the steering wheel," I say. "What would happen to you if I'd died? Would you get in trouble? Would you be given a kneecapping for that?"

The driver opens his mouth. He wants to defend his technique, which is a start. If I can get him to argue with me, then we'll be getting somewhere.

"What did they tell you about me?" I ask, feeling the tires spinning beneath the car. "Did you actually believe it?"

The younger man's jaw has tightened. He wants me to shut up, he doesn't think he should have to hear my voice. He was fine with earlier, with tracking my car, chasing me down the road, bracing for the crash. This part, though, isn't exciting.

"My son is four years old. Did they tell you that part? He could have been in the car with me. Would you have hurt him?"

"No," says the driver, rolling his hands on the wheel.

"I believe you," I say. "Will you help me?" Neither of the men looks at the other, but a silent argument is under way up there, between the pair of them.

The driver turns down another road. Thick hedgerows block the view, then we come around a bend. I can see a house ahead, a gray bungalow in some fields, and my breath catches. I'll only have a second to tug the door open, throw myself onto the road, and start screaming. My fingers are on the lock, ready to pull, but the driver is downshifting and turning onto the bungalow's drive. No one is going to hear me, the only house in sight belongs to them.

The two men climb down onto the gravel, and the younger one takes my arm and walks me toward the front door. I feel something like vertigo from all the open space around us, the broad fields stretching beside the bungalow. Even if I can twist out of his grip, there are no woods to swallow me up, no walls to crouch behind, no neighboring houses to shelter me. Behind the bungalow is a hill with electric pylons up its side, black wires strung between them. I can hear the pylons humming, a ringing in the empty air.

The bungalow has a rock garden and lace curtains in its windows. It looks like someone's granny's house. A statue of a fawn stands outside it. My mam would love the statue, it would look right at home in her front garden.

The men push me through the doorway, and the air goes out of my chest. The bungalow has been stripped to its floorboards. It's a safe house, a war room. The ordinary front is only a facade, to distract anyone driving past on the road. Someone from the IRA bought that fawn statue and stuck it in the garden, which I might find funny under other circumstances.

I can see a card table and plastic chairs, a portable generator, rolled-up sleeping bags, a box cutter. The younger man walks me into a back room and lifts a shackle attached to the radiator.

"Please help me," I say, looking in his face. "Please."

"Which leg?" he asks, avoiding my eyes, and when I don't answer, he closes it around my left one, snips the zip tie on my wrists, and leaves the room.

I stand alone in the middle of the room, the collar of my dress stained with sweat and blood. When I step forward, the chain pulls tight, the metal biting into my ankle. There is a mattress on the floor, and bare walls with thick sprays of black mold.

The window is boarded over, but there's a crack between the boards. I press my face against it and look out at the low hill behind the bungalow, and the electric pylons climbing over it. Those pylons will lead to a town, to other houses. I work my fingers into the gap between the boards, trying to tug them loose, but their nails are hammered deep into the wood. The pylons aren't far off the bungalow, and I wonder if I can use them somehow. Snap one of their wires, start a fire, so a repair crew is called in. I've no idea how, though, from in here.

The fear is total now, obliterating, a white room with nothing else in it, and something about that means I'm able to move and think inside it. It's like that absolute silence after a loud blast of noise, everything else blown clear of it.

I study the radiator, like my sister would, and the wiring in the ceiling fixture, for anything that might be useful. There are no lamps, but a yellowing plate with two electric outlets, and I might be able to weaponize them. I'm forever telling Finn to be careful around outlets.

I run my hands around the shackle, feeling for a catch in the metal. The band is loose at my ankle. Sized, I'd imagine, for a man. I rock back onto my heels. Already I can fit two fingers inside the band, and my ankle is swollen from the heat. If I can bring down the swelling, maybe I'll be able to slip my foot loose.

I start rubbing at my ankle, working my hands under the shackle. I remember this from pregnancy, pressing down hard with my thumbs to drain the fluid. When nothing happens, I grow frustrated, pummeling hard enough to leave bruises.

Finally I sit back against the wall under the spray of black mold. The men are talking on the other side of the door, but I can't make out the words. This would be easier if I knew what they wanted. Or if I had something sharp.

I need to warn Marian. She's working today, though. They won't risk going after her at the air-ambulance station.

I blame the heat wave. I made this so easy for them, driving out to the countryside. If they'd come for me in Dublin, I would have stood a chance. I would have taken a knife from the block on my counter. They're stronger, but they'd expect me to hesitate, and I wouldn't have hesitated.

But Finn might have been in the house, and I'd rather be locked in here than fighting them in my kitchen with Finn looking on. If he saw that now, he would remember it for the rest of his life.

I wipe the sweat from my forehead. This room is sweltering, with no vents and nothing shading the roof. They haven't given me any water. I move toward the window, feeling for a draft, but there's no wind outside, either. On the hill, the pylons are so bright that looking at them makes my eyes sting.

In another life, I would be swimming at Art's Lough now, diving under the cold water by the boulders, looking out across the valley. I put myself in this position. Driving out, alone, for a swim. I'd stopped being scared of the IRA in the daylight. Stupid, unbelievable logic. Over the past few years, Marian and I have both grown careless of ourselves in certain ways. Nearly all of our worries are attached to the children instead, the way you put sun cream on them and not yourself.

We should have seen this coming. Having a bad thing happen once doesn't make it less likely to happen again. If anything, it's the opposite, at least where we're from.

Three years ago, the IRA interrogated me and my sister at a farmhouse in south Armagh. Seamus Malone asked us if we were informers, if we were working for the British. I have trouble remembering exactly what happened next, except in scattered images. Marian rising up, a hairpin clenched in her fist, blood running down Seamus's throat, the two of us sprinting through the snow.

We faked our own deaths, and started new lives across the border, in the republic. I have long bangs now, darker hair. People often think they recognize me, but never from Belfast, only because I have one of those faces.

I sit very still, straining to hear sounds, listening for movement outside the bungalow. What evidence was left of my abduction today? Some trampled wheat on the side of a road, a few drops of blood drying on the tarmac and clinging to the wheat. It won't be enough. Though that man sent messages from my phone. If he made a mistake, if he didn't sound like me, mam and Marian will be suspicious.

Of the pair of them, Marian is more observant than mam. That message is sitting in her phone. I will my sister to read it again, to think, No, that's not right, to try ringing me, to call the police in Belfast and the Gardaí here in Dublin when I don't answer.

I picture a police convoy racing toward the bungalow across the countryside, and a briefing in an incident room at Harcourt Station. Some senior officer describing the situation to a group of gardaí. "Tessa Daly, thirty-six. Her sister Marian Daly was in the IRA but turned informer, and Tessa helped her pass messages. MI5 dropped them when their cover was blown, and the Belfast police helped them settle in the republic under new identities." If I were an officer hearing all that, I wouldn't be optimistic. What's the life expectancy of an informer from Belfast? It can't be long.

I close my eyes and try to breathe slowly. My clothes are clinging to my skin, and I pull at my dress, adjust my bra. The underwire digs into my ribs, and my eyes blink open.

I work my bra off under my dress. The bra is white cotton with a blue rosette and two wires under its cups, and I bite at the fabric, making a hole big enough to slide out the underwire. The wire feels sharp when I test it against my thumb. It could puncture skin, with enough force behind it. I put the bra back on, and slip the wire inside one of the cups, within easy reach.

This should be simple enough. I'm only in a room in a bungalow, of course there's a way out, I think, but then my mind runs into a wall, again and again. I'm so tired. Finn still isn't a good sleeper, and I'd been expecting things to get easier soon. Though this past year has not been, it occurs to me, so hard. Let me go back, I think, and I won't complain, I won't mind waking during the night, cooking a dinner my son refuses to taste, cleaning underneath the table afterward, picking up a hundred peas one by one. What, exactly, about all that had seemed difficult?

An elasticated sheet is pulled over the mattress in the room. Earlier this week, I was trying to make the bed in my room, while Finn kept tugging the corners loose. "That's enough now," I said, irritated, and remembering that makes me as homesick as anything else.

At some point, I shift my body toward the mattress, close enough to run my hand back and forth over the ridges of the elasticated sheet, feeling them bump against the pads of my fingers. The one at home, I tell myself, would feel exactly like this.

Two

HOURS PASS, and slowly the light drains from the gap in the window boards. It's late. I picture Finn asleep at the cottage in Donegal. Tom must have tried ringing me, but he won't be concerned that I didn't answer. His mind doesn't tend toward worry. Finn must have been confused, though. I always say good night to him when we're apart.

Finn had a mother when he went to bed tonight, he might not have one when he wakes up. The thought feels like a cardiac arrest, like stopping my heart in my chest. It can't come true.

Sometimes, during the night, a storm passes over our house. Rain thuds on the roof and the windows, above where my son sleeps, and then moves away, without waking him. This will be like one of those storms, Finn will never even know it happened.

I'm not leaving him. I need to pour his milk and find his blue bunny at night, I need to tuck the blanket over him, and I need to hear his feet running down the hall in the morning. I need to hold his hand at the school gates, and I need to be the one to collect him. On Finn's first day at playschool, when I picked him up, he said, "Mama came back," quietly, more to himself than to me, sounding surprised.

"Of course she did. Mams always come back," said his teacher, and I nodded, desperate for her to be right.

I AM SITTING against the mattress when floorboards creak behind the door. I stare ahead at the mold on the wall, my whole body liquid, terror melting through me. They're going to shoot me. One of the men is on the other side of that door, chambering a handgun, slotting a bullet into place. Strange that a bullet can hold that much death, enough to end an entire lifetime.

Suddenly I feel calm, but I know it's not a real calm, the way the last stage of hypothermia is feeling warm. Somehow, it's like Finn is here, sitting on my lap, curled against me, his bright golden head nestled under my chin. I close my eyes, clasping my arms around him, pressing my mouth to his hair.

"Mama," he says, and I press my eyes tighter, hearing the sweet, high sound of his voice. I can hear all his questions. Finn talks constantly, he asks me questions all the time. The hardest part about persuading him to brush his teeth is getting him to stop talking for thirty seconds. He always starts speaking halfway through anyway, lowering the toothbrush, too impatient to wait. "Mama, can you read me this book, can I have pasta for dinner, is tomorrow a school day? Mama, when will I be five?"

Across the room, the door is creaking open. I don't look up. That man's face won't be the last thing I see. "Next year," I tell Finn. "You'll be five next year." I lace my fingers over his head, covering his ears so he won't hear what happens next, stretching my fingers so hard the webbing between them burns.

Nothing happens. No gunshot, no blow. Someone is crouching down in front of me, close enough for me to hear him breathing.

"Tessa," he says, and my eyes fly open. The man is pale and wiry, with a long, bony face and hair cut close to his scalp.

"Who are you?" I say.

"You don't recognize me?" he asks. "That's all right, I'm not offended. They've been long old years, haven't they?"

"Eoin?" I say, the recognition dropping into place, and he nods. Eoin Royce grew up on our estate in Andersonstown. His face is thinner now, and harder.

"You'll be needing ice on that cut," he says, gesturing toward my mouth. "You shouldn't have resisted. If you hadn't resisted, you wouldn't have been hurt."

"Would you have resisted?" I ask.

Royce laughs. "Yeah, I would have done."

He unlocks the shackle and leads me to the table in the front room. A battery-powered lantern sits on the table, filling the room with artificial light. Behind him, through the gaps in the lace curtains, I can see the darkness outside. It must be the middle of the night, but the two other men don't look tired. They don't even yawn, and I wonder if they've taken something, an amphetamine. They are both leaning against the kitchenette at the back of the room, with their phones out. Neither of them will look at me.

Royce hands me an ice cube for my bloodied mouth. "How's your mam?" he asks. When we were children, mam used to mind him sometimes for his mother, her friend Sheila. I remember a shy, pale boy, sitting in our paddling pool, patiently lifting his head so mam could rub sun cream on his face. Mam used to give out to us for not being as polite as him.

"She's fine," I say carefully. I press the ice to my mouth, the cold numbing the split on my bottom lip. "I thought you were in prison."

"Early release," he says.

"How did you manage that?"

"The prison chaplain supported my petition," he says, leaning back in his chair and clasping his hands between his knees. His large, light eyes fix on me.

"And you went straight back to the IRA after prison?" I ask.

"Oh no, I never stopped," he says. He was directing terrorism from inside prison, he tells me. He is a brigade commander now, promoted while inside Portlaoise.

"How's your own mam?" I ask.

"Grand."

"Did she visit you in prison?" I ask, and his mouth twitches.

"Yeah, she did," he says, running the flat of his hand over his scalp. "Every visitor's day, she was there."

"That must have been nice. A bit of home comfort for you. It can't have been an easy trip for her."

"They've a bus, actually. Right from Andytown to Portlaoise," he says, and god that's depressing, that my old neighborhood in Belfast needs a direct route to the prison where IRA members get sent.

"My mam always liked you," I say. "She said she wished we'd half your manners."

Royce nods, fidgeting, jumping his foot on the floor. "She's a class act, your mam. And your sister and I went to the same sixth form, did she ever tell you that?" he asks, and I nod, even though Marian never mentioned him at the time. "Marian was the only student in our year who was sound to me."

I lift my head, surprised. "Were you bullied?"

"Mostly I was left alone, but no one besides Marian was decent to me, do you know the way? They just ignored me."

"I'm sorry you'd a hard time at school," I say. I can feel the ice cube melting, dripping down my upturned fingers, sheathing my wrist like a gauntlet.

"Ah, no, it's all in the past. It doesn't mean anything," he says, and I nod, neither of us believing him. Royce was bullied as a teenager. He should never have been allowed to join the IRA, he should never have been allowed anywhere near it. The IRA should have known what giving someone like him a gun would do.

When he was twenty-nine, Royce was arrested outside the holiday market in Belfast with a duffel bag full of automatic rifles. No one from the organization had approved the attack, he'd planned it off his own bat. I don't know how he won his way back inside their ranks after that. He must have offered them something good.

"How did you manage in prison?" I ask.

"Oh, fine. I kept busy, did an Open University course."

"On what?"

"Philosophy," he says. Stop trying to be nice, I can hear my sister telling me. Stop being polite. You won't change his mind by making him like you, it won't work. I can't remember what Marian said to Seamus during our interrogation three years ago, to needle him, to shift him off-balance. All I remember is the way she sat, holding her hand out in front of her, casually, like she was looking at her nails.

Boxes are stacked along the wall. Royce notices me looking at them and lifts one from the pile, carrying it back to the table. "Military ready meals. You can buy them online. They became a hobby for me in Portlaoise," he says, and I think, of course he's interested in military history. "You can find ones from the Boer War, the First World War. Edible, even now. Imagine, you're eating what those lads ate in 1916, in the Somme. Want one?"

"No, you're all right."

He cracks open the lid, and the smell of the gravy turns my stomach. "Which country do you think has the best ones? Guess."

I shake my head, and he spreads out his hands. "Seriously?" He twists around to look at the driver, leaning over his phone at the back of the room, who shrugs. "France," says Royce, and I nod. He hunches over the tin, forking up beef soaked in gravy. After finishing the tray, he unwraps a little foil bar. "Chocolate," he says. "Keep the lads' spirits up. You don't want them deserting. Or, worse, going over to the other side."

He pushes back his sleeves. I can see the veins on his arms, raised ridges the same color as his skin. Part of myself is watching him and part is casting around the house, toward the doors, the windows, measuring all the distances. Royce doesn't exactly look like he spent his sentence exercising in the prison yard. I'll be faster than him, I think, I'd put money on it.

"Did you ever consider joining us, Tessa?" he asks.

"No."

"But your sister did," he says. "Do you see much of her these days?"

"Yes."

"I wouldn't, if I were you," he says. "I'd cut her right out."

"Do you not believe in forgiveness, then?" I ask.

"No," he says. "No one does. Not really."

I sit facing Royce across the card table, with the lace curtains drawn over the front windows. Their pattern will have this room cut up into holes, too small for anyone passing outside to piece together.

"Do you like living in Dublin?" asks Royce. I watch the tendons in his neck shifting when he speaks, the twitch of his fingers. Royce's cheeks are gaunt. He's only in his thirties, but IRA members do tend to age early. Most of its leaders are on statins, since so many die of heart attacks.

"Yes."

"I'd hate it, for myself," he says. "For me, it would feel like being buried alive. No one knows you there. You don't matter, you're nothing to do with the place."

"Well, there are upsides to that. I couldn't breathe in Belfast anymore. I don't know how anyone can."

"It's not giving me any trouble. I'd never be anywhere else," he says. "You know, I laughed when I saw your street."

"Did you?" I ask, smiling, like we're sharing the joke.

"It couldn't be more ordinary."

"Is that a bad thing?" I ask, and he shrugs. Royce seems brittle, in his voice, his movements. A burner phone rings, and the younger man says, "Yeah, we're fine. No, we'd no bother on the way."

"When," I ask, "were you on my street?" Royce doesn't answer. The fear keeps changing pitch, rising and falling. I can't get a handle on it, I can't pull it under control. I am almost fainting from it, while Royce sits a few feet away, unconcerned. He's not scared. He has no doubt about his odds of walking out of this house, and really he should know better.

Under the dress, my bra is lopsided on my chest. I can feel the upright wire tucked inside its cup. If Royce lunges toward me, I'll push the wire into his throat.

"Can I have a glass of water?" I ask.

"Say that again. Say that word."

"Water?"

"Can you hear that? Does it not bother you? You don't sound like you're from Belfast anymore. You've lost your accent." Royce lights a cigarette, leaning back in his chair. "So how does it work, Tessa? You agree to betray your people, then what happens?"

"I was never an informer."

"Don't start, Tessa," he says. "Don't fucking start. I know what you are. If we can't even have an honest conversation, then you're finished."

"I'm not a tout. I never worked for the security service."

Royce flicks an object onto the table. A small, shiny black orb, like the button eyes on Finn's soft toys. I reach forward to pick it up, turning it in my fingers. "I've never seen this before," I say, even as my pulse speeds faster. It's a camera, a tiny surveillance camera.

"We found it in the private bar at the Balfour Hotel," says Royce. "Have you ever been to the Balfour?"

"Of course, everyone from Andersonstown has been there."

"When was the last time?" he asks.

"I don't remember."

"It was your cousin Aoife's wedding," he says. "One of the lads saw you and your sister alone in the private bar. You planted this."

I remember Marian pressing the camera behind the eye of a deer head on the wall, while I watched the door, jumping back behind the bar and splashing tequila into glasses right as a man stepped inside. We thought we'd gotten away with it, a near miss, a lucky break. So that was how they discovered us.

"I've never seen that before in my life."

Royce raises his hand, and the younger of the two men steps forward with a roll of plastic sheeting. They're going to spread the plastic under my chair and then shoot me.

Behind me, I can hear the plastic crackling as the man rolls it across the floor. Royce sits watching me, and the younger man steps back, the plastic sliding under his shoes. I'm trapped between the two of them.

I reach across the table for his pack of cigarettes, and Royce signals to the younger man to return to the back of the room. I put a cigarette to my mouth, and Royce leans toward me to spark his lighter. I sit back, inhaling, and blow out a long stream of smoke. "What do you want?" I ask.

"What do you think I want? I spent eight years in prison because of you," he says.

"I didn't give you up. I knew nothing about you back then."

"You know what I mean. I went to prison because of touts like you," he says. "How did it start?"

I hesitate, but Royce already knows about Marian. I can tell him the truth. "Marian started informing in the spring, and she asked for my help. Your internal security unit was watching her, so she couldn't meet with her handler herself. She asked me to pass messages to him."

"How did you arrange meetings with your handler?"

"He gave me a gift card. He was watching the balance, if I made a purchase that was our signal to meet the next morning." At the edges of my vision, I can see a distortion, like rippling water, from the battery lamp reflecting off the plastic sheet.

"Where did you meet?"

"On the beach in Ardglass."

"Did he ever bring anyone else with him? Did he have security?"

"No, he was always alone."

"What about his house? Did you ever meet there?" asks Royce, and I shake my head. "Did he pay you?"

"You think I would have risked this for money?" I say. "They didn't have to pay me. I agreed to inform because the IRA's off its fucking trolley."

"Mind yourself," says Royce.

"You were meant to be protecting us," I say. "But what makes you any better than the loyalists? Can you tell me the difference?"

"Between the IRA and the UVF? Are you joking me? They're gangsters," he says. "And we're trying to unite a nation."

"Right, and this is going to free Ireland, is it?" I ask, pointing at my bloodied mouth. "This will get the Brits out?"

"At least I'm trying," he says. "What've you done for your people?"

"My people? Who do you mean?" I ask, which Royce doesn't answer. We're both from Catholic families, from west Belfast. He thinks the answer is obvious. I say, "Your ancestors weren't all born here. You know that, right? The oldest human remains found in Ireland are from two thousand BC, but that was before a five-hundred-year winter, which none of his descendants could have survived. You're not his, so whose are you? When did your family come here?"

"Are you defending colonialism?" he says.

"No, I'm asking you for a little nuance in your analysis."

"Who asked for your opinion? You're nothing, Tessa. The security service doesn't care about you. When we kill informers, they don't even look for your bodies," he says.

It's time. Marian showed me how to do this, once. She showed me how to survive. I just need to remember. I hold my hand out in front of me, turning it over, like I'm studying my fingernails. Without looking at him, I say, "Your mam never visited you in prison. Not once."

I glance up in time to see his eyes flare. "Want to hear what Sheila told our mam, after you were arrested? She said she didn't have a son anymore."

Sheila said she'd never forgive him. Children were riding on the carousel at the holiday market he'd tried to attack.

"Stupid bitch," he says. "You think I care about your mam running her mouth?"

"Did you write to her from prison? Did you try to change her mind? I mean, she is your mam. How could she never want to see your face again, for the rest of her life?"

He's raging. Almost there, almost time to run. The front door is maybe ten feet away from this table. If Royce signals to the younger man again, I'll bolt. Already I've unsettled him, frayed his concentration.

"What about yourself, Tessa? Are you close with your son?" asks Royce, and I tilt my head, confused by the question. Finn's four years old. Close doesn't even begin to describe it.

Royce says, "Is four old enough?"

"For what?"

"To remember you," he says, and I try not to flinch. "The card you used, to signal your handler. Do you still have it?"

"No, I threw it away when we moved here."

Royce stubs out his cigarette slowly, taking his time. Then he leans back in his chair, digging his hand into his pocket, and draws out my wallet. Cold sweeps through me. He uses the edge of his nail to flick through the cards, then draws out a gold gift card and tosses it onto the table in front of me.

I should have known. He's going to make me use the card to signal my handler. Tomorrow morning, I'll be on the beach in Ardglass, and when Eamonn appears, they'll swarm over the dunes and ambush him. They're going to use me as bait.

Royce watches me, and I say, "It's been three years. He could be anywhere in the world by now. Even if he somehow sees the signal, he won't come."

"You better pray he does," says Royce.

"No, I'm not doing it," I say, and shove the card back across the table toward him. "I'm not helping you murder him."

Royce stares at me for a moment, then laughs. "You're telling the truth, aren't you? You'd die for some MI5 pig."

"No, I'd die before being anything like you. I'd die before making my son wish I was never his mam."

"Well, look, luckily for you, I don't want you to murder him," says Royce. "I want you to turn him."

"Sorry?"

"Here's what you're going to do," says Royce. "You're going to meet with your handler and offer to inform again. And you're going to convince him to work for us."

"Do you actually think an MI5 agent will work for the IRA?" I ask.

"If you apply the right pressure."

"And what's that?"

"You know your man better than I do, I'm sure you'll figure it out," he says. "The security service has five hundred handlers working in Northern Ireland, and we can't identify a single one of them. They might as well be ghosts. We need someone from their side."

"Why are you asking me?"

"No one in MI5 will suspect you. You were never in the IRA," he says. "You're just someone's mammy."

I let out a sort of laugh, and he says, "Speaking of, give Marian my congratulations."

"Stay away from her."

"Marian's trash," he says. "She's nothing. I'm not about to throw away my chance at a handler to go after her. But your cousin Aoife just had a baby, too, isn't that right?" he says. "She lives on Clondara Street in Belfast. Number Thirty-Nine. And you've other cousins in Toomebridge and Magherafelt. If you run, if you call the police, if you tell anyone, we will kill them."

"How would he work for you?"

"Tell us about MI5's targets, tell us about their communications, tell us their long-term plan for the North," he says.

I stare at Royce, the cigarette burning down between my fingers. "Okay."

"Okay?"

"Yes, fine," I say, trying to sound calm. "I'll do it." It's impossible. What Royce is asking me to do is impossible, but I'm not exactly going to say that, not when it's my only chance of leaving this house.

"What has you so confident?" Royce asks, like he sees straight through me. He can still change his mind and order me to be shot. This is an audition. He knows that what he's asking me to do barely stands a chance. If I fail the audition, they'll move on to the next tout. They might have already gone through other informers before they reached me, and disposed of them. More trash.

"My handler trusted me. We had a good relationship."

"Were you riding him?"

"Is that your only definition of a relationship? I thought you did a philosophy course in prison," I say, careful not to actually deny that I ever slept with my handler, leaving the idea in Royce's head. If Eamonn slept with me, then he's already compromised, already closer to persuasion, or blackmail.

"Tell me about the relationship."

"He liked me."

Royce smirks. "He was a handler. It was his job to make you think he liked you."

"I know that, I'm not an idiot. I'm saying he didn't have to work at it," I say, which is true. There was an affinity between Eamonn and me, it sprang up without either of us trying, to my surprise, and I think to his, too. "I knew that he liked me, the way I know that you don't like me. And that you wouldn't like me, no matter how we met."

Royce's mouth twists. "Right, okay," he says. "Why don't I like you, Tessa?"

He is auditioning me, after all. Testing me, seeing how well I can read people, how well I might manage with my handler.

"You think I'm spoiled. You think I grew up believing I was too good for Andersonstown. You think I'm ungrateful. You think I look down on you for not going to university," I say, and Royce listens, tapping his fingers, slightly bored. This isn't good enough. "I remind you of being a child, and you hated being a child," I say, and his fingers stop tapping. "You couldn't wait to be done with it, done with school, done with the other kids, done with the whole joke of it. You couldn't wait to be taken seriously. You hate that I remember you as a skinny little kid in our paddling pool. You hate that I remember the way you used to dress, which was fine, by the way, just old-fashioned. I make you self-conscious about your teeth and your ears—"

"Enough. Fucking enough," says Royce, holding up a hand, and I can tell he's thinking about the two men behind us, who have gone stock-still, listening. Royce's ears are bright red. For a moment, none of us move.

"Did I pass?"

Three

IT HAS STARTED TO RAIN. A fine drizzle, fizzing in the air, brushing against my hair and bare arms. A deep, rich smell rises from the fields surrounding the bungalow. The driver throws the Range Rover into reverse, and from behind the tinted window I look at the bungalow, stark in the headlights against the dark fields, its lace curtains illuminated behind the glass.

We skid backward down the drive, then the rear tires bump onto the laneway, and the driver whips the car around, accelerating, the bungalow disappearing behind us. This ride will be an exercise in not losing my head, I already understand that. For miles, all I can see outside the car are black hedgerows, shadowy leaves, the dark glint of a stream, and then suddenly we reach the motorway, a bright river flowing north toward Dublin. I look at the row of halogen streetlamps angled above the motorway from the concrete median.

"How much did MI5 offer to pay you?" asks the driver.

"Why? Are you thinking of touting?"

"Come on now. How much did they offer?"

"Not fucking enough," I say, and he laughs. My control is cracking apart, though. I can't keep playing this game for much longer.

On the motorway, I can see a handful of other cars, their headlights wobbling in the rain. It is three in the morning. Being up at this hour is familiar from nursing Finn. The 3:00 a.m. night feed was always the hardest to wake myself up for, the last one he dropped.

I barely recognize Dublin as we drive through the outer suburbs. Is this where I live, is this my home? The driver pulls up outside a church at the south end of Ranelagh, and the headlights find the churchyard gate, bleaching the rails white against the darkness. We climb out, and the sound of our heavy doors closing thuds through the quiet. He walks me between the gates, up a gravel path toward the church. Gravestones ring the church, mossed and tilting in the long grass. In the dark, I can see the shape of the church and the black yew trees standing to its side. Above us, the stained glass in the church looks like oil, glossy and dark. The driver hands me my tote bag. "Your car's parked on Northbrook Road," he says. "The dent's not too bad, but you'll be wanting to bring it to a mechanic. You don't want rust getting in."

That was an apology, I think, or as near to one as he will ever give me. "Right, okay."

"Stand there," he says, pointing to a yew tree, and I put my back against its trunk. "Wait until I've left, all right? Count to a hundred."

He walks back down the path, with an easy, confident stride, like this night took nothing from him. The Range Rover is hidden from view, but I can hear the engine start, and see the red stain on the road from its taillights. I listen as he drives away. Above me, the yew branches creak in the wind.

I start counting. I make it to ten, then dig into my bag for my phone and dial 999. "Emergency services," says the operator. "Which service do you require?"

Police, I think. Leaving the bungalow, I memorized the registration plates on the Range Rover before climbing inside. All I need to do is recite the number, and the police will track down the driver. An armored van will block the road ahead of him and another will swerve behind him. I remember the driver reaching his arms through the open window of my car, grabbing onto me, and I can nearly taste it, the moment when he feels that terror for himself.

And I can describe the bungalow to the police. A property somewhere between the N11 and the Wicklow Mountains, along a row of electrical pylons. With satellite maps, the detectives will be able to find it in minutes. They can send in a special unit to surround the property. Royce will see the armed officers and know that he is trapped and that I'm the one who did it. What wouldn't be worth that, what wouldn't I give for that moment?

"Emergency services," says the operator again. "Can you hear me? What's your name?"

I open my mouth to answer. It will be so easy, I can see it all spread out in front of me, tingling at my fingertips, unscrolling like a lit-up map. A few words in the next couple of seconds, and Eoin Royce will be back in prison.

"Stay on the line," says the operator. "Don't end the call, all right? It's fine if you can't speak, we're tracing your location now, we'll be sending a vehicle out to you." Her voice is brisk and direct, reassuring. This isn't my problem anymore. Other people were trained to deal with it, they'll be taking over now. I feel the weight taken off me, an actual physical release, lifting my shoulders. Except then, someday soon, my cousin Aoife will open her door in west Belfast, and a gunman will shoot her in the face.

"Sorry," I say, hearing my voice from a distance. "Sorry, I must have rung you by accident." I hold my breath with the phone clamped against my ear, part of me hoping the operator won't believe me. One more question and I'll buckle. But then she is telling me to have a good night and ending the call, and I hear a groan leave my throat, a strangled sound fading away into the rain and darkness.

I can't move. It's as if the driver tied me to this tree, and I have to wait until someone comes to cut the rope. It seems important to stay in this position, like I need to preserve the evidence, but the police aren't coming, this isn't a crime scene. No one will ever know I was here.

Tomorrow morning, the priest will give mass inside the church, and nothing will seem any different. The parishioners won't look twice at this tree. I've the urge to throw a brick through the church window, less out of anger than respect, like a signal. They'd want to know, too, wouldn't they, that the IRA is using their church as a dumping ground.

Instead of bricking a window, I tear a strip of loose fabric from my dress and drop it on the ground under the tree. Someone will see it, someone will wonder where it came from, and that will have to be enough, for now.

The roads in Ranelagh are deserted, the orange streetlamps glowing on the parked cars and quiet houses. My feet feel swollen inside my shoes, and damp. Something has happened to my balance as I drag myself up the road toward my house. Anyone looking out their window will think I'm leathered. The last time I was out this late, I probably was. Years and years ago. My vision would have been shuddering then, too, though from vodka and not fatigue, or shock, or whatever you'd call this.

I weave up Sallymount Avenue, not looking before crossing the roads, since there's no sound of a motor anywhere nearby. In the darkness, the bloodstains down the front of my dress look like tar.

Something is yawning open inside me, deep and dark as an ultrasound screen. I'm alive, they've let me go. I limp past houses where my neighbors are sleeping, and grip my doorknob for balance while turning my key in the lock.

No one sees me come in, no one knows where I've been. Inside, I don't turn on any lights, like I'm the one committing a crime, breaking into my own house. In the darkness, I strip off my dress, dropping it in the hamper, and wrap a towel around myself. Finn is in Donegal with his father, but I go into his room anyway. I kneel beside his bed, the way I do every single night after he has fallen asleep. I hold one of his muslin blankets to my chest, breathing in its smell, then I curl up on the rug under his bed. A few minutes, I think, then I'll take a shower, make coffee, figure out a plan.

Four

I WAKE ON THE CARPET next to Finn's bed. When I sit up, the towel slips, and I can see black bruises down my rib cage. The bruises feel soft to the touch, with blood swelling under the skin. Slowly I turn my head around the empty room.

It's already dawn. I need to leave, now. I need to drive to Donegal and find Finn, and pay a fishing boat to bring us to Scotland or France. Royce might have someone watching the airport and the ferry terminal, but there are thousands of fishing boats moored along the west coast. One of them will take us away.

I stand up too fast, and my head spins. How quickly can I pack a bag with our passports, spare clothes, some cash. I'm crouching on the floor of my closet, reaching for a holdall, when my hands stop. Even if I warn Aoife, they will find someone else to punish. That wasn't an empty threat. A few years ago, an informer from Ballymurphy managed to escape abroad. The IRA murdered his older brother, a teacher in Claudy who had no part in the conflict. He was coaching a football practice when the men came to shoot him. The last thing he did was shout at the children to run.

The holdall drops from my hands. I rock back from the closet, with frustration choking my throat. We're trapped. After searching through my bag for my phone, I open my messages. That man, yesterday, sent mam and Marian the same message from my phone. "Heading home, talk to you tomorrow x." They must think I sent it. Mam has replied, asking how seeing off Finn went, and I feel unfairly betrayed that neither of them realized the messages weren't really from me.

My black swimsuit is still stuffed inside my bag, rolled up in a towel. Both of them are clean and dry, but I put them in the wash anyway, like I did actually spend yesterday swimming at Art's Lough.

In the bathroom, I take pictures of the bruises and the split on my mouth with the Polaroid camera Marian gave me for my last birthday. Without watching them develop, I put the photographs in a box and hide them in the back of my closet. If the police ever find the bungalow, my fingerprints and DNA will be across it, and they might think I went there to meet Royce on my own. These photographs are my insurance. Proof, if I ever need it.

I run a shower, holding my stiff body under the warm water. Afterward, I sit on the edge of the bath in my bra and knickers, rubbing arnica ointment onto the bruises. I want them gone, I don't want Finn to ever see them. I wrap a compression bandage around my torso, to hold my cracked ribs in place. It hurts to breathe, but I know how lucky I am. Those men could have killed me last night. I kick away from the thought, like I'm trying to surface from the mangle of a wave.

In my bedroom, I put on a white cotton top and a navy wrap skirt long enough to hide the scratches on my legs. I swallow two Nurofen and walk down to the kitchen to make coffee in the filter. While the water boils, I look around at the sky-blue cover of a *Dublin Review* on the table, the stacks of mismatched china cups, the thick cookbooks stained with grease. All of it mine, all exactly as I'd left it yesterday morning. I don't know why I feel guilty, why it feels like I committed a crime yesterday. Not reporting something that happened to you is not a crime.

On the fridge is a snap of Marian, holding Finn on her lap at a restaurant. I look at my sister's laughing mouth, her clever eyes. This is her fault, I think. She brought these men into our lives.

"If I were you, I'd cut her right out," said Royce. The thing is, I thought I'd forgiven her. Last spring, the two of us were watching a film at my house, and Marian said, "Sometimes I wish you'd do something really bad."

"Like what?"

"I don't know. Kill someone in a hit-and-run by accident, not a nice person, obviously, and ask me to help you hide the body."

"What, to balance things out?"

"Yes."

Without looking away from the screen, I said, "Just pretend I did. To be honest, it's probably only a matter of time anyway, given the traffic in Dublin."

Marian gave a hollow laugh and turned back to the screen. After a few minutes, I said, "It could have been me and not you. If you'd left Belfast and I'd stayed, I might have been the one who joined."

Anyone who'd met us as teenagers would have expected me to join the IRA before Marian. I was the stubborn one, refusing to go to mass, getting into shouting rows with our uncles over politics. I was almost expelled during the 2002 abortion referendum for showing up to our Catholic school with a repeal shirt on over my uniform. Marian had never seemed interested in politics. She'd always liked painting, she could have gone away to art college in Glasgow or London.

"Do you really believe that?" asked Marian. "That it could have been you?"

"Yes."

But Marian stayed in Belfast, while I was the one who left for Trinity. Often I stayed working at the library in the Arts Block until late at night. When Marian called me, I'd text back, "In the library, want me to go outside?" She always wrote back, "No, you're grand," and then when I called her on my walk home, she often didn't pick up.

While I was in my fourth year at Trinity, Marian met Seamus Malone. He was a familiar figure around Andersonstown, a tall, thin man in a corduroy jacket, with red hair. I'd seen him before, browsing in the record store, drinking in the crowd at the Rock bar, standing at the edge of the hurling field.

He started calling round to Marian's flat, asking her out for coffee, helping her paint her walls. He gave Marian books to read and invited her to join a political discussion group. We were reading some of the exact same books that year, ones about colonialism, power, class, except I was reading them in a library carrel, and Marian was reading them with terrorists.

She still fights me on that word. Marian won't call the IRA terrorists, which makes me lose the absolute run of myself. I agree with her that the Irish Republican Army weren't always terrorists, but we're not in 1916 anymore. We're not even in 1971. Since Brexit, the IRA has only become more brutal. Something inside the organization has warped and hardened.

That doesn't make me a colonialist, whatever Royce thinks. I'm outraged that the British still control the six counties of Northern Ireland. That I was born in the world's oldest British colony, with all the problems of a colony. The partition of Ireland is as unnatural as the Berlin Wall, but this version of the IRA won't be bringing it down.

We had years of peace after the Good Friday Agreement, but it never felt stable. By the time the conflict reignited in 2019, I'd graduated and moved back to Belfast. I remember standing in my flat one night when the kitchen suddenly filled with smoke. I grabbed the pan off the cooker, thinking I'd burned something, before realizing the smoke was coming from outside. I stood at the open window watching ash drift across the city, stinging my nose and eyes.

A riot had begun. Some lads had hijacked a bus and set it on fire, and the cloud of smoke was spreading over Belfast. I checked the news on my phone and thought I'd be fine, the riot was miles away, those lads would need to burn down half of Belfast to reach my building. I turned away from the window and finished cooking my dinner.

I kept a journal during those first weeks of the conflict. I thought what was happening around me was interesting, historic. I wrote down what people bought out of the supermarkets, and what the helicopter searchlights looked like over the city, like a Blitz diary. I described watching a Molotov cocktail burst on the road, the flames leaping from the petrol as soon as the glass broke, like a magic trick.

When a curfew was announced, it was exciting at first, like a holiday. Everyone was let off work early to get home in time, and the roads were empty, with police helicopters hovering overhead. In fairness, I wasn't the only person who felt restless, energized by the disruption. Most of us did.

I stopped keeping the journal after three weeks. I didn't write down the first death in the conflict, or the second, or the third, or any of the ones afterward, and the thought of that journal now makes me sick with myself. I shouldn't have been looking out at the helicopter searchlights anyway, I should have been looking at my sister. I remember watching the news with her and mam, when the unrest still seemed likely to blow over. I said, "The Troubles are over."

"Ours aren't," said mam.

Five

THE WALK TO my sister's house will take twenty minutes. Marian lives in the Liberties, in a row of old maltworkers' cottages behind Bride Street. Heading up Clanbrassil Street, I try to walk normally, but the bruises make my legs feel constricted, like the front and back of my thighs are being pinched together.

Storm clouds are banked over Dublin, pale at the top and darker on the bottom, like bands of dripping watercolor, as I turn onto her road. Guidebooks tell tourists to avoid this area after dark, which helps Marian more than them. No one wants a group of trolleyed tourists shouting outside their house late at night. The worst crime Marian has ever seen in the neighborhood, she says, is when one father accidentally took another's empty pram outside the Fumbally, then returned it a few minutes later.

I've a key to Marian's house, but this morning I press the bell. I wait, listening to the traffic on Bride Street, looking at the arch of red bricks above her doorway. Down the terrace, one of her neighbors comes outside with a terrier, stepping over the lead to stop it tangling around his ankles.

Marian opens her front door in a saffron-yellow corduroy dress, with Saoirse at her shoulder. She says, "Have you taken the day off work? Want to come to a baby music group?"

I shake my head. "Of course you don't," says Marian, "but what if I take you to brunch afterward?"

"Marian," I say, but she is already turning away.

"I left the kettle on," she says, and I follow her down the hall, stepping over loose shoes and heaps of laundry. I thought Marian would know something was wrong from my face, but instead she's switching off the hob, chatting about hiring a pub in Bray for mam's birthday. I won't tell Marian, not yet. I'll give her a few more minutes before destroying her peace.

"How's the bairn?" I ask, and she swivels to show me Saoirse, asleep, her mouth gaping open. Saoirse has on a striped cotton suit and a pair of white socks rolled down twice to fit over her feet. She looks so small, which I know better than to tell Marian. I reach out to touch her socked foot, my chest aching.

I look at the piles of post, the dirty dishes and sticky pools of jam on the kitchen surfaces. "This place is a tip."

"Isn't it disgusting?" says Marian cheerfully. "Seb left on Saturday night."

Her husband works as a cameraman on film sets. He will be away for the next three weeks filming on Inishmore, in the Aran Islands. "How's the shoot?"

"Grand. Apparently they're doing quite a lot of karaoke over there."

"Ah, no, Seb." I reach into the open bag of Hula Hoops on the counter, suddenly ravenous. "And this is what you've been eating?" I ask, crunching them between my teeth.

"Mostly," says Marian. "And ready meals."

Seb does the cooking in their house. During holidays, Seb and I are insufferable about the food, inordinately ambitious, working on lobster thermidor, homemade linguine, parmesan soufflés, while mam and Marian drink white wine and mind the children and shout at us to hurry up. Seb is like Marian, calm about most things and then absolutely nuts about others. He hates going to IKEA, not for the normal reasons, but because he loves it so much that he can't bear for the trip to end.

They met through a work friend of hers two years ago. At first, Marian wouldn't tell me anything about Seb except that I'd meet him soon. I could picture him—everyone she has ever fancied looks the same—but when we met, Seb was nothing like the others, warm where they were cold, silly where they were aloof, cheerful where they were moody. His large, lovely north Dublin family has welcomed Marian as one of their own. You'd think she has known them all her life.

Marian takes two chipped mugs down from the shelf. "Are you still coming over for dinner tonight?" she asks, and before I can answer, she says, "Mam's not coming anymore, she has a date."

"With Joe?"

"No, the other one, the one from her ballroom group."

"Martin?"

"No, she's seeing him on Tuesday."

"Gerry?"

"That's the one."

"Jesus, what is she like?" I say, and Marian shakes her head. I have to tell her, but I need a few more minutes of talking with her like this first, of knowing what we're about to lose.

"What about yourself? How was your date on Thursday?" she asks, and I shrug.

"It was fine," I say. Once a month, I download a dating app and arrange to meet someone for a drink after work. Afterward, I delete the app on the bus ride home, relieved to not have to look at it for another month. A one-hour drink, and home in time to do Finn's bedtime. I've not yet met anyone worth missing a bedtime. "He's an actor. He's in a show at the Abbey, and now he thinks he's going to be the next James Bond, do you know the way?"

"God loves a trier," she says. "Did you shift him?"

"Jesus, are we fifteen?"

We did kiss, actually. I do sometimes kiss on these dates and, less often, have sex, mostly because I don't want to have forgotten how when it counts, whenever that might be.

"You should give it one more go," says Marian, and I nod absently. She says, "Will you really?"

"No."

"Of course not," she says. "Stubborn cow."

I can feel an ache against my skull, the start of a pressure headache. Marian spoons honey into her mug. She pours the tea, and we carry our mugs into her front room. Before sitting down, I shift the usual mess of baby clothes and board books and mallow lotion from the end of the sofa.

"Marian," I say, but she is distracted, fixing her pillow, settling the baby against her. "Marian," I say again, and she turns toward me. Aside from Finn, Marian has my favorite face in the world, the one I know best. I find her face calming, the way a forest is calming.

"Two men stopped me while I was driving in Wicklow yesterday," I say. Marian nods, like I've asked her a question, and she is still nodding as her face collapses.

"Did they hurt you?" she asks.

"No."

"What happened to your mouth, Tessa?"

"It's nothing. They didn't hurt me," I say, out of pride, or stubbornness. Royce will be expecting me to fall apart today, and even though he can't see us, I don't want to give him the satisfaction.

"They brought me to a house," I say, and my voice is level, but Marian closes her eyes anyway. I don't have to describe the zip tie, the shackle around my ankle, she already knows, the knowledge is ripping through her. "Eoin Royce was there."

"Is he not in prison?"

"Early release," I say, and Marian says, "Whose brilliant idea was that?"

"They want me to start meeting with Eamonn again. They want me to convince him to give them information about MI5."

Marian's forehead creases. "How? Do they already have something on Eamonn to blackmail him?"

"No."

"Then how do they expect you to bring Eamonn under control?" she asks, and I shake my head. "I'll do it," she says. "Not you."

"He won't take you for it, Marian. He thinks Eamonn will be more likely to trust me than you."

"Too bad," she says. "Royce can take me instead, or we'll run."

"If we run, they'll kill Aoife. He knows her address," I say. "And if she runs, too, they'll find someone else from our family to punish."

Marian lifts her head, staring at the ceiling, and I watch her struggling to breathe. "Are you going to tell Seb?" I ask, and the question seems to make Marian exhausted. "Of course I'm going to tell Seb," she says.

"We're going to need help, Marian. We should tell the police," I say. "The IRA won't find out."

"They always find out," she says, and something echoes, something chimes down the years. "How do you think they found us? They might already have someone inside the police."

For a while we sit in silence. Marian's right. The IRA might be blackmailing an officer, here or in Belfast. I should have thought of that earlier, but all these rules feel unfamiliar, and my mind isn't working properly.

Finn had croup earlier this week. I woke in the middle of the night, hearing him cough, and crouched with him on the floor of the shower, hugging him while he inhaled the steam. Those are our problems now, mine and Marian's. Croup, strep throat, drop-offs and pickups. Not this, nothing like this. I understand our mistake now. It was a child's logic. The IRA haven't gone away, after all. We'd only stopped thinking about them.

"Mam might have let something slip," I say. "Or Tom."

Aside from the police, the only people who know the whole story are mam and her siblings, Tom, and Seb. Seb is quite possibly the least discreet person I've ever met. He's the middle brother in a family of five, and an absolute gossip. He's terrible at keeping secrets, but he would lay down his life for Marian. There's not a chance he told anyone about her past.

"Has anyone from the North tried to contact you?" I ask.

"No," says Marian, then her voice falters.

"What? What is it?"

"I've been sending money to Niall in prison."

"Sorry?" I search Marian's face, confused. Niall O'Faolain was in Marian's active-service unit, and he's still a member of the IRA.

"Just small amounts, so he can order books and things," she says quietly. "He has no one else." Niall joined the IRA when he was seventeen. He'd grown up in care, he'd no family.

"Come here to me, Marian. What were you thinking?"

"I grew up with him."

"No, Marian, you grew up with me, you spent your childhood with me," I say, pressing my hands against my eyes.

"Niall doesn't know the money is from me."

"Of course he knows it's from you, Marian. Who else would it be from? He must have told Royce."

"No, he'd never do that."

"You don't know him anymore," I say. "You've no idea what the past three years have done to him. Niall must have told someone that you were alive, after he got the cash in prison, and then they could have sent someone to follow Tom. He's down twice a month to visit Finn."

Saoirse wakes, fussing, and Marian settles her to nurse. I look at the baby docked against her, nursing steadily. "If Finn had been with me yesterday, what would they have done?" I ask, and my voice sounds hoarse. I can barely finish the question. "Would they have left him strapped in his car seat on the side of the road?"

"No. No, they wouldn't have done that."

"Should I send Finn to stay with Tom until this is over?"

"It might take months, Tessa."

"At least he'd be safe."

"He'd be confused," she says. "And anyway he's safe with you. They won't harm a child."

She's right. The IRA needs lookouts, cars to borrow, safe houses to hide inside. If they were to deliberately target children, that support would vanish, their community would turn on them.

"Where was the house?" asks Marian, and I hesitate. "What? Do you think I'm going to drive out there?"

"Yeah, I do, actually." I picture her stalking up to the bungalow with petrol and a lighter, burning the place down. "Will you?"

"No," says Marian, while rubbing her daughter's back. "If I were to go, though, maybe I could have a conversation with Royce. Maybe I could talk him out of this. What if I don't go alone? What if I bring Sheila?"

"He'd kill you, Marian. Humiliating him in front of his mother," I say. "I only mentioned her to him and he was raging."

"If she forgave him—"

"He's not thick. He'd see through that, too."

Marian thinks, brushing her hand over the sofa arm, making the velvet bristle. "I still want to see the house."

"It's a bungalow in some fields, in west Wicklow."

"Any landmarks?"

"Electrical pylons, and a hill behind the property. And a fawn statue in the front garden."

"If no one's there, I can bug it."

"What's the point? We already know what they want."

Marian raises her eyebrows. "Aren't you meant to be the clever one? We only know what Royce told you they want, that's not the same thing as what they actually want," she says. "Did you ask him what he wants Eamonn to do, after you've turned him?"

"He said they want information from him."

"On what, Tessa?"

"They might not even know yet."

The velvet on the sofa darkens and lightens as she brushes her hand back and forth. She says, "Seamus was obsessed with MI5. He was desperate to identify a handler. It drove him mad, not knowing

46

who they had working in Belfast. He spent ages trying to get some-one into their offices as a cleaner."

After what happened to me yesterday, it feels good to dissect the IRA, to take them apart, turn them over in our hands like this, and I wonder if Marian feels the same, and that's why she's telling me all of this.

"And Seamus wanted to send me to a culinary institute in Lon-don," she says, "on the tiny, tiny chance that MI5's canteen was staffed off it."

"That's demented," I say. "You're the worst cook I've ever met."

Marian nods. "He was convinced I could learn. He was always thinking about how to get inside their building."

Listening to her, chills sweep down my neck. Marian once told me that Seamus was a fan of Agatha Christie. He built his opera-tions like puzzles, dismantling them and putting them back together a hundred different ways.

"Maybe this was Seamus's plan," I say, and my voice sounds hol-low. This idea, using an informer to turn a handler, sounds exactly like him. Seamus might have been the one who first suggested it, years ago. Maybe he told someone on the army council that they needed to go after handlers, and that the best way would be to make informers do the work for them.

Marian's face turns pale. "Yeah," she says, after a long time. "Yeah, I think it is his plan." Three years on from his death, and Seamus is getting his revenge.

Neither of us knows what to say. In Marian's lap, Saoirse has fallen asleep nursing, and Marian gently slides her finger into the baby's mouth to loosen the latch.

"I need to leave for work," I say, and I expect Marian to protest, to say I should go home and get some rest, but she already knows that this is how informing works. You have to act normal, and today is a normal working day.

"What if Eamonn's not in Northern Ireland anymore? MI5 might have brought him back to London, or sent him to a new posting," I say, while standing from the sofa.

"I doubt they'd pull him from Belfast. They wouldn't want to lose his contacts," she says. "Can you wait to signal him? We need to work out what you're going to say to him first."

"What, though? Ask him if he fancies betraying his country?"

"It might not be that complicated. I mean, what happens to him if you video him and upload it on social media with a caption saying, Look at this MI5 gobshite?" says Marian. "His career would be finished, he'd be kicked out of the inner circle. That might be enough, depending on why he's in the job."

I nod, bending to kiss Saoirse goodbye. "Hang on," says Marian, handing Saoirse to me. She disappears into the bathroom, returning with a bottle of prescription tablets. "For the pain," she says.

"I told you they didn't hurt me."

"I know what arnica smells like, Tessa," says Marian. She's the one who told me to put arnica on bruises, like she told me to use valerian root for sleep and evening primrose for stress. "How bad is it?" she asks. "Will you let me take a look? As a paramedic, not as your sister."

"I'm fine," I say, gently lowering Saoirse into her Moses basket. Marian waits, and finally I untuck my top and roll it up over my torso. Her face falls. "Oh, christ. Can I?" she says, and with cold, quick hands, she does a trauma exam, running her fingers up my spine and palpating my stomach to check for internal bleeding. "If you start feeling nauseated or dizzy, go straight to hospital, okay?" she says, and I nod.

After a moment, I say, "Royce said I shouldn't have resisted. He said I wouldn't have gotten hurt if I hadn't resisted."

"He's going to pay for this," says Marian simply, like she's stating a fact, and that's how I know the conflict will never end, because despite everything I say about peace and reconciliation, I hope she's right. I hope he does pay.

Six

OUTSIDE MY SISTER'S HOUSE, I'm disoriented by the row of cottages, expecting to see tall brick terraces. For a moment, I'd thought I was back in Belfast, outside Marian's old house on Adelaide Avenue.

You could see the Black Mountain from the end of her old road, rising on the edge of Belfast. I could see it from our council estate, too, and from my secondary school. I used to sit in class, watching the rain and clouds lashing the mountain, with longing tugging at my chest. The mountain is so large that looking at it was like looking at the ocean, its shades constantly changing.

When we left the North, we tore our lives apart, starting over with nothing. Not one friend, not one plan. I had to build it all up again. Find a job, a place to live, a playschool for Finn. Introduce myself to my new coworkers, to the other parents on the playground, under my new name, and wait to see if we'd grow a friendship. And we have done, I've new friends here, but they're not my mates, not yet. Mates piss in front of you. I remember my old mate Clodagh dropping onto a toilet in a pub stall without even breaking conversation. None of my new friends would do that, not yet. Sometimes the thought turns me grief-stricken, that I might never again have the sort of friend who will reach over and take a sip of my drink without asking first.

And I miss my old job at the BBC, and the high-wire act of producing a radio show live on air. I was good at it, too, really good at it.

I owned a small house in Greyabbey that I'd fixed up myself, tearing out the insulation, ripping up the floorboards, putting in a new boiler, spending all that cash and all that time, because I'd planned to stay. I'd planned for Finn to grow up in that house. I'd even chosen the doorframe where I'd mark Finn's height every year. We only got to one measurement, the one I drew on his first birthday, when he must have been about two feet tall. He'd only just learned to walk. I remember him standing against the doorframe, proud, wriggling, while I held the book straight above his head, and if the new owners have painted over it, I'll hang for them, I swear to god.

We could have stayed in Northern Ireland, for all that leaving helped us. It didn't keep us safe, after all, the IRA have found us anyway.

I remember walking in Greyabbey on the green lanes behind our old house, past sheep pastures and potato fields, with Finn in his front carrier, kicking his feet against my thighs. I was happy then, with my baby snug on my chest, and I want to go back to that exact moment. If I could, I'd do every single thing differently.

BEFORE REACHING THE OFFICE, I duck down a laneway behind Molesworth Street, lined with blackened exhaust vents and restaurant service doors. I ring Tom, and ask to say hello to Finn. "I'm in the middle of making breakfast," says Tom.

"Please, Tom. Two minutes."

A few scuffling seconds of quiet, then a high, bright voice says,

"Hi, mama." I lift my face toward the sky, love thundering through me. "Hello, sunshine."

"I'm making pancakes by myself with dada."

"Are you? Very good. And how's the beach? Have you been swimming yet?"

"And bellyboarding," says Finn. He chats to me about the beach, and warmth runs through my veins. He sounds cheerful, contented. Four more days to go. Before we hang up, I say, "Finn, sweetheart, can I talk to your da?" When Tom comes on the line, I say, "So everything's going well?"

"We're good. You sound exhausted, by the way."

"Thanks, mate," I say. "Tom, have you ever told anyone where we live?"

"Of course not. Why?"

"No reason," I say.

"What's going on, Tessa? You sound awful."

"Nothing, sorry," I say. "Where's the cottage?"

"It's great," he says. "It's really close to the beach, maybe a couple hundred meters."

"Lock the door at night."

"You think Finn is going to open the door and sleepwalk two hundred meters down to the beach?" asks Tom.

"Maybe."

"Has Finn ever sleepwalked in his life?"

"Will you just lock the door, Tom?" I ask. He tells me not to worry so much, like he usually does, and I tell him he's right, that I'll try to relax a bit.

After hanging up, I stop into Buswells Hotel, turning my face away from the clattering tea room, since some of those tables will be people from my office, and head straight for the toilets to straighten myself out before work. I expect my face to look bruised and raw from last night, for my eyes to be bunched up and blackened, and I do look terrible, but not in that way, more like someone suffering through a migraine. My mouth is strained, my eyes bloodshot. I take my hair down and try to soften the pinched set to my forehead. I dab more aloe onto the cut on my bottom lip, and check that none of the scratches on my legs are showing below my skirt.

On the way out, I walk through the tea room, as a sort of rehearsal. I recognize a few faces from the office. None of them takes much notice of me, even though I feel like I'm dragging something across the carpet. And then I'm pushing through the door and out onto Kildare Street, with the parliament looming across the road behind tall black iron gates.

Inside the parliament courtyard, a cameraman from RTÉ stands checking his phone, waiting for his reporter, and a few senators are climbing out of their cars. The senators can park in the courtyard for free, their very own parking spot in the center of Dublin, a privilege they seem to hold more dear than their actual senate seats.

I walk up Kildare Street, past the parliament, to the *Irish Observer* building. The morning is still overcast enough to see the strip lighting glowing inside the offices. I scan my badge by the security turnstile. "Hi, Stephen," I say to our front clerk. "How's things, how was your weekend?"

"Grand," he says. "The wiring is still banjaxed, though. It's going to be boiling in here again today."

"Ah, look, I'll take that over baltic." I climb the stairs to the open-plan office, making my way between the desks. After settling at mine, I start mousing through the first copy to arrive this morning, a long story on economic indicators around Ireland.

Our production editor, Joanna, says, "Sorry about the heat, everyone. I've asked for more fans, but I've seen neither head nor tail of them yet."

A few people start to complain, and Emer catches my gaze above the desks and rolls her eyes. She advises the newspaper on legal questions. Today Emer has on tracksuit bottoms and a gray sports top, and a pair of thick athletic sandals. She has never once followed the newspaper's dress code, but no one minds. Emer's brilliant. I doubt anyone has ever even tried to have a word with her about her clothes, too worried she'd piss off to a private law firm, which would pay ten times her current salary.

Emer was the top law student in her class at UCD. "It wasn't a fair competition," she once told me, as we circled around Merrion Square on our lunch break. "Both my parents were alcoholics, I'd more that I needed to block out than the other students." We'd only been working together for a few weeks at that point, but people often tell me their secrets. I don't know why. I'm not nearly as outgoing as Marian, or as approachable. When strangers stop the two of us on the street, they look at my sister while asking for directions, not me, and at a party, whoever is telling a joke will often look at Marian, expecting her to laugh, which she does easily. People tend to tell Marian jokes, but they tell me what they worry about.

"Nice shoes," I mouth at Emer, and she winks back at me.

I spend the rest of the morning editing copy for the news desk. The atmosphere in the office soothes me, the constant stream of voices, of laughter and arguments, the squeak of dry-erase markers. I can feel twinges in my ribs and a stiffness in my neck from the whiplash, but they're submerged, snowed under the painkiller.

I look around the other desks. If I were to tell any one of my co-workers about what happened yesterday, they would each tell me the same thing. They would tell me to go to the police. And maybe they'd be right. I don't have to do what Marian says. The main garda station on Harcourt Street is only a few minutes away. The city center will be busy at this time of day, I might be able to slip inside without being seen. I wouldn't bet my life on it, though. Or Marian's.

At half two, Oisín says, loudly, "Christ on a bike. Emer, have you seen this?"

"What?" she asks.

"Nesbitt and Hooper is threatening to sue us," he says. "For the Fianna Fáil piece."

"Pricks," says Aisling, and everyone nods. Protecting the newspaper from getting sued is the hardest part of our jobs.

By four in the afternoon, the office is stuffed with heat, and the painkiller is wearing off. The temperature isn't doing me any favors. I should have ice packs on my ribs, to bring down the swelling. Instead, they're throbbing with heat.

A piece on a bank robbery in Ballymore still needs a headline, but my mind has gone blank. This one should be a doddle, but I can't think of a single clever heading. Normally I like writing them. I've a collection pinned above my desk of classic headlines from vintage newspapers. My favorite is for a match between Celtic and Caledonian Thistle, "Super Caley Go Ballistic, Celtic Are Atrocious."

Whoever wrote that would have no trouble writing a headline for a bank robbery. I rub my temples with my thumbs, and when I look up Joanna is watching me. She turns away quickly, tapping on her keyboard. Minutes pass, in which I focus on staying upright in my chair. Finally, I type, "Bank Robbed in Ballymore" and send off the copy, shame flushing my cheeks.

At five, I say goodbye to Joanna, in the midst of the others as they troop out the door. "Pub?" says Andrew, once we're down the corridor.

"I've to finish some work," says Oisín.

"Wagon," says Andrew, and turns toward me. "Same," I say, and as the others walk down the road toward Toners, I sag against the rails of Merrion Square to wait for the bus. The air is cooler out here than in the office, and carrying a green scent from the trees overhead. None of the others were surprised that I'm not joining them. I never do, too nervous about blowing my cover by saying something stupid after a few glasses of Rioja down the pub.

I call Marian from the top deck of the bus. "You okay?" she asks.

"I'm on the bus."

"Get some rest, then. You'll be back at work tomorrow," says Marian, and I know which work she means. She's right, too. My mind is grinding to a halt under the exhaustion.

"How're you?" I ask. "Did you have any visitors today?"

"Only Seb's sister," says Marian. "She dropped off a lasagna, since she knows I'm on my own with the baby."

"Which sister?"

"Orla," she says, the youngest one of the five. "Seb says it'll be inedible, but wasn't that lovely of her?"

"Yeah, she's a dote."

"Where are you now?"

"Leeson Street," I say, and Marian talks to me about nothing much for the rest of the bus ride home and up to my front door, like she's holding my hand.

Without Finn, the air in the house feels thin, like the difference between fresh and salt water. It's strange to move around the rooms without bumping into him, apologizing, touching my hand to his hair, to brush my teeth without Finn following me into the bathroom, tangling around my legs. Being away from Finn now is like being out in a city with your phone about to die, that slight hum, that sense of something askew.

Upstairs, I fill the bath with lukewarm water and lower myself in. I sink under the water, feeling my dry hair floating on the surface for a moment before the water swallows it under. Finn's not home, but a part of me is listening for him anyway, circling around and around, like the beam of a lighthouse. After toweling off from the bath, I set my wet head on the pillow and let the beam rotate.

Seven

I'VE SLEPT FOR ELEVEN HOURS STRAIGHT, and my mind feels cold and clear. Downstairs, I wrap an ice pack in a cloth and carry it out to the back patio. The air brushes against me, sweet and mild, with mourning doves cooing from the roofs.

Someday I will need to consider what happened to me on Sunday. For now, though, I have to act as if those hours in the bungalow, with the lace curtains and the smell of gravy, happened a long, long time ago, and like I've already recovered from them, which doesn't seem difficult, somehow. Those hours don't exist in normal time anyway. They're deep in the past and waiting in my future. They're not tied to Sunday, by any means, or to this week, to the month of August, they're not lashed down to a calendar date. They're much too large for that.

Sitting down on the back step, I hold the ice pack against my side and think about Eamonn. I'm ready for it this morning, the long hours of sleep sharpening my mind like a knife.

Eamonn used to meet me on the beach at Ardglass. I'd pass along whatever information Marian had told me, about arms drops, robberies, targets, then he'd leave and I'd swim in the sea, my cover for being at the beach at that hour. When I think about those meet-ings, I think about the shock of cold water pressing against my eyes.

I adjust the ice pack, listening to it crackle. Eamonn told me he was born in Northern Ireland, but his family moved to England when he was twelve. He worked in counter-terrorism for MI5, with a post-ing in Hong Kong before he was sent to Belfast. Nothing else, noth-ing about his personal life. Once, he did up the zip on my wetsuit, but I'm embarrassed that I even remember that, years later.

I shift the ice pack higher on my ribs, and feel the cold tingling in my bones. Eamonn swore the security service would protect us. Marian had a tracker hidden on her, and Eamonn promised that if we were caught, if anything went wrong, they'd send in an extrac-tion team for us. I believed him. When the IRA caught me and Marian, I expected a special-forces team to storm the building. I remember listening for tactical officers to surround the farmhouse where we were being held, waiting for them to appear from behind the trees. But no one came.

My ribs are fully numb now. I breathe in and feel nothing, only an icy shimmer where the pain had been.

Six months of meetings, of risk, of trusting him, and Eamonn left me to be shot in the head by the IRA and dumped on the side of a road. Which, you could say, means I owe Eamonn nothing, abso-lutely fuck all.

WHEN I WALK INTO THE OFFICE, the new fans are going at full tilt, rotating on their stands, rifling the papers on the desks. "Jesus, the actual sound of them," says Aisling, dropping her bag under her chair.

"White noise," says Oisín brightly. "It's been doing wonders for my focus, actually."

"Piss off, Oisín," says Aisling.

For her office wear today, Emer has chosen a pair of long, silky rugby shorts and a nylon shirt, and the sight of her gladdens my heart.

I carry an iced coffee to my desk, watching the cream attack the glass. At half ten, I start a software update on my computer, leaving it open on the monitor for anyone to see. Then I take the lift down to the basement. The basement is original to the building, a warren of old cellars and tunnels. One tunnel supposedly leads to a bomb shelter under Merrion Square, though I've yet to find it.

The ceilings are low, the light dim, and you can tell from the damp air that you're far underground. We've had flooding down here, and some of the others have seen rats. I listen, but no one's coming behind me.

I take the few short steps down toward our archive, and continue past it, and the first storerooms. I step into the third storage room, switching on the light to illuminate metal shelving units of old electrical equipment. Broken printers, mostly, and projectors, and a few shelves of old loaner laptops.

I carry one of the loaners back up to an empty conference room. Editions of the paper are delivered here at dawn every morning, and the whole room smells like newsprint.

Using a proxy server, I set to work like I'm fact-checking copy, like someone has written a feature on traitors in the British security service. The stories about defectors don't appear easily. Someone from MI5 has tried to make them disappear, burying them far down in the search results. They can't whitewash all the stories, though, and soon a list starts to grow. I don't know what to call them all, exactly. Whistle-blowers, moles, defectors, some incompetents. People who did one on the security service, basically.

By the time I finish, MI5 seems about as impenetrable as a colander. I'd always thought of the security service as a fortress, but now the place seems rotted through, filled with employees with the same petty issues as in any office, plus other more grievous ones besides. I make a list in my head of reasons MI5 agents have given up their secrets. Ideology, bribery, love, revenge.

At five o'clock, I rush to Marian's house, and start talking before she has even closed the door behind me. "It's not easy, working at MI5," I say.

"Right," says Marian warily. She lowers herself to the rug, where Saoirse is lying on her play mat.

"The work's isolating, the pay's shite, and it's corrupt. They kept secret files on the committee who oversaw them, can you believe that? They were ready to blackmail any politician who tried to rein them in," I say. "And they do mad things. They spy on students, and environmentalists. They tried to assassinate Gaddafi, all on their own, no one in the government even approved it. They ended up killing three civilians instead."

Marian leans over to hand Saoirse her rattle. "Eamonn never seemed disillusioned to me. Did he seem that way to you?" she asks.

"I don't know. Maybe not back then, but maybe he is now, after three more years of being undercover in Belfast. Maybe he hates MI5 now." After everything I've read today, I've convinced myself that Eamonn will be grateful for the chance to stick two fingers up at them.

"Then he'd quit. Go work in a bank or something."

"Not necessarily. Other handlers have defected to the enemy instead. This one handler sold secrets to the Russians because he was so upset at not getting a promotion. Another did because he was having an affair with his coworker in MI5, and she dumped him," I say, and Marian tilts her head, listening. "Another sold classified information to four different buyers, because he needed the cash. And one handler started working for the Stasi, but he was an alcoholic, so he might have been too much of a mess to even realize he was being a double agent—"

"Eamonn doesn't have a drink problem," Marian interrupts.

"Will you just listen to me for a minute? This other handler leaked stories to a journalist, because he thought his bosses were incompetent."

"Grand," says Marian. "So, what, you'll sing 'Four Green Fields' to him until he decides to volunteer for the IRA off his own bat?"

"It worked on you," I say quietly. "I'm not trying to start a fight here, I'm just saying, it worked on you."

Marian seems to shrink in on herself. She hates talking about this, about her recruitment. "I was twenty-one, Tessa. Eamonn's, what, forty years old?"

"Exactly. Plenty of time to get disappointed with his life. On balance, your average forty-year-old man is much angrier than some young lad. He's just better at hiding that, until it erupts."

Marian frowns. "Are we talking about Tom here? Because Seb's not like that."

"No, Seb's lovely. He'd also cut off his own arm before joining MI5, so he's not relevant," I say, my voice rising in frustration. "Maybe Eamonn's lonely."

"And you can convince him the IRA are his mates?"

"Why not? Eamonn's from Northern Ireland. He was born in Strabane."

"No, he told you he was born in Strabane. He's probably actually English."

"Come here to me, Marian. No one would have thought grooming would work on you, either."

"When will you meet him?" she asks, her voice brisk.

"I'm going to signal tonight and drive to Ardglass tomorrow morning," I say. Finn's still away in Donegal with his father, and I can call in sick to work.

"What if Eamonn doesn't show up?" she asks.

"Then I'll go to the British embassy and offer to inform," I say. "And we'll do all this with whoever they assign me as a handler."

"Maybe we won't actually have to do any of this. Maybe things are about to change," says Marian. "Did you see the news today?"

"About the priest?" I ask, and she nods. Some unnamed priest from west Belfast told a journalist that he is working with an Anglican priest from east Belfast as mediators between the IRA and the UVF. "And you believe him? He's a priest."

"Maybe you can find out more from Eamonn," she says.

"No. I don't care about their talks, I care about surviving this."

"Okay," says Marian, finally. "So you'll meet with Eamonn, offer to inform again, and try to work out if he's disillusioned or not. We can start with that, and if it doesn't work we'll try my way."

"Which is what?"

"Blackmail."

Eight

I DRIVE THROUGH A ROUNDABOUT, my headlights flashing off the reflector arrows, and onto the motorway. It's four thirty in the morning. A few lorries thunder alongside me, and taxis heading north toward the airport.

Past the airport, a sign over the motorway says THE NORTH. I look up at the sign, and then the car is whipping under it, racing toward the border. The drive to Ardglass will take two hours. Around Dundalk, gray light starts to lift around the road, and the Mournes appear ahead of me, the mountains trembling with the car's movements.

I tighten my fists on the steering wheel, watching the needle on the speedometer vibrate. Thick green trees stand alongside the road, power lines swooping between them, and then the trees thin, giving way to broad fields. I come around a bend, and ahead of me soldiers are waiting on the road.

A soldier in a heavy bulletproof vest steps forward to take my passport though the window. Other soldiers are standing at the border checkpoint, with rifles across their chests. One leads a sniffer dog around my car while the first soldier flips through my passport.

"Where are you coming from?" he asks, studying my face while I answer.

"Dublin," I say, trying to stay calm while he examines my passport. It's genuine. The Belfast police had it processed for me, in my new name. "Where are you going?" he asks.

"Ardglass." To the east, cloud shadows are spilling down the slopes of the Mournes, and the same wind is surging over the fields, making the soldier's fatigues ripple.

"What for?"

"To see a friend."

"Staying overnight?" he asks, and I try not to look at the smooth plastic of his rifle. I can hear the dog panting as he presses his snout against the car door. The soldier has a Yorkshire accent, and I wonder if he's scared of never making it home to England. Every border checkpoint is an IRA target.

"No, I'm driving back later today."

"Long drive for that," he says, and I think he's going to detain me. "What happened back there?" he asks, cocking his head.

"In Dublin?" I say, confused.

"What happened to the back of your car?"

"Oh," I say. "Some prick drove into me."

The soldier looks past me into the car, running his eyes over the picture books on the floor, and Finn's empty car seat. He hands me back my passport. "Enjoy your visit to Northern Ireland, ma'am."

Slowly I slide the car back into gear. As I drive away, I glance in the rear mirror. A few soldiers and a portacabin surrounded by fields, and that's it, that's the border. To me, over the past few years, it has felt more like Northern Ireland was behind a great stone wall.

I hadn't known if I'd ever see the North again in my life, and now I'm here, I'm back in County Down. Mist is coming off the damp green hills, tangling around the apple trees in the orchards. The countryside looks peaceful. How could this place be dangerous, I think, but then I reach the first town, and every road is hung with flags. Even the curbstones have been painted, in case anyone has any doubt over whether the neighborhood is Catholic or Protestant. My heart sinks. Campaign posters for a local election are fixed to the streetlights, and every candidate has its eyes gouged out, the town lined with row after row of demonic councillors.

Even on the roads without flags, something seems off. Nothing is out of place, but everything feels askew, the way your house looks different right after you've watched a horror film. I drive past a group of lads in tight tracksuits, messing in the town's park. They can't be older than fourteen, fifteen, and already the paramilitaries in this town might be grooming them.

At the crossroads, the names of towns have been struck out with black spray paint, to confuse or intimidate the British soldiers. Somewhere toward Crossmaglen, two army helicopters are beating through the air.

Most of the mist has burned off by the time I reach Ardglass, the last vapors blowing over the dune grass. Stepping out from the car, the smell of the place hits me in the chest, the scent of sand and warm wooden decking from the footpath through the dunes.

Beach roses grow along the footpath, twining around the sign warning of riptides. That same sign was here three years ago, draped with old polystyrene ship's buoys, which must have blown away in the last big gale. I look at the diagram of a swimmer in a riptide, her arm bent above the waves, and then step onto the footpath.

No one has seen me. I can turn around. All I want is to drive back to my ordinary routines, to work and playschool, the supermarket and the playground, to the children's birthday parties, the errands, the bedtime stories and bath times.

I don't know what to expect in the next hour. Eamonn might not come. Other agents might come instead and bring me to be questioned. They could charge me with treason, or conspiracy to commit terrorism.

I've been reading a few pages of *James and the Giant Peach* to Finn at bedtime. If the next hour goes wrong, we won't finish the book together. I'll never do another one of his bedtimes, ever.

This place looks nothing like the bungalow in Wicklow. I'm out in the open, but it's the same. It's just another trap.

The wind lifts suddenly, whipping my hair around my face, nearly shoving me off the path. For a moment, I can't hear anything over the wind and the blood roaring in my ears. Eamonn might already be here, waiting for me. I follow the decking through the dunes and step down onto the sand.

Part Two

SAFE HOUSE

Nine

AHEAD OF ME, the beach is empty, a layer of marine fog hanging a hundred meters offshore. I sit down on the sand to wait. The wall of dawn fog over the sea is sun-shot and golden, glowing. It looks like a portal, like you could swim under it into another world. I keep thinking I see sailboats ghosting through it. My face feels hot with anticipation, nerves snapping through me. Any minute now.

Last night, I used the gift card from Eamonn to buy a small bottle of amaretto from the SuperValu on Ranelagh Road. On my way home, I tipped the amaretto down a sewer, breathing in its fumes. I've never liked the stuff. It seemed important to buy something I don't actually use, that has nothing to do with my real life.

Small waves collapse on the shore. I can hear their sound receding down the beach and the dry rustle of the dune grass behind me. Near the water, a rusted lobster trap has washed onshore, tangled with sea wrack. The last time I came here was in winter, three years ago, and the sea was frigid then, heaving and gray, the sand frozen underfoot.

Eamonn will be here soon. We always met at seven. I wonder if he will look different, if these three years will have changed him. I stare down the beach until my eyes start to ache.

I force myself not to check my watch, and by the time I do, it's half past ten, and the fog has burned off, leaving acres of flat, featureless water stretching to the horizon. My eyes are dry, razed from the sun, and Eamonn isn't coming.

You stupid woman, I think, you stupid, stupid woman. Coming here with your plan all wrapped up and ready to go, as if you've ever been in control in any of this. I didn't sleep last night, not for one minute. I was too worried about missing my alarm. I lay awake, and for what? So I could sit here alone on a beach, making a mockery of myself. The truth, probably, is that Eamonn saw my signal, but what happened with me meant so little to him that he can't even be arsed to come see me.

WITHOUT THINKING, I turn north out of Ardglass instead of south toward the border. Out of habit, I'm driving toward Greyabbey. Soon I'm on the lough road, and something is swelling and rising through me. To my right a low stone wall stands covered in moss below gnarled green trees, their branches knotted above the road, and god, this place is every bit as beautiful as I'd remembered.

I look at the wooded islands in the lough and the vast expanse of silver water flooding around them, the tide fast enough to make whirlpools. The Vikings who sailed here thought the whirlpools sounded like snoring, and I can't believe I'd forgotten that sound. The road curves back and forth alongside the lough, and then the Orange Tree House comes into view. When we lived here, I could hear the music at its weddings from our garden.

I turn up my road and park outside our old house. This is

Eamonn's fault. Strangers are living inside my house because of him, because he failed to protect us. I sit in my car, biting the inside of my cheek to stop myself from crying. Wise up, I tell myself. It's only a house. And not up to much, either, as houses go. Four walls. Bit of garden. Small rooms, doors that always jammed.

But I gave Finn his first bath in that tub. Two weeks old, right after his umbilical stump came away, and he was small enough to fit in my cradling hands. I still remember the face on him, when he felt the warm water slipping over him for the first time, his small bowed legs, his wariness, and then his bliss, rotating his head to feel the water moving against it.

Even if we'd stayed in Greyabbey, Finn would still be growing up. It wrecks my head, how fast he's changing. Staying here wouldn't have slowed that down.

When Finn was two years old, mam said, "He will never remember living in Northern Ireland," and part of me refused to believe her. None of his first year? None?

I was pregnant with Finn in Greyabbey, I brought him home from hospital to Greyabbey, to sleep in a bassinet beside my bed. I spent hours walking down the lanes behind my house with him in his front carrier.

When we left the North, Finn was just learning to walk. I remember watching him pull himself up to stand, holding on to the stone wall at the bottom of our garden. He pointed out across the field toward the sheep, smiling, turning his head back to show me.

On our last morning in this house, I lifted Finn into his high chair and fastened a bib around his neck. "Are you hungry?" I asked, and he kicked his feet in the air. I was carrying a bowl of porridge toward him and then the thread snapped.

Two men in black ski masks were standing behind my garden

wall. They agreed to let me bring my son to my neighbor's house before they took me away. I unstrapped Finn from his high chair and carried him out of the room, stepping over the mess of porridge and pottery shards on the floor. The men had guns. If I tried to escape, they said, they'd kill both of us.

Finn was one year old. We won't be able to pick up where we left off. I'll never set that bowl down on his high-chair tray. That morning is over, it's done, it's finished. There is no other life in which Finn learns to talk, and to drink from a glass, and to ride a bicycle in Greyabbey and not Dublin. I don't know why I keep thinking I'll be able to do his childhood over again, but this time somewhere safe.

Ten

AT HOME IN DUBLIN, I strip off my sticky, crumpled clothes and find a clean pair of jeans. A train slides past on the tracks while I'm changing, and I step out of view of the bedroom window, tugging a cotton shirt over my head. The raised tracks run behind our terrace of small brick houses, level with our upstairs windows.

We live on Dartmouth Terrace, a quiet lane below the canal in south Dublin. We're only a fifteen-minute walk up to the city center, though the roads on this side of the canal feel like a village, with brick terraces and hidden parks, and the mint dome of the church on Rathmines Road rising above our roofs.

I'm renting the house. I can't afford to buy anywhere in Dublin, since this place has lost the absolute run of itself. Dublin is now more expensive than Paris, which people tend to say with pride, like we've won a competition and not lost one.

The terrace was built two hundred years ago, and before we moved in I scraped the plaster down to the original stone walls to let the years of damp dry out. Now the walls are whitewashed, hung with small oil paintings from secondhand shops. There's a small fireplace in the front room, with an ivy garland carved in its mantel, and another upstairs in my bedroom. A tiny kitchen, a tiny bathroom, and a small, paved back patio.

Nearly all the money I have or ever will have goes to the rent, but I can leave the office on Kildare Street and be home for Finn in fifteen minutes. Ten at a run, twenty if snow or ice are covering the footpaths.

A message arrives from Marian while I'm cooking dinner. "How was your date?" she says, and I wonder why she's asking me about Ardglass in code, who she thinks might be reading our messages. "He didn't show up," I type back.

"Give it a few days, then try calling him again," she says. "Don't worry, though. Plenty of fish in the sea."

Before bed, I stand at my window, breathing in the humid air. The sun set hours ago, but my bedroom is still warmer than blood temperature. This presents a problem, since I always close and lock our windows at night.

I lean forward, pressing my hands against the warm metal of the window screen, like I'm testing its weight. It's nothing, I could put my hand through it with barely any resistance. The screen leaves soot on my fingers, dust from the traffic and trains around our road. The downstairs windows will be locked, at least. I picture our house from the road. A small brick terraced house, the red standby light on the alarm system bouncing back and forth.

Eleven

Tom is bringing Finn home from Donegal this evening. I hurry out of work, and then spend the hour before they arrive cleaning the house, putting fresh sheets on the beds, sweeping the floors, hoovering the stairs. The dryer cycle ends, and when I pull out the clothes, the clean laundry gives me shocks of static electricity. The shocks feel good, they feel like something I need right now, like a defibrillator, like a stronger version might restart my stalled heart.

When Finn runs in the door, it's like sunshine pouring through the windows, like the house warms by ten degrees. He launches himself at me and I let him tackle me to the floor, laughing, ignoring the hard screws of pain in my ribs. "I missed you," I say, with my forehead against his. I lie on the floor with my son clamped to my front and close my eyes, tears sliding into my hair.

Tom hovers by the door. "You all right?" he asks, and I nod, barely listening, still breathing in the clean, canine smell of Finn's hair. "How was your week, Tessa?"

"Oh, you know. Quiet."

Finn is busy at once, untidying all his toys, setting them on the floor, getting to work. He bowls over to me to ask if I want an ice cream. "Strawberry, please," I say, and he shakes his head sorrow-fully. "Vanilla?" asks Tom. "No, we're out of vanilla," says Finn, since this is his favorite game, shopkeeper out of stock.

I look at Tom's broad frame, his light brown hair and beard. Tom is friendly and affable, and he cheated on me when I was two months pregnant. I don't hate Tom for cheating, I don't wish we were still married, but it's his fault that Finn doesn't have both his parents in the same house, and I'll take that grudge to the grave.

Tom tells Finn he'll ring him from Belfast. His voice is cheerful, but I can see how reluctant he is to leave and drive home without Finn. He says, "Right, I'm double-parked. I should head on."

"Safe trip home," I say, closing the door gently behind him.

IN THE MORNING, I'm making coffee when Finn wanders by in only his underpants, strumming a ukulele and singing loudly. Funny age, four. It's playdates and swim classes, tantrums and the time-out stair, colds and stomach flus. It's wearing me out, it's sending me near the end of my rope, and then suddenly not. For a long time, Finn was shorter than the doorknobs in our house, now his head is level with them. He is stubborn and curious and silly, and I'd like him even if he wasn't my son.

I wipe down the kitchen surfaces and scrape the coffee grounds from the plunger, nodding my head along to Finn's singing. "I've a surprise for you," I say.

Yesterday I bought a cheap inflatable paddling pool for Finn. The child has just spent a week at one of Ireland's most beautiful beaches, you'd think a pool in a Dublin back patio wouldn't impress him, but Finn is delighted. He barely leaves the pool for all of Saturday, and I sit with him, cross-legged, in my black swimsuit, the warm water slopping around my waist, with the trains going past above us.

I cup water in my hands, chatting with Finn about whatever runs through his mind, looking at his wet lashes and freckled nose. "I think rain is faster than people," he says.

"I think you're right."

In the afternoon, we walk down Ranelagh Road for ice cream. I get two scoops of pistachio and hazelnut, he gets a vanilla twist, which melts onto every inch of his person, trickling down his arms and smudging his shirt.

ON SUNDAY MORNING, I pull on jeans and a sleeveless linen top. "Is this the right way?" asks Finn, with a shirt tangled around his shoulders, and I fix his sleeves.

"No shoes," says Finn, hiding behind the sofa.

"Of course shoes," I say, finishing my coffee and pushing my own feet into a pair of woven leather sandals by the door.

Outside, I use my keys to bolt the locks. Finn runs ahead of me up the road while I follow, shouting, "Too far." He waits for me at the corner of Dartmouth Road, and I take his hand, a sprite in red shorts skipping at my side. We turn onto the footpath along the canal. Office blocks rise to the north side of the canal and buses trundle through Ranelagh to the south, but the canal itself is pastoral, like an old millstream deep in the countryside. Under the willows, sparks of sunlight flash on the water, their reflections climbing the green branches. Ahead of us, cars and cyclists cross the rounded stone bridge, and joggers trot down the path. I like to run on the canal path, too, when I have time, which I never do.

"How do helicopters work?" asks Finn, and we chat as we walk toward the Liberties. The large clouds over Dublin have a pink tinge in the heat. I can feel the sun flushing my cheeks, and I scoop my hair from my shoulders into a knot. We turn up Clanbrassil Street, into the cool shadows of its buildings. When we reach the playground at St. Patrick's Cathedral, Marian is already there, pushing Saoirse on the baby swing. "Hello, Finn, how are you, you well?" says Marian, bending down to tackle him.

"Can I go in there?" asks Finn from inside his aunt's embrace, pointing at the baby swing.

"No, sweetheart, you're too big," I say, and his brow lowers. I tickle Saoirse's feet as she swings toward me, and she squawks with laughter. Finn climbs onto the next swing, and he looks so tall beside her, so grown.

I push Finn on the swings, far below the cathedral's gothic spires. On the ground, the shadows of the swing's chains thin as they lengthen, darkening as they sweep back toward me. The cathedral lawn is filled with couples and groups of friends, and children's voices bounce across the playground. High above us, gargoyles cling to the stone vaults of the cathedral, screeching into the air above the city.

Today Marian has on a blue dress with a pattern of tiny daisies, cheap sunglasses pushed up on her head. We are standing together, chatting, pushing our children on the swings. Anyone glancing over at us will see two smiling, tired women.

We don't talk about Eamonn. There's nothing to say yet anyway, not until I signal him again, and we don't talk about what Royce will do to us if we fail. Instead we talk aimlessly about the heat wave.

Every so often another parent waves to her across the playground, and Marian calls out, "Hiya, how are you, how's things?" Some of the other parents know that Marian works for the air-ambulance service in south Dublin. They will bring their child over to her after a fall or a scrape, and Marian will run through a set of steps, talking to the child all the while in her lilting, reassuring voice. The parents are always grateful and apologetic. None of them know the truth, that Marian was a terrorist.

I look at the daisies on my sister's dress, at her strong arms. When she was twenty-one, Marian joined the IRA in west Belfast. She spent seven years working in an active-service unit, and I'd no idea, not one clue. Somehow Marian kept her involvement hidden from me and our mam. That was years ago, though. Another lifetime. Finn drops toward me on the swing, and I raise my hands to propel him back into the air.

Saoirse starts to cry in the baby swing, and Marian scoops her up. The pair of them have the same eyes, though I can see a bit of Seb's in the baby's, too. I hold the chains steady so Finn can hop down, and he races toward the climbing frame while I follow Marian to a bench in the shade of an oak tree.

Around the cathedral lawn, the old oaks and elms stand heavy in the humid air, their thick leaves casting dark shadows. My eyes chase Finn around the playground, tracking his bright orange shirt as it flashes in and out of view. Marian is rocking Saoirse when an alert pings on her phone, and she cups her hand around the screen to read through the glare.

"Oh, god," she says, and the back of my neck stiffens. Above us, the oak leaves have started to shiver, like a thunderstorm is coming.

"What is it?" I ask, and she hands me the phone, her hot fingerprints still smeared on the screen. Under the loops and whorls of her fingerprints, I can see a news photograph of a small cottage in Ballynahinch. The start of the article says "An IRA brigade commander was seen leaving a County Down property owned by a rumored loyalist leader early Sunday morning."

"Jesus christ," says Marian. "You know what that means, right? That means they're talking about a joint ceasefire."

"It won't happen," I say, and Marian's mouth opens, then closes. "Or the IRA and UVF will call a ceasefire, and then one of them will wreck it before the peace talks even get going."

"When did you give up?" she asks, and I turn away from her, looking across the lawn. I say, "Did you even read the rest of the article? The threat level for Northern Ireland was raised from severe to critical."

In the past, the days and weeks before a ceasefire have often been the bloodiest, with each side trying to weaken the other before negotiations start. It's as if any limit, any line of decency, disappears. Not long before the 1994 ceasefire, the IRA held a man's family hostage and forced him to drive a bomb into an army camp. They call those operations, the big ones, the ones that make headlines around the world, spectaculars. One will be coming now, too.

Beside me on the bench, Marian's body is bristling with energy. She looks, somehow, like she wants to be there, in the North, part of the action. I don't know why this surprises me so much. Marian left her active-service unit years ago, but maybe she hasn't really changed. She named her daughter Saoirse, after all. Her daughter's name means freedom.

Twelve

As we leave the cathedral lawn, Finn says, "My legs are tired."

"Already?" I ask, swinging him onto my hip. "Here, you're heavy. Put your arms around my neck."

I clasp my arms under Finn, carrying him home past the crowded shops and restaurants, squinting at the traffic with the sun in my eyes and loose strands of hair falling over my face.

A group of men is drinking pints outside Devitts with their shirts off. One of the servers says, "Lads, will you put your kit back on?" Their whole table groans in disbelief at the request, or the heat, and I smile at the server in sympathy.

After Finn's bedtime, I move through the house, draining his bathwater, gathering his crumpled clothes from the floor, scraping our dinner plates into the bin. I pour a large measure of red wine and lean against the kitchen counter, holding the wineglass in one hand and my phone in the other, reading the news from Northern Ireland. All the commentary, all the analysis. If a joint ceasefire might be called, what one might mean. It makes me furious enough to want to throw my phone at the wall. Stop acting like this will change anything, stop giving people false hope.

When I remember being an informer now, the part I find hardest to believe isn't the threat to my life. It isn't even that my sister had joined the IRA. It's that I ever believed a peace process could happen. No one in the North is going to surrender. Not the IRA, not the UVF. They've made that clear, they've said so themselves, in countless releases and communiqués. It was my own fault for not listening to them.

I drain my wine and set the glass by the sink. Even now, hours after a huge, blood-red sunset, the temperature has barely dropped. I'll have to sleep with the windows open again.

Lying in bed, I picture a man in a black ski mask silently climbing the downpipe at the back of the house, toward my open window. I spend some amount of time trying to work out if the downpipe would be strong enough to support a man's weight, before telling myself to cop on and rolling over.

WHEN I WAKE in the middle of the night, I wonder if Marian is up, too, sitting beside her daughter's crib, like she's keeping watch. It wouldn't be the first time.

Six months ago, Marian sat in a small room on the fourth floor of a northside hospital. She had come to the maternity hospital after starting to bleed, though the bleeding had stopped. She was still in her own clothes, leggings and a loose shirt, chatting with Seb, eating a chocolate bar.

During the ultrasound, the doctor's face didn't change. She pointed at the monitor and said, "There's your baby."

"Ah," said Marian, craning up her head, relieved. But then the doctor was standing from her chair, asking a nurse to prepare an operating room. She pointed at dark patches on the ultrasound screen.

"See these? The placenta has detached. Your baby won't be getting enough oxygen."

Marian changed into a hospital gown, neatly folding her clothes on top of her shoes. A nurse shot an injection of ceftazidime into her thigh to prevent infection during the surgery. She gave Marian another injection in her back, a steroid for the baby's lungs. Marian took off her necklace and wedding band, and Seb tucked them into his pocket.

The doctor told her the cesarean normally took about forty minutes, and then they waited for the steroids to work, or the antibiotic, or for an operating room to be ready. Someone had told them, but when the medics spoke, they were both too busy nodding and trying to stop their heartbeats galloping to hear the words.

On the operating table, Marian lay back, answering the anesthesiologist's questions, listening to the monitors, the surgical trays rattling, while Seb stood beside her, holding her hand. Eventually Marian began to hear something different, some new sound, and realized it was shoes sticking to a wet floor. An alarm attached to one of her monitors started to ring. Her blood was splashing onto the floor, sticking to the surgeons' shoes. She saw her daughter being lifted into the air, curled up, her knees tucked into her stomach. Then the neonatologists blocked the baby from view, and Marian felt her eyes roll back in her head.

Hours later, Marian was conscious again, weak from blood loss, hauling herself across the neonatal intensive care unit. She had a drip port taped to the back of her hand, and her hair was damp with sweat. A doctor told them that an intravenous line had been placed, that the baby was at 60 percent oxygen supplementation. Saoirse was asleep between rolled-up blankets, with a cannula and a heart monitor. She weighed less than three pounds.

Her milk came in on the third day. Every two hours, Marian walked into a small windowless room, unbuttoned her shirt, and assembled the parts of a pump. She sat with her head bowed, watching milk splashing into the bottles, the white liquid rising. She was scared of long-line infections, oxygen desaturation, necrotizing enterocolitis.

Once the bottles were brimming with milk, she twisted on the yellow caps, marked her name with a pen, and slipped them into the fridge. She bent over the sink, scrubbing her hands until they turned red, her hair sliding over her face, and walked back onto the ward.

She wasn't thinking about her past at all, except a part of her must have remembered, because on the first night, before leaving at handover, she found the ward nurse and said, "My husband's right over there. If anyone else comes in saying he's the father, he's lying. Don't let him take the baby."

The nurse didn't even blink. Calmly, she tapped the band on the baby's ankle, and said, "She's not leaving here with anyone but you."

Saoirse was in the NICU for thirty-eight days. Every night, I dropped food off at their house, with ingredients meant to help Marian recuperate. Bone broth to restore her blood, chicken and red dates for iron, custard with honey and chamomile for sleep.

In the morning, Marian and Seb arrived at seven when the unit opened to parents, rubbed alcohol gel onto their hands, and listened to their daughter's ward rounds. Seb brought in a small blanket that he'd slept beside so it would smell like him, and tucked it inside her incubator. Each movement required concentration, to lift Saoirse from the incubator without disturbing the tubing and cords, to fold her miniscule nappy.

Marian wasn't exactly in hiding. She was on the top floor of a northside hospital, with her shirt unbuttoned, talking with other mothers while pumping milk for her baby, who was not well. She could have told the other parents the truth. She could have said, "I'm from west Belfast, I joined the IRA in my twenties, then became an informer, and moved south when my cover was blown," and they would have nodded and said, "So is your daughter on Optiflow or a CPAP mask?"

Saoirse wouldn't have cared, either. All she wanted was her mam. Marian sat in a chair with Saoirse on her chest for hours, her shirt wrapped over the two of them. Saoirse's heart rate calmed when she was being held, and her oxygen levels steadied. Marian could see it happening, she could watch the numbers change on the baby's monitor. Those numbers on the monitor were proof, evidence of how much Saoirse needs her.

They will kill her anyway, I think. If I fail to turn Eamonn, they will kill both of us.

Thirteen

I wake to the sound of Finn running to launch himself onto the bed. "What did you dream about?" I mumble, tucking my arm around him.

"I don't know," he says crossly. Walking downstairs, he holds on to the banister, sliding his socked feet off each step. I rush around fixing our breakfasts, putting on a clean dress and tying my hair back, frowning in the mirror at my tired face, shadowed eyes. Finn stands outside the bathroom with his hands clasped, his small shoulders rounded. "I don't want to go to school."

"We have to, *mo leanbh*. I need to go to work."

"Why?"

"I like working," I say, which makes him so angry he throws a shoe across the room. Wrong tactic, apparently, but I want him to like his work, too, one day.

I pack his lunch and fill his water bottle. "Where's my rhubarb?" says Finn, peering in his rucksack.

"What?"

"I have to bring in a rhubarb today," he says. I forgot. His playschool sent a note home, asking all the children to bring in rhubarb for a summer ceremony. We do not, currently, have any rhubarb. "Right, okay, we'll stop at the supermarket, but we need to leave right now." Five minutes ago, actually.

"Are you angry, mama?" asks Finn, as we start down our road.

"What? No." He walks at my side, his hand in mine. "I'm not angry. I'm a little frustrated, but not with you. It's nothing, it's normal."

Finn doesn't seem particularly concerned, but shame seeps through me. He has been home for, what, two days, and already I've failed to hide this from him.

His playschool classroom is bright and noisy, swirling with other children hanging up their bags, saying goodbye to their parents, slamming the doors on the toy kitchen. "I'm nervous," Finn whispers.

"What are you nervous about?" I ask, crouching down to his level.

"I'm nervous about not knowing what to do first," he says, ducking his head and tangling his feet.

"That's all right. You'll be grand once you get going, you know that." I hand him his bag to shove into his cubby, and wish I could stay in the corner of this room all day, watching Finn and his classmates draw and read books and sit in a circle of carpet squares having a singsong. As I leave, Finn waves to me from the window, his small head barely visible above the sill. I wave back, blowing him kisses, until he skips away into the room.

I'VE JUST SETTLED in at work when an article arrives from the news desk for me to copyedit. Another sighting of an IRA leader, this time at a property in north Antrim. The house is owned by a Belfast property developer who has been seen playing golf with the Northern

Ireland secretary of state. "The sighting has fueled speculation about secret talks being held between the IRA and the British," says the article. I move my cursor through the document, fixing errors, and send it to Joanna. Afterward I sit at my desk, chewing the edge of a pen, then walk into Joanna's office.

"That piece on the IRA leader sighting in Antrim. Why are we publishing it?" I ask, and Joanna takes off her glasses, looking up at me from her desk. I say, "It's not news. It's gossip."

Joanna frowns. "You don't think possible evidence of peace talks is newsworthy?"

"No, because none of it's real," I say. "The IRA are playing us."

"How do you mean?"

"They want us publishing this sort of thing. They want us to make it seem like they're actively pursuing a peace deal with the British, so they can carry on killing and maiming people. They're making us look like fools." I stop, folding my lips shut between my teeth. Joanna studies me, her eyes searching my face.

"Sorry," I say, rubbing my forehead. "I just meant to say none of this seems substantiated to me. If we publish it, the property owner could sue us for damages."

"Thank you," she says in a measured voice. "I'll run it past Emer, okay?" I nod, and retreat to my desk, wondering what just happened.

At pickup, Finn runs out in a bright torrent of children, his face splashed with poster paint. "I painted a pine cone," he announces.

"Did you?" I say, taking his hand, listening to the other parents shepherding their children away from the school gates. My friend Caroline catches up to us and says, "Want to come over to ours for dinner?"

I rub my eyes. "I didn't sleep much last night, I might not be good craic."

"That's fine, I'm not in top form, either. These two will do enough talking for both of us," she says. Behind us, her son, Rory, and Finn are whacking each other with their rucksacks.

"Fair enough," I say, and the four of us go around the corner to her house on Alma Terrace. We start peeling potatoes while the boys play at our knees. Caroline says, "Lads, will you not take every pan out of the drawer?"

"But we need them for our restaurant," says Rory, while Finn freezes, holding a pot lid, waiting to see if he'll be told off.

"Fine," Caroline sighs, and the boys race into the other room with their equipment. Caroline rummages in the fridge, then says, "Ah, no, we're out of butter."

"I'll go pick some up," I say, ruffling Finn's hair on my way to the door. "Don't wreck the place while I'm gone, okay? Yes? Good."

At the supermarket, I find the butter, then add a bottle of white wine to my basket, and a box of chocolate biscuits for good measure, sliding them through the self-service tills.

I'm leaving the shop with the plastic bag hanging from my wrist when something makes me lift my head. The air around me seems to heat suddenly, like it does right before a thunderstorm. Eamonn is standing across the road. I can feel the looser and tighter strands of hair in my ponytail, the soft pockets of my dress against my bare legs.

Eamonn tilts his head down Ranelagh Road, and slowly I turn and start moving in that direction. I'm not prepared for this. I was ready, on the beach in Ardglass, but now I'm in disarray, my palms damp, slipping on the plastic bag. At the crossing, I turn off the main road and follow the lane toward the railway overpass. I don't look back, but every inch of my body knows Eamonn is following me. Under the railway tunnel, I turn around, and Eamonn stops a few feet away. I'd forgotten the force of his presence, the way being near him seems to draw a ring around the two of us.

"You look the same, Tessa," he says.

"No, I don't." It has been three years. My hair is darker now, cut into a different shape, with long bangs, and I've creases at the corners of my eyes and across my forehead.

Eamonn doesn't look the same, either, not quite. His skin seems to have grown thinner somehow, drawn down slightly under his eyes and over his cheekbones. And something has happened to his right eye. A sunspot, a small white flare, so the black line around his iris is broken, not making a full circle.

"Has someone threatened you? Is that why you signaled?" he asks.

I shake my head. "No, it's not that. I'm fine." Even in the heat, the underside of the tunnel smells damp. Eamonn looks at me, and I'm aware of the weight of all the stones suspended in the air over our heads.

Being near Eamonn is flooding my senses, so I can feel a train coming in the distance, setting faint vibrations in the bridge, and hear each voice down the road, and even though he's standing a few feet away, I'd swear I can smell that his shirt was ironed recently.

"I'm sorry for not getting to Ardglass in time on Wednesday," he says.

"No, I understand. I figured it'd be a stretch," I say, and even though we're both speaking softly, our voices echo against the tunnel, lapping back to us from the corners. I always thought that if I saw him again, Eamonn would look guilty, but his face is filled with some expression I can't decipher. He doesn't look guilty. Why, I think, why on earth doesn't he look guilty?

A train is above us now, running over the bridge, all those bodies and electricity passing a couple of meters above our heads.

"You left us to die, Eamonn."

"I'll explain," he says. "But we can't talk here." Eamonn tells me the address of a safe house in Stoneybatter. "Will you meet me there tomorrow?"

Fourteen

THE NEXT AFTERNOON, I pass through the security turnstile at the office and turn onto Kildare Street, walking through the city center to the river. The Liffey looks greasy and gray today as I cross above it on the footbridge. Over Dublin, the light is flat and muddy, the sort of stark light that picks out the marks on skin, so all the faces coming toward me on the bridge look wrecked in one way or another, and I'm sure mine does, too.

I have on a striped shirtdress and flat mules, ordinary work clothes, clothes that Eamonn would be hard-pressed to read any sort of intention into. Almost no makeup, either, like if I turn up in lipstick he will know I've been put up to this. I've already seen how the security service treats its regular informers, I can't even imagine how they'd punish someone attempting to turn one of their own.

I walk across the northside and into a residential part of Stoneybatter. The address Eamonn gave me is a new-build house, plaster with PVC windows, and two wheelie bins in its front area. The whole road is lined with neat, anonymous houses. Anyone who can afford one of them will be working long hours, which must mean no one will be hanging around here during the middle of the day, keeping an eye on their neighbors.

Eamonn would never tell me where he met his other informers. I've always wondered about MI5's safe houses, picturing everything from tower blocks to country mansions, but of course they're on a road like this, the sort you might catch sight of from a bus or taxi and immediately forget. I turn my head slowly, taking in the road, and the curiosity sees off my nerves well enough to get me up the two stairs to the front door and ringing the bell.

Eamonn opens the door. He has on a denim shirt and dark canvas trousers, like roughly half the men his age in Dublin. Before yesterday, I'd only ever seen him on the beach in Ardglass, in jogging gear, never in ordinary clothes, and these suit him better.

Stepping past him into the house, I notice that Eamonn smells the same. Months ago, someone walked past me on the street and I caught that same warm scent, like cedar. I whipped my head around, certain it was him.

He closes the door behind me and leads me into a front room with flat-pack furniture and a vintage cycling poster. "Did you get here safely?" asks Eamonn.

"It's been three years," I say. "Can you be more specific? How far back do you want me to go?"

"I meant, were you followed?"

"No." My nerves feel like caffeine poisoning, like drinking black coffee on an empty stomach. I drop onto an armchair, looking around the room. "Nice set dressing," I say. "The poster's a good touch."

Eamonn smiles. "Want a coffee?" he asks.

"Sure," I say, and watch him in the open kitchen down the hall, pressing a capsule into the machine, waiting while it brews. He returns with two small white cups balanced on saucers.

"Was it hard to get away from work?" he asks, and I shake my head.

"No, I'm working on copy for the weekend supplement. I can finish it tonight." Yesterday, under the railway bridge, being near Eamonn sent sensation flushing through me, but now my body barely seems to exist. I can't taste the coffee at all, I might as well be drinking water. Right now, I'm only mind, breaking down the words leaving his mouth, turning over what he's saying and what might come next.

"Do you like working at the newspaper?"

"Ah, here. I think we're beyond all that carry-on now, don't you? You don't need to pretend to be interested anymore."

Eamonn sets his cup down on the saucer, like he needs to focus on the movement, nearly tipping over the coffee. I can't tell if he's genuinely nervous or pretending to be, for some reason. I breathe in, trying to remember everything Marian and I worked out for me to say. "Why did you contact me?" he asks.

"Because I might need your help," I say. I force myself not to touch the cut on my mouth, or the bruises on my legs. Eamonn can't know the truth, he can't know that Royce sent me here to meet him. Luckily the cut on my bottom lip is almost healed, and the bruises on my legs have already faded. Some of them were deep enough to leave behind bumps of scar tissue under the skin, like ropes. "Did you know Niall O'Faolain is in prison?" I ask.

He takes another sip of coffee. "Yes."

"Marian has been sending him money."

Eamonn's brows lift. "Why?"

"Niall was like her younger brother. He grew up in care, he has no family. Marian feels responsible for him. She thinks she could have gotten him to leave the IRA back then, if she'd tried harder."

"Does anyone else know about this?"

"I don't think so. But the police will find out, won't they?"

"Depends. How has she been sending the money?"

"Cash, with no note or letter. She always sends it from different post boxes in the city center. And she wears gloves, so no finger-prints."

Eamonn says, "Does she know what Niall's been spending the money on?"

"Books and food, she thinks."

"Is she sure about that?" he asks. "Because depending on what he's using the money for, she could be up on charges of funding ter-rorism."

"But then you'd have a word with the prosecutor, right? And the charges would be dropped."

Eamonn shakes his head. "Her immunity from prosecution isn't a blanket agreement, covering all crimes. Marian wasn't working with us when she sent him the money, she did that on her own."

Part of me is disappointed at how easily Eamonn is taking the bait. If he had any decency, he'd be offering to help Marian without asking for something in return, and that's not where we're heading.

"Has Marian spoken with Niall since leaving the North?"

"No," I say. "She has different priorities now. She's working for the air-ambulance service, she's married, she has a baby. She's not still wrapped up in the conflict."

Quietly, Eamonn says, "Funding terrorism has a minimum prison sentence of six years."

"Right, okay," I say, and I don't need to fake the indignation in my voice. "Then let's hope no one finds out, since you won't be help-ing us."

I rise from my chair, and Eamonn stays seated, watching me. I start toward the door, and he says, "Look, there is one thing we can do." I fold my arms over my chest, waiting. "Marian can ask to visit Niall in prison."

"Catch yourself on. Why would she do that?"

He says, "If Marian gets information from Niall for us, then we can say she was working with us all along, and sending the cash was to warm him up. She'll be protected."

I shake my head. "We've spent three years in hiding, and you want her to toss that away?"

"Where is Niall serving his sentence?"

"Castlerea."

"So all the way out in Roscommon. Medium security. What was he arrested for?"

"A cashpoint robbery in Dundalk," I say, and Eamonn nods. He says, "Castlerea's small. I doubt another IRA prisoner is in there. And visitors can ask for individual rooms if there are any safety concerns."

"Even if no one else sees her, what about Niall? What if he decides to tell someone?"

"You said that Marian was like his family. Would he do that to her?"

"I can't believe you'd ask this," I say, which is true enough. "Do you've no shame, Eamonn? How do you sleep at night?"

"I don't much, to be honest," he says, and fair enough, his face does look weary.

"Why can't you talk to Niall yourself? Why do you always make other people take the risk?"

"What exactly do you think I've been doing here for the past five years? Do you think I've been safe all this time?" he says. Five years, then. Eamonn has been in Belfast for five years, which I didn't know before. It's small, but it's not nothing.

"Castlerea's two hours from Dublin. Marian doesn't need to tell Niall her address, or her new name. Visiting him wouldn't exactly narrow down her location. You should give her the option," he says, and I let out a bitter laugh.

"Every time I give Marian an option, she wrecks my life."

"I thought you'd forgiven her," says Eamonn.

"So did I."

Eamonn listens with his elbows on his knees, leaning forward. Earlier, when I came inside the house, Eamonn stepped forward and lifted his hands slightly, like he was about to hug me, then thought better of it.

I knew I was attracted to Eamonn before, but I'd assumed the way things ended three years ago would have doused any chemistry, that my mind would override any attraction. Apparently that's not how it works. A large part of me doesn't trust Eamonn, and another large part wants him to sit closer to me.

"We're getting ahead of ourselves here. Let's slow down," says Eamonn. "Tell me about Niall."

"Do your own research."

"Right, correct me if I'm wrong on this," he says. "Niall's younger, and he joined the IRA when he was a teenager. Mostly he did their driving on the robberies." I wait, listening. Marian said Niall was a good dancer, she said he could have become a professional, if any adult in his life had the cop-on to notice.

"You met Niall on five separate occasions, and you were terrified of Seamus but never of him. You thought Niall seemed sweet."

"This isn't a game, Eamonn. You don't get points for your memory," I say, which Eamonn ignores.

"Since Niall was a driver, he could have been moved anywhere in the IRA, after their active-service unit broke apart with Seamus's death and Marian's disappearance. He could have been a driver for the army council," says Eamonn. "When he was arrested, Niall didn't turn state's evidence, clearly. He kept his mouth shut, which means all his links in the organization are intact."

I pull my focus tighter, since this is the weak part of the plan, the creaking stair that I have to force myself not to rush over. This next part has to go perfectly, not a single mistake. Eamonn has to agree to meet with me instead of Marian. "My sister won't speak to you," I say. "She hates you."

"What, more than you do?" asks Eamonn gently.

"You didn't turn me into a murderer," I say. "Marian killed Seamus at the farmhouse because you'd left us to die."

"Tessa—"

"We were raised Catholic, Eamonn. She thinks she should go to hell for killing him," I say, which is not true. As far as I can tell, Marian feels guilty about everything in her life except Seamus. "She'll never agree to work for you again."

"Then we can't help her," says Eamonn. "Try asking her to visit Niall in prison. And she doesn't have to meet me, she can pass along any information to you."

I don't answer. Now that I've offered him the idea, Eamonn needs to talk me into it. I have to act reluctant, which isn't so hard. I can think of a dozen reasons this is a horrible idea.

"You're asking me to risk my life."

"How many locks are on your front door?" he asks. "Three? Four? But it's only been three years, so you remember what it's like to feel safe," he says, and I picture pushing Finn in his pram, the sunshine pouring down on us, not looking over my shoulder, just walking.

"You're right, I do remember feeling safe. It was before I met you."

"You want the conflict to end, Tessa."

"It doesn't matter what I want," I snap. Parts of this conversation are fake on my end, and parts must be fake on his end, glittering, artificial shards, but surging under and around those shards is something real, a strong, dark tide.

"That's exactly what Seamus would want you to say. He'd be delighted to hear it." Eamonn rubs at his jaw. "The last time we met in Ardglass," he says, "the IRA had just called a ceasefire. Do you remember? You were walking on air."

"What good did it do? We're right back where we started."

"We're not," says Eamonn, his voice steady.

"You can't have me believing we're on the edge of a peace deal, not again."

"We're not where we started anyway," says Eamonn, but I don't believe him. I know, in my bones, that the conflict won't end in my lifetime. We're all trapped in it, caught in lockstep.

He says, "You knew, back then, the ceasefire was down to the work you'd done, and Marian, and all the other informers."

"This isn't my job, Eamonn. You're the one who signed up for it. Because, what, you'd watched too many films? You thought it'd be exciting? An interesting life?"

"Come here to me, Tessa. You know that I was born in Northern Ireland," he says. "My childhood was a lot like yours."

"Are you saying you joined the security service because you were traumatized? Even if that's true, which I doubt, we're not the same. I've a son."

"And you're all right with Finn growing up in a house with extra locks on the door?"

"Don't you dare. My son feels free as a fucking bird, I make sure of that."

Eamonn's eyes are intent on mine, and for a moment I forget

about Royce, I forget that this is staged, I forget my actual reason for being here, like somehow the conversation has spat us out onto some vast, icy plain.

"What happened, Eamonn?" I ask. "When you were a kid."

"I can't tell you the specifics, but you can imagine, can't you?" he says, and I don't think he's lying. I can imagine it, of course I can. A shooting, or a stabbing, or a bomb.

Eamonn says, "If you don't think the conflict's going to end anytime soon, that's all the more reason for Marian to get her situation sorted."

"Get herself backed up by you again, you mean," I say, and Eamonn nods. And there we are. There's our plan, with Eamonn thinking it was his idea. I close my eyes, like the reality of the situation is just now coming home to me.

"Well, look, I hope your team are delighted, Eamonn. Is this like a freebie, is it? Digging the two of us back out of the rubbish heap you threw us on."

Eamonn breathes hard down his nose. I realize that I've never seen him angry before, not once. He says, "I was there, Tessa. I was outside the farmhouse."

"You're lying."

"I was outside the farmhouse with twelve special-forces soldiers. They were ready to storm the building."

"No. I would've seen them."

"It was an SAS unit, Tessa. It's their job not to be seen."

"If that's true, then why didn't you send them in?"

"A siege would have been dangerous," he says. I shake my head, even though I'd had the same thought at the time, running through the positions, the crossfire. I remember huddling on the mattress, thinking that if there were a siege, we'd be killed.

"It was already dangerous."

"We thought Seamus was bluffing. Marian had been interviewed by the IRA before and released, I was confident she knew what to do. But then the two of you were taking off across the field, and I was about to send our men in when the building went up. We were ordered to stand down."

"I don't believe you."

He says, "The river behind the farmhouse was frozen solid, do you remember? I was running across it when the farmhouse exploded."

I picture Eamonn standing on the frozen river, watching the debris raining down, while on the other side of the farmhouse I was sprinting, tearing away across the field, the snow scalding my bare feet.

"Then why didn't you come and find me afterward? Why didn't you send me a message?"

"We don't contact informers once they've left, for their own safety," he says. "I did ask to visit you, but the request was denied. My supervisor said it was an unjustifiable risk for you."

"Right."

Eamonn lifts his gaze toward the ceiling. Slowly, he says, "I made thirty-six requests to see you."

I blink at him. He says, "Are you not going to ask the question, Tessa? Are you not going to even ask?"

"What question?"

"How do you think I saw your signal? I've been checking the balance on that card every day for the past three years."

Fifteen

A TRAIN IS TICKING PAST OUR HOUSE. Finn watches it with his hands pressed to the glass, and I lean beside him, my arm around his shoulders. Anyone looking out the train will see us, a small boy and a woman with dark hair, for a second, two, before the train is gone, gliding south across Dublin. They won't know who we are, or why we're here. Our window is only one of the thousands they will pass on their way home.

"Right, time for bed," I say, as Finn yawns. "Off we go." He turns from the window, padding down the hall to his room. After reading aloud from Roald Dahl, I reach over to switch off the lamp. Finn rotates his muslin blanket until he finds its tag, tucking it against his chest, and I close my eyes, resting my forehead against my son's. Soon his breathing slows and deepens, and I feel sleep coursing through his body and into mine, some deep frequency, like sonar.

Unwinding myself from the bed, I tuck the blanket around his shoulders and step into the hall. What I'd like to do tonight is pour a large glass of red wine and watch television, but I need to catch up on the work I missed this afternoon while meeting Eamonn, so instead I carry my laptop to the armchair in my bedroom and open a document.

While I work, darkness falls over Dublin, shadows folding over the roofs and sheds and garden walls. Past my bedroom window, trains slide past on the elevated tracks, the gaps between them growing longer as the night wears on. Not trains, technically, light rail. They're almost silent, only a whistling sound, a faint clacking of their carriages on the tracks.

I am typing in the document when something makes me lift my head. A train is stopped just behind our house. It's late, past midnight, this must be one of the last trains of the night. My fingertips flex away from the keyboard. Trains never stop here.

The train hangs on the tracks outside our house, its strip-lit carriages glowing in the darkness. I blink, and when my eyes open, I expect to see two men in black ski masks standing at the train doors. They must have pulled the emergency brake to stop the train here, and now they will force open the doors and start crawling down the high stone wall into my patio.

The laptop tilts on my knees and I catch it in midair before it crashes toward the floor. No one's standing at the train doors. I can't see a single passenger onboard. It's a signal problem, probably. Moments later, there is a sound of pressure being released, and the train eases forward on the tracks, gliding out of view.

The watch on my wrist pings. Sit down, it says, take a breath, because it thinks I'm sprinting, it thinks that's why my heart is racing. Piss off, I think, undoing the clasp and dropping the watch to the floor. I rub my forehead, telling myself it's all right, I'm only tired. I save my document and walk down the hall to check on Finn. He is asleep with his head tipped back on the pillow, his mouth parted. He's fine, we're grand, we're safe. Those men aren't here. The IRA wants something from me now, they're not going to hurt me.

MARIAN MEETS ME on my lunch break in Merrion Square. She arrives late, breathless, pushing Saoirse in her pram. "I saw Eamonn yesterday," I say, as she drops onto the bench beside me.

"Jesus," says Marian. "What did he have to say for himself?"

"He told me he was at the farmhouse. He said armed officers were ready to extract us."

"He's lying."

"I'm not thick, Marian. I know he's lying." The only reason Eamonn didn't look guilty when we faced each other under the railway bridge is that he has so much practice pretending.

"He wants you to visit Niall in Castlerea," I say, and Marian nods. The weeks start to unfold in front of me. Marian meeting Niall in prison, myself meeting Eamonn at the safe house, Royce checking on my progress, breathing down my neck.

"How am I meant to keep them apart?" I say. "What if they both turn up at my house at the same time?"

"Eamonn never came to your house before."

"But this might not be anything like last time."

"Eamonn might not even recognize Royce," says Marian. "He can't know the faces of every single IRA member, and no one thinks Royce is important anyway. He was let out of prison after turning religious, all that clabber." The police must think Royce is some sad case, living in a tower block and going to mass every day. Both of which are true, probably, fitted in alongside his other activities.

Saoirse starts to fuss in the pram, and Marian says, "Here, she wants me to walk." We leave Merrion Square, wandering toward Dawson Street, and then through the gate into Trinity. We cross Front Square, circling under the college's worn stone halls. "How was it anyway?" asks Marian. "Seeing Eamonn."

"I gave out to him, like we'd talked about. I think it came off, he didn't seem suspicious or anything. But I lost track of what I was doing a few times."

"Don't worry about that. You wouldn't want to seem like you'd already run it through."

"He seems different. Eamonn was confident before, do you know the way? I remember thinking he was out of his mind not to be scared."

"He seems scared now?" asks Marian sharply.

"No, it's not that. I can't put my finger on it yet, but he's different," I say. I lean my head back, looking up at the slate roofs and stone chimneys.

"Ah, no," says Marian. "I bet he's every bit as confident as he was back then, and he only wants you thinking he has changed. He's playing at something here."

Marian leaves to bring Saoirse home for a nap, and I stand outside the Arts Block, surrounded by students. During my fourth year at Trinity, Marian came to visit me. The visit was not, by any measure, a success. One night during her visit, while I was cooking us dinner in the tiny communal kitchen of the student halls, Marian said, "I thought you were a Marxist."

"I am," I said, taking a box of spaghetti from the press, leaning down to spark the flame under the pot.

"Then why are all of your friends rich? Their parents all have second homes."

"Not all of them," I said, though Marian was right. I was often invited to stay in their guest rooms, to swim in their pools and drink their wine. I was a good guest, easy company, putting a load of wet beach towels in the wash, bringing back fresh figs from the local market. I was always invited back.

When the water boiled, I dropped a fistful of spaghetti into the pot. "Where was the last one?" asked Marian. "Majorca?"

"Formentera. It's one of the islands past Majorca," I said, and turned away, using a spoon to press the upright spaghetti down into the pot.

"You've won the lottery, mate," she said.

I frowned, stirring the spaghetti. "You're making it sound permanent. Those trips are nice, but I'm their guest. It's not like I get to keep anything when I leave."

"Of course you do," she said.

"Do you think my friends' parents give me money?"

"Yes."

"You've lost the plot, Marian."

"I mean, on a practical level, how much money have they spent on your meals at restaurants? Four hundred euro?" Marian asked, and I stared at her, steam rushing from the wooden spoon in my hand.

"And that's just to start. Do they ever ask about your coursework? Or what you want to do after graduation? They're going to help you find a job."

"Right," I said, "and you can't find a job because you don't have the right friends?"

"I do have a job. And I never said you have the right friends."

I shook my head, wrapping the pot in a tea towel and carrying it toward the sink. "What's wrong with my friends?"

"Don't burn yourself," said Marian, because I was looking at her, ignoring the pot of scalding water in my hands. I bashed the pot against the colander, and she said, "Sorry, I didn't mean to insult your friends. They're just different."

"Different from what, Marian? From Andersonstown?" I said. "You're the one being shallow here. We've plenty in common."

We ate the spaghetti at the table with garlic bread and a two-euro bottle of wine. I twirled spaghetti onto my fork in neat twists, and noticed my sister trying to imitate the gesture, her own fork clumsy in her hand. I tore my garlic bread in half. "What if you come with me, the next time I'm invited away?"

"I've to work."

"At the dry cleaner's? You're not planning to stay there forever."

"I'm not a Trinity student, Tessa. It's not that easy for me to find work."

On the last night of her visit, we went to an Italian restaurant in Portobello with a group of my friends. I was across the table from Marian. My hair was piled up on my head, and I had on a dark sweater dress that one of my friends had loaned me, and burgundy lipstick, which also wasn't mine. I was talking and laughing when I heard one of my friends ask Marian, "Are you at university in Belfast?"

"No, I work in a dry cleaner's."

"Are you saving money to go traveling?" he asked.

"No," she said, and he cleared his throat, then coughed. I tried to catch Marian's eye across the table, but she wasn't looking toward me. "What's it like, living in Belfast?" he asked, reaching over to re-fill her glass.

"How do you mean?"

"It's fairly rough, isn't it?"

Marian shrugged. "No more than Dublin. You'd twelve people killed in drug feuds here last year."

"Not in the city center."

"Do you not leave the city center?" she asked.

"I mean, am I going up to Finglas? No," he said, and Marian said, "Why not?"

He laughed, like she hadn't been serious. "Were any of your family in the IRA?" he asked, and Marian frowned, looking down at her lap.

"Our great-grandfather fought in west Cork," I said.

After dinner, the two of us walked back toward the college. We were passing Stephen's Green when Marian said, "So is that the bargain, then? You tell your friends about the IRA, and they let you borrow their expensive shampoo."

I stopped walking, stung. Without looking at her, I reached up and wiped the lipstick off onto the back of my hand, leaving a dark smear like a bruise. Marian said, "I bet you don't know the name of the woman working in the canteen today."

"Her name's Ruth. Jesus, is that what you think of me? We have the same mam, Marian."

Why, I should have asked, do you care about the IRA? But I was stupid, too offended to think clearly. Before bed, Marian wiped off her makeup while I watched clips from a royal wedding. "Turn that shite off," she said.

"Why?"

"Because the British royal family is a symbol of white supremacy."

"Who told you that?" I asked, and Marian recoiled. She said, "I worked it out for myself, which wasn't that hard, to be honest. Do you think only Trinity students have opinions?"

"Jesus, no," I said, yawning. "Most Trinity students don't have any opinions."

Sixteen

TONIGHT I NEED A DUVET on the bed. September has brought a cold front, which comforts me for some reason, like I'll be safer in colder weather. In the morning, I fold back the duvet as Finn appears by the bed, and he climbs in beside me. "Is it a school day?" he asks.

"Yes," I mumble into his hair. "But it's still early, let's go back to sleep." For a few moments, Finn is quiet. Then he says, "I'm hungry."

While I'm washing our breakfast dishes, Finn says, "I coughed somewhere."

"Oh, right, okay."

"I coughed in there," he says, pointing at my coffee mug on the counter. "I'm sorry, mama. Are you going to throw it away?"

We need to leave in three minutes. "Ah, no, it's probably fine," I say and finish the coffee, which might explain why I'm forever catching his colds.

After work, I bring Finn to his swim class at the leisure center on the South Circular. He splashes in the pool, and I sit in the stands with the other parents, barely noticing the time passing. I couldn't grow bored this evening even if I tried, I'm unable. I could sit here watching Finn and talking about school catchments for hours and hours.

As we walk home, I look at the trees, thinking how you can tell that the season's turning, even though the leaves haven't changed color yet. Finn runs ahead of me, rounding the corner onto our road first. When I come around the bend, I see a thin man smoking a cigarette in front of our neighbor's house, and my heart stamps. Finn runs straight past Eoin Royce, trailing an arm's length away from Royce's hands.

I hurry after him, one strap of my bag hanging loose from my shoulder. "What are you doing?" I ask Royce, forcing my voice down. Finn is ahead of me, already at our doorstep, tugging at the handle.

"Aren't you going to invite me in?" asks Royce.

"You're off your trolley."

"Calm down now, I only want to hear how you're getting on." Royce blows out a gray stream of smoke, and I hold my breath, not wanting to swallow anything leaving his chest. "Not doing anything stupid, Tessa? Not calling the police?"

"Of course not." I can feel the wet swimming things pressing against my side, soaking through the bag. The sharp smell of chlorine rises into the air. Finn is looking back at us now, calling for me as he swings on the door handle.

"Have you made contact yet?" asks Royce, and I nod. He tells me to meet him at a pub near Glasnevin Cemetery tomorrow morning, and turns away down the road.

I unlock the door, my hands shaking. Finn trots into the kitchen, asking for water, for crackers, for pasta with pesto sauce. He doesn't seem bothered, but during dinner he says, "Who was that tall man?"

Royce is not particularly tall, but I can see how he'd seem to loom higher to Finn. "Oh, I don't know him very well. He's someone from when I was little."

"When you lived with granny?"

"Yes."

"Where was I?" asks Finn.

"You hadn't been born yet, sweetheart," I say, the fact of which Finn absolutely will not brook. "But I wanted to be there," he says, and I answer, grateful the conversation has taken an existential tack.

THE PUB IS BUILT INTO the wall around Glasnevin Cemetery. When I told my sister that Royce had asked me to meet him at the Gravediggers, she said, "Not very subtle, is he?"

Gravediggers working in the cemetery used to buy pints through a hatch in the pub's back wall. The hatch is gone, but otherwise the pub seems unchanged by the centuries, with low ceilings and a fireplace and a long wooden bar. The pub is nearly empty, except for the barman and a few old regulars leaning over their pints. The regulars glance over at me for a few seconds, long enough to identify me if anyone ever comes asking questions, I think. Royce is at a table in the back corner, eating a fry-up. Marian's right that Eamonn might not notice him. Your eyes skim right past him, a thin man in a pilled gray jumper.

When I sit down across from him, Royce doesn't look up from his plate. The last time we sat together, in the bungalow, I was in a cotton dress, with a split lip and blood on my chin. Today I've on jeans and a black leather jacket, thick as a stab vest.

I scrape my chair toward the table. "What was that yesterday?" I ask.

"I was only checking in," says Royce, wiping the corners of his mouth with a napkin.

"If you ever come near my son again, I'll kill you," I say.

Royce stares at me across the table. "That's odd," he says. "You're not sure if you really mean that. You think it's an empty threat, but I don't. I think you do mean it." He hunches back over his plate, using his knife and fork to cut into a black sausage. "Did you really never consider joining the IRA, Tessa?"

"No."

"You're very angry," he says. "You're much angrier than Marian ever was. She was a good recruit, but you could have been something special."

He digs into his pocket and hands me a burner phone. "I can't have that in my house," I say.

"So don't. As long as you're checking it once a day, I don't care where you're keeping it. You can keep it up your hole for all I care," he says, and I drop the phone in my bag.

Behind his head, the yellow paint on the wall is shiny, bulging with damp. "How's your man?" he asks. "Do we own him yet?"

"We had our first meeting. He wants Marian to visit Niall in prison, but we can give him something else if you've a problem with using Niall."

"Fine by me. Niall was never going to amount to much, even if he hadn't been lifted. He was cannon fodder."

"Is that what you tell all the lads when you recruit them?"

"Yeah it is, actually," he says. "They never believe me, though. They all think they'll be something special. You try convincing an eighteen-year-old he's going to die."

A wave of sickness passes through me. For a few seconds, it's like each of those lads' mothers is inside me, looking out at Royce through my eyes, spitting with rage.

"When are you meeting your handler again?" he asks.

"Next week, after Marian visits Niall. Should she tell Niall you're behind all this?"

"Sure," he says. I look at his long fingers, the yellow nicotine stains on his nails.

"Are you not worried about Niall telling someone?"

"No, he's sound. The police beat the shite out of him when he was lifted, and he kept his mouth shut. If he didn't squeal then, he's not going to now," says Royce.

"What should I tell my handler?"

"Tell him the prisoners are talking about a hunger strike. That'll get his knickers in a twist."

"Are they?" I ask, alarmed. Mam said the hunger strike in '81 was the darkest year of her life, the worst year of the Troubles, like all of Belfast had joined a death cult. Everyone watching these young lads wasting away, and no one, not the IRA, not Thatcher, telling them, That's enough now, you can stop. "Are they really planning a hunger strike?"

"Not a chance, the lads today would be too soft for it," says Royce. "That generation was made of stronger stuff."

But I don't want to put the idea of a hunger strike in anyone's head. Once those words are out, we won't be able to take them back. They might come true, and a hunger strike now would pitch the North into pure madness.

Across the pub, drizzle fogs the windows, blurring the view of the road. Rain is falling on the pub and the graves in Glasnevin. Under my boots, the floor feels crooked. Drainage might be a problem here, so near the cemetery.

Coming to this pub on my own some evening, I would have loved everything about it, the low ceilings and the fire in the grate, the scratched floors, but Royce has turned this place sickly, yellow as the nicotine stains on his teeth. This pub is lovely, but that's no match for him. If I'm not careful, he'll cast the same pall across all of

Dublin, until I hate the place, and can see nothing good or natural in it.

"What else do you have for me?" asks Royce, as he starts on the black pudding. He begins chewing, and I notice how his bones, his jaw and cheekbones, seem too big for his face.

"He let slip that he's been in Belfast for five years. And he said he joined MI5 because something bad happened during his childhood."

"Find out what."

"I will."

"What about his personal life?"

"He's not a parent," I say. I was watching Eamonn's eyes when I mentioned my son, and nothing slipped across them.

"Is that all? Come on, Tessa. Tick tock."

"He'll know if I try to rush this."

"Does he drink?"

"I don't know."

"For god's sake. Is he religious? Does he go to church?" asks Royce, and I say, again, "I don't know."

"Did he offer you anything? Did he offer to pay you?" he asks, and I shake my head. "Ask him for money. I want to see how he gets it to you."

"I can't, he knows I wouldn't do that."

"What, he thinks you're above that? You're a fucking tout," says Royce. "You're trash, he knows that well enough."

"I can't ask for money," I repeat calmly.

"Then find out what else they're selling. I want a catalog, okay? Everything they're offering. Ask where they'll set you up if you get caught," he says, pushing away his plate and lighting a cigarette. "You did well for yourself the last time. Nice place in Dublin, nice job."

"No one got me either of those," I say, though the Belfast police helped with our first year of housing and new CVs.

"Whatever you need to tell yourself, Tessa," he says. "Is your handler a looker?"

"Sorry?"

"How attractive is he? Above average? Below average?"

"Above average," I say, my skin prickling.

"Shame," says Royce. "No offense, like. You're fine, but your job would be easier if he were desperate."

"Grand. If you're looking for a honey trap, pay some model to do it and leave me out of it."

Royce shakes his head. "Anyone too attractive they can see coming from a mile off."

This conversation would have wrecked my head when I was twenty, but luckily for me I'm thirty-six and the only reaction I can muster is an eye roll.

Royce is still openly studying me, and I wait for him to tell me to go on a diet, or buy new clothes, or dye my hair. I'm a woman in Ireland, which means I've spent my entire life hearing this from all quarters, but the thought of even the IRA wanting to have a word with me about my appearance strikes me as a bit much.

"What did you wear, when you went to see him?" asks Royce.

"No, we're not doing that," I say, in a quick, cold voice.

"Did you make any sort of effort? No? That's all right. He's probably a lonely bastard. Friendship might get at him more than sex anyway."

Seventeen

WHEN MAM TAKES FINN to the chipper that night, I zip the burner
phone in a freezer bag and push it down the hollow of an oak tree in
Dartmouth Square, around the corner from our road. As I walk away,
I'm aware of the oak leaves rustling behind me, and the phone buried inside the tree, pulsing, waiting for a message.

Tonight I need to do Finn's bedtime, catch up on work, make a
grocery list, pay bills, scrub the toilet. I remember this from before,
how nothing else slows down to make room for the informing. You
have all the same responsibilities as ever. There is a violence to it, to not
having any spare time. I can't catch the flu, with my life as it is. There's
no room for error, for sick days. So how will informing work, exactly?

I love my son and I love my work, and sometimes right before
falling asleep at night, I think, Oh, god, I have to do all that again
tomorrow. The days are so full, they don't seem like something to be
repeated five times in a row. I'm already at the limit of my capacity.
Or past it. Or, more likely, well beyond it.

Every evening after work, I will stop in Dartmouth Square to
check the burner phone. The days are already growing shorter. Soon

the square will be fully dark by the time I arrive, the oak branches black overhead as I reach into the hollow.

On Saturday morning, I take Finn to his gymnastics class, where he grips the rope swing, and somersaults down a mat, and stops at the edge of the long trampoline, waiting to be sure I'm watching before flinging himself down its length.

Finn and I both look forward to his class all week, and I hate Royce for occupying my mind, trailing after me, even now, while I clap for Finn on the balance beam. Royce might as well be here, standing at the back of the room, staring me down. He'd be hard-pressed to imagine why I care so much about this class for preschoolers, in a tatty old leisure center on the South Circular. Finn wobbles on the balance beam, sticking out a foot to right himself. Royce would have me missing all of this. It means less than nothing to him. Leave us alone, I think. Give my head peace.

After gymnastics, we meet Caroline and Rory at the playground. I push Finn on the swings, looking at his snub nose in profile, his bent knees. Another mother shouts at her son, "Be a good friend, ask him questions about himself." I snort, and at the next swing Caroline says, "In fairness, though, that is good advice."

"When I was that age, I don't think my mam even knew my friends' names," I say. She was a single parent, working long shifts as a cleaner.

"What age?" asks Caroline.

"I don't know, maybe eight?"

"I've met your mam. She definitely knew your friends' names when you were eight."

I lean forward to push Finn back into the air. "Did yours bring you to playgrounds?"

Caroline frowns. "Were playgrounds even around back then?"

"I only remember playing on our estate." Marian and I played outside on the road, and when we were hungry, we made dinner for ourselves. My favorite was a frozen potato waffle, with butter and a can of spaghetti hoops on top. And when mam came home, we ran down the hall and she threw her arms around us. She always smelled like Je Reviens, even after a twelve-hour shift.

"My mam never complained," I say.

"Don't compare yourself," says Caroline.

"What? I wasn't comparing myself. Do I complain a lot?"

"I meant things are different now, parenting was easier back then," she says. "It can't have been harder, can it?"

I don't remember mam ever complaining about being busy, or tired, though she must have been. She never seemed pressed for time or distracted.

Our boys leap down and run toward the slide. An older woman holding an expensive handbag looks at us over the playground fence. "Enjoy every single moment," she says to us. "You'll miss this when it's over." We both smile tightly, then Caroline mutters, "For fuck's sake."

Neither of us needs to be reminded that our boys' childhoods are going too fast. Sometimes I look ahead to primary school, when our days will be at a slower pitch, but mostly I think about how much I will miss these years, the stickiness of them, the color. Every night, I check on Finn sleeping, and am surprised at how much of the bed he takes up now. He's not a baby anymore, he's not a toddler, and he never, ever will be again.

A shout comes from the far end of the playground, and when we walk over, Finn and Rory are shoving each other, red-faced and teary, and need to be pulled apart.

"Stop that, we don't hit," I say, which isn't true, the boys hit each other all the time, they shove and bite and kick and pull each other's hair.

"He hit me first," says Finn.

"That doesn't matter," I say. "You both need to apologize." Finn shakes his head, kicking at the gravel. "It's fine, okay? Just say you're sorry, and you can keep playing."

"Rory?" says Caroline, and he turns away from her, stormy. Five minutes pass that way, an absolute age. Finally Finn shouts the word, and Rory mumbles it, and they return to their game.

On our way home, Finn tries to ride his scooter in the bus lane. When I stop him, he shouts, stamping his feet. I kneel on the road facing him, but he's too upset to even hear me. Some of the people walking by ignore us, a few give me a sympathetic nod.

"Look, I understand that you're frustrated. You're very frustrated because you wanted to ride your scooter in the bus lane," I say, because I've read it's something you're meant to do, repeat back whatever mad request they're making, though it only seems to infuriate Finn. "It's okay to get frustrated," I tell him in a bright, false voice.

After Finn falls asleep, I gently close his door. I lift my hand and bite down hard on the base of my palm, then drop my hand, surprised. I stand in the hall, my bitten hand hanging at my side, thinking, It's okay to be frustrated.

Eighteen

WE'VE BEEN INVITED for Sunday lunch with Seb's family. His parents live in the house where he grew up, in East Wall. Their road looks similar to Marian and Seb's in the Liberties, a terrace of red-brick houses.

Seb's older sister, Nicola, opens the door, in heels and a printed dress. Seb's family always dresses up for Sunday lunches and holidays, giving the proceedings some glamour. "Hiya," says Nicola, giving me a kiss, as Finn patters up the stairs toward Seb's nieces and nephews. "The big ones are letting the little ones watch them play FIFA," says Nicola. "Isn't that good of them?"

I laugh. "Finn will be delighted."

The front room is crowded with Seb's family. Marian is on the sofa, chatting to Seb's granny. She's talking, gesturing with her hands, but her eyes are too bright, and she's already holding a drink. Marian was in a visitor's room at Castlerea prison yesterday. A stream of Seb's relatives surges around me, dropping kisses on my cheek, saying, "Is that your Finn, what a dote, he's gorgeous."

I squeeze down the hall toward the kitchen, saying hello to some people, touching others on the arm as I pass, and hand Seb's mother,

Eileen, a bunch of cabbage roses. "Oh, they're lovely," she says, hugging me. By the counter, Seb looks exhausted. He's only home for the weekend, returning tonight to the Aran Islands and the last week of the film shoot.

"Can I help with anything?" I ask Eileen.

"Ah, no, go relax."

"She'll be happier in here, mam," says Seb, his tone uncharacteristically terse. His mam frowns at him, and I say, "I do like to cook, he's right."

"If you're sure," says Eileen, and hands me a recipe before going out the back door to check on the barbecue. I start arranging fingers of shortbread in a glass bowl for the trifle, while Seb works a knife up and down through the herbs. "You're going to lose a finger," I say, because he's not minding himself at all.

"Want to know what I did yesterday?" Seb asks. His eyes are red and bloodshot. "I drove my wife to a prison."

"Ah, Seb. I'm really sorry."

"She'd told me this might happen, before we got married. I should have seen it coming," he says, working the knife faster. "I couldn't even go in with her. I had to sit in the car park and wait."

"She was safe in there."

"I know that. I know she's able to look after herself, but dear god." He takes a swig from a bottle, and my stomach drops. Seb catches my eyes on the bottle and says, "It's nonalcoholic. You thought I was off the wagon? Jesus, that's the last thing I need right now."

Through the back doors, I can see his mam in the group of people, talking and laughing around the barbecue, and smell charcoal smoke. Family snaps are pinned on the fridge. His parents have been married for over forty years. All those holidays and birthdays and weddings, the seven of them crowded around various tables. I take a gulp of my prosecco. If Finn weren't here, I'd want to get absolutely leathered.

Marian comes in holding an empty glass. "Is there more sherry in here? Your granny's out."

Seb reaches onto the top shelf to hand her a bottle, and Marian twists off the foil. "How was seeing Niall?" I ask quietly.

"It was awful," she says. "He screamed at me the whole time." She describes the visit, then says, "This isn't going to work. He won't agree to see me again."

"Yes, he will," I say. "What he did yesterday sounds like one of Finn's tantrums."

"So?"

"Finn has never once had a tantrum at school, a lot of kids don't. They only have tantrums with people they trust," I say. "If Niall's having a tantrum, he wants you to hear him."

Seb listens to us with his face turned to the ceiling and his arms dropped at his sides, exhaling huge breaths. He looks ready to start crying. While we talk, Marian moves beside him, wrapping her arms around his waist, and he puts his arm around her shoulders.

Marian tilts back her head, looking at him, and I turn away to give them privacy. After a few minutes, Marian lifts the sherry bottle and carries it back into the front room. Seb sighs. "What about you, Tessa? Are you able for this?"

"I don't have a choice, Seb."

He nods, looking down at the flecks of green herbs sticking to his wet hands. The patio door slides open, and the crowd from outside comes into the kitchen, carrying platters of short ribs. The two of us return to our cooking. I beat brandy into cream, heaping it into the glass bowl with the shortbread.

We eat at several tables shoved together, close enough to knock elbows. Nicola tells a story about a camping holiday in Spain, and Seb's father laughs until he cries. Finn sits on my lap, wolfing down his food so he can run back upstairs with the other children. Seb eats with one hand, the other holding Saoirse at his shoulder. Farther down the table, Eileen and Marian fall into a long, urgent conversation about ambulance wait times.

After lunch, Seb's father hands around tall glasses of coffee with whiskey and white caps of cream. I'm pressed onto the sofa beside Seb's youngest sister, Orla, and we click glasses. "Slainté," she says, and I sip my coffee. "Do you fight with your sisters?" I ask, and Orla nods.

"Oh, god, yeah. We row all the time," she says.

"What about?" I ask.

Orla thinks for a moment. "Nicola's always late, we all give out to her about that. And Caoimhe forgot to get mam a birthday present last year," she says, and I nod, taking a long sip of my drink.

Soon afterward, I carry my empty glass into the kitchen, and thank Seb's parents for having us. Marian comes outside with me while Seb goes upstairs to extract Finn from the pack of other children. Marian and I wait on the road, with our arms crossed over our chests, mirror images of each other. "Are you okay?" I ask.

"Seb's terrified," says Marian. "He's worried about me, and he's pissed off. He feels the way I would if he'd relapsed."

"It's not your fault."

"Of course it's my fault," she says, lifting her hands to scrub at her face. "And you've seen his family. Nothing in his life has prepared him for this."

Ahead of us are the glowing windows of the house, with Seb's family inside, talking and laughing.

"Seb's sober, Marian. It's not like his life has been perfect."

"His drinking was never so bad. He reined himself in before things were desperate," she says. "He's been happy all his life. Even when Saoirse was in the NICU, he was absolutely convinced she'd be grand. How is he meant to deal with this? Jesus, what a mess," she says, scuffing the toe of her shoe on the pavement. "When are you meeting Eamonn again?"

"I'll signal tonight, so we'll meet tomorrow afternoon," I say. "Did you find out what Niall was spending the money on?"

"He said it's none of my business."

"What's he been doing in prison?"

"Absolutely fuck all, as far as I can tell," says Marian, which is strange. IRA members always keep busy in prison. They're inside studying for Open University degrees, or teaching themselves law, or weight-training until their bodies are armored with muscle. It's a point of pride, part of their image, reading Chekhov while they're banged up.

"He can't be doing nothing," I say. The thought of Niall in Castlerea, staring at the walls, turns the back of my neck cold.

Seb appears in the doorway with Finn balanced over his shoulder like a plank. Beside me, Marian watches her husband with a fierce, protective expression, and I'm suddenly anguished for all of us. Seb rotates so that we can see Finn's giggling face, and says, "I promised to carry him to the bus stop."

Marian and I follow them toward the main road. I say, "Did I tell you what Royce said to me at the Gravediggers? He wanted to know if I'd be punching above my class with Eamonn, looks-wise."

Marian shakes her head. "I can't wait to put manners on him."

Nineteen

AT THREE ON MONDAY, I leave the office and walk to meet Eamonn in Stoneybatter. I have on a tartan dress knotted at the side, and a black umbrella holding off the rain. On my walk across the north-side, I pass lads walking bareheaded through the rain, and middle-aged men hoisting the back collars of their jackets over their heads.

Eamonn comes to the door in dark trousers and a white shirt with the sleeves folded back, and I wonder how he looks so clean despite the rain. "Did you get here safely?" he asks.

"Yes, I got here safely," I say.

He gives a little nod. Eamonn has never once told a joke in my presence, but I can tell from his mannerisms, from little shifts in his expression and his voice, that he has a good sense of humor, which he is actively suppressing when he's with me. He won't tell jokes. Maybe that's part of his training, or maybe he's holding back out of respect for the situation, the risks we're both taking. I know Marian would say I'm giving Eamonn too much credit, that I'm inventing his sense of humor without any evidence, but I'm certain of it.

We sit in the front room, behind a window that might be fitted with bulletproof glass. Light from a lamp runs across the floor-boards from me to him, like a cup of water knocked over at my feet. "Marian visited Niall in Castlerea on Saturday."

"Anything I should know?" he asks.

"He said the prisoners at Portlaoise are planning a hunger strike."

"Jesus, okay. That's really useful. Thank you, Tessa," says Eamonn. "Did Niall say when?"

"No," I say, alarmed over the unintended consequences of even discussing this, the chance of us kicking off a hunger strike.

"That's all right, these things take time," he says, and my heart drops at the thought of doing this for months, through the rest of the autumn, past Christmas, into the new year.

"How did Marian get Niall to talk?" asks Eamonn, and my face starts to flush. Part of his training must be working out when someone is lying.

"She could barely get him to stop talking," I say, shrugging. "They've been planning it for months. He was bursting to tell someone."

"But why tell her? I hadn't expected him to forgive her yet."

"It's Marian," I say. "She can talk her way out of anything. I forgave her, too."

Eamonn looks at me for a moment, turning this over, then nods. "Have you been back to Belfast?" he asks, and I shake my head. "Does your mother ever visit Belfast?"

"Yes, to see her siblings."

"She's not nervous?"

"No. I mean, she's nothing special, is she? There are plenty of other parents of informers walking around Belfast."

"Has anyone ever given her any trouble? Or asked her about you or Marian?"

"No, they either think we're dead, or they're our family, and they know they need to pretend we are," I say, trying to keep my voice level. "Why? Have you heard something about us?"

"No. Just tell her to mind herself on those visits," he says, and I nod, wondering what he's not telling me. "Do you still swim?" he asks.

"Sometimes," I say, and we talk for a while about the swimming rocks around Dublin.

"Do you want something to drink?" asks Eamonn. "A beer?"

"Are you allowed to drink?" I ask, and he nods.

"My cover job is still working in restaurants," he says, and I follow him toward the back of the house. We stand in the gleaming kitchen, under a row of strong track lights for cooking. Rain taps the windows, a light glows on the espresso machine. I sit on a stool at the kitchen island, running my hands over the veins in the fake marble. Eamonn levers off the caps on two bottles of Moretti, and hands one to me with a clean pint glass. I watch him tilt his own glass, pouring the beer. "There's a fair amount of drinking in the industry."

"Which one? Restaurants or the security service?"

"Both, actually," he says, lifting the glass to his mouth and swallowing. "I meant restaurants, though."

"So what's real?" I ask. "Do you have to drink for your cover story? Or did you actually want a beer?"

"I did, yes." He wipes his wet hands on his trousers, and I look away, lifting my drink. If we were in different circumstances, I'd enjoy glancing at Eamonn, watching how he moves and stands and talks, but I can't do that because we're the only people in this room, and he's nearly always looking back at me. This whole time, I've felt a growing frustration that I can't get a good look at him.

"Did you buy this beer? Or did someone else buy it for you?" I ask.

"I bought it."

I fold back the foil on my bottle. "I'd have thought someone else did the shopping for a safe house."

Eamonn looks amused. "No."

"For security reasons?" I ask, and Eamonn frowns. "No, so they don't buy the wrong brand of beer. I'd lose my head," he says, and I laugh. That was it, then. The first time he has tried to make me laugh.

He might do the shopping nearby. There's a Lidl on Stoneybatter Road, but I can't ask him where outright. I'd like to know, though. Instead, it's like Eamonn vanishes into thin air anytime he leaves this safe house. I've no idea where he goes, or what he does.

"What about the wheelie bins? Who takes those out?" I ask. "Is that also your job?"

"Sometimes," he says. I'm nervous, the glass turning damp from the heat of my hand. I can't even imagine how to ever ask him the question. Will you betray your country, Eamonn, will you give up your entire identity, will you work for the IRA? It's all right, though, for now. The process has begun, at least.

"Tell me about working at the *Irish Observer*," he says. "When did you start?"

"Two years ago."

Eamonn listens as I describe my work, and I'd forgotten about the depth of his attention, about this huge sympathy coming from him in my direction. I used to feel it whenever we met on the beach at Ardglass, this tolerance.

It's working, I think, crossing my legs on the kitchen stool. This is working. I barely even have to try. Both of us need the other to like us, to trust us, and the strange thing is that the trust already exists. I wonder if it has confused him, too, this affinity between us, if he'd expected to have to work harder.

We chat about Dublin, and the Temple Bar food market. "It's no St. George's, though," I say. "I miss the dulse from St. George's."

"Nowhere else comes close," says Eamonn.

"You visit it?"

"Of course," he says, and it's strange to think we might have run into each other. I'd never once imagined bumping into Eamonn when I was in the North. Or here, in Dublin.

"Is that not a security risk?" I ask, and for a second a look of discomfort passes over his face, vanishing before I can decipher it.

"No more than most places," he says, and starts to tell me about visiting the night markets when he was working in Hong Kong.

Eamonn walked me to the door last time, and already I'm wondering if eventually I might hug him goodbye when I leave, in a casual way. That's a thing people do after seeing each other, I think. I wouldn't need to make a habit of it. Even if I only did it once, at least then I'd know what it's like to embrace him. The idea of not knowing, for the rest of my life, seems sad and impossible.

"Have you been in Belfast this whole time?" I ask, and he nods. "Is it like an army deployment, though? Do you get breaks to go home?"

"Home?"

"I don't know. London?"

"Belfast is my home."

I never knew if he was telling the truth or not, about being from Strabane. He fit, on the beach in Northern Ireland, he seemed at home, but maybe it was a pretense, maybe he was actually born somewhere in England. "Is this your real voice?" I ask, and he laughs.

"Do you know how hard it is to fake a Northern Irish accent? Even actors can't do it."

"And you're not an actor?" I ask slowly.

He takes a swallow of his beer, and I watch the bubbles sliding behind the glass. "No, Tessa. I'm not."

Twenty

WHEN I ARRIVE AT the Gravediggers the next morning, Royce is sitting at the same table in the back with a fry-up. "I hope you're not here to disappoint me again," he says.

"Do you want to know something? MI5 doesn't threaten its informers. It doesn't turn up at their homes, or kick their ribs in."

"Don't be stupid," says Royce. "Of course they do. That just didn't happen to be their approach with you."

"You want to run informers on the British, but you're doing this wrong. No one will do good work for you if this is how you act. They'll be too scared to think straight."

"Are you too scared to think straight?"

"No, but I'm special, remember?" Under the table, I press my knees together to stop myself from shaking. Royce dabs brown sauce onto the edge of his plate. "So how do the British run their informers?" he asks.

"They treat it like a relationship."

He pauses with his fork in the air. "A relationship? You told me you weren't riding him."

"For god's sake," I say. "I meant their handlers take an interest, they ask after your job, your family. They act like a friend."

"That sounds manipulative."

"It works."

"So, Tessa," says Royce. "Tell me about your job."

"I work for a newspaper. I'm a subeditor."

"How much do you make? Did you make more as an informer or less?"

"I told you, they never paid me. Does that make you hate me less?" I ask.

"Not really. Are the hours hard on your son? Children need their mammies at his age," he says, and I force myself not to flinch.

"Did your parents neglect you?" I ask.

"No, not at all."

"And look at you now."

Royce smirks. "Have you thought much about your future yet, Tessa?"

"Sorry?"

"When this is done, you know, we'll pardon you. You'll be free to move home."

"I live here now."

Royce considers me across the table, his knife and fork resting in his hands. "A lot of the other prisoners in Portlaoise did AA," he says. "When you give up alcohol, you have to avoid certain things that you associate with drinking. People, places, things. You miss those more than the alcohol, apparently. What are your people, places, and things, Tessa?"

"I don't know what you mean."

"Of course you do. A certain song, maybe, that you have trouble listening to?"

I dig my fingers into my palms, shaking my head. He says, "I don't believe you. What reminds you of home?"

Sheep, I think. I miss watching the sheep in the field behind my house in Greyabbey. I miss how steam rose from our laundry vent when I'd a load of washing on, I miss hearing the sound of my neighbors dragging their bins out to the road at night, I miss the poppadoms from the Indian restaurant in the village, and drinking a gin and tonic during the interval of a play at the MAC theater, and spending Christmas Eve in a house in west Belfast crammed with my aunts and uncles and cousins. I miss the other staff at Broadcasting House. Often, working at the BBC, I felt like I was at the very center of the world.

"What's his name, by the way? Your handler."

"I'm not telling you that."

"But you met again yesterday?"

"Yes." I tell Royce about our conversation. "And we drank together, he gave me a beer. So he's not sober, and he doesn't have a drink problem." I could be wrong. Maybe Eamonn had another ten beers after I left yesterday, but I'd doubt it.

"Okay," says Royce. "Where does he live?"

"I don't know. Somewhere in Belfast."

"Get him to invite you to his house," says Royce, and I laugh.

"You're serious?"

"Come on, Tessa. You can do better than this," says Royce, and the strength drains from my legs.

"I told you, I can't rush it."

"Well, you need to," says Royce, stabbing a sausage with his fork.

"Do you want Marian's house?" I ask. She'd mentioned offering it to him.

"Sorry?"

"There's a mortgage on it, but you'd make a profit anyway," I say, and Royce stares at me over his plate.

"How much profit?" he asks.

"Two hundred thousand euro, about. Maybe more, in this market."

Royce looks at me for a long time. "Is that all you think you're worth?" he says, and frustrated tears rise to my eyes. I thought I'd found a solution, a way out for me, for Eamonn.

"How much, then? How much to leave me alone?"

"Do you think I care about money, Tessa?"

"Yes. I know from Marian how hard it is for you to fundraise." I stare out the fogged window, thinking. "Here, do you want to know something? My mam used to work as a cleaner for this couple in Bangor, the Dunlops. They're art collectors. They own a painting by Agnes Martin."

Royce looks at me blankly. "Never heard of her," he says.

"The painting is worth ten million euro." Royce doesn't believe me. He doesn't believe a painting by a woman could be worth that much. "It's called *The Islands*. Look up the valuation."

Royce reaches into his pocket and hands me a pen. "Write down that name."

I write down *The Islands*, Agnes Martin, and push the napkin toward him. "Grand," says Royce, leaning back from the table and slapping his hands on his thighs, like I'm a waitress and he has just finished his meal.

I stand to leave, then stop myself. "Why did you say that I need to rush? What's the hurry?"

"We're in talks with the government."

"What is this, the seventh time? Nothing ever comes of it."

Royce balls up his napkin and throws it onto the table. "This time's different."

"How? How is it different?"

"The prime minister," he says.

"What are you talking about? Rebecca Main's a hard-liner."

I met Rebecca Main years ago, when she was interviewed on our program at the BBC. I remember the excitement in the building when she arrived at Broadcasting House. She was the justice minister back then, and already every speech she gave was drawing crowds. She came to the BBC with a team of close-protection officers, wearing a bulletproof vest under her suit. "She built her entire career around being hard on national security."

"You studied politics, Tessa. You tell me why Rebecca chose to present herself that way."

"Are you joking me?"

"This was always her endgame," he says. "She wants peace. All that hard-liner shite was for show."

Something is toppling through me. Rebecca Main pretended to be a war hawk, since that was the only way she could start negotiations with the IRA, or ever convince the government and public to accept a peace deal. She had to seem tough. I want to start laughing. "God almighty. What a con."

"I know. We couldn't have planned it better ourselves, to be honest with you," says Royce. "She's ready to draw up a peace deal as soon as we call a ceasefire."

Dizziness sweeps through me. "So call a ceasefire."

"We can't, not unless the loyalists call one first. Otherwise they'll use that time to go on a rampage."

"Then tell the loyalists to call a ceasefire."

"They won't unless we call one first."

I grip the edge of the table. "Are you hearing yourself? What's your plan, then? This just goes on forever?"

"The loyalists will surrender."

"They'll be out saying the same thing about you. Jesus, you're like children."

Royce shrugs. From the corner of my eye, I can see the fog blowing at the pub window. Something has been nagging at me, something I've been trying to ignore, to stop it from complicating matters, but then Royce wipes a little spill of coffee from the table and the thought drops into my head fully formed. He wasn't a cruel child.

"You'd a pet rabbit," I say, before I can stop myself, and Royce shoves his plate hard across the table. "What was its name?"

"Piss off, Tessa. Whatever you're trying to do, piss off."

"I'm not trying to do anything, I just can't remember its name."

If I'd learned now that Royce had a pet as a child, I'd be terrified for the creature. But it was grand. He built the rabbit a hutch in their back garden, and an open run. He's not a sociopath. However he is now, he wasn't born like this.

Royce stares past me, and I say, "What happened to you? Was it just being bullied at school?"

His eyes have gone blank. "We're done here," he says.

I stand to leave. As I'm pulling on my bag, Royce watches me, with his arms folded over his chest and his jaw tight. "You missed out, Tessa. You were meant to join the IRA," he says. "It's in your blood."

"What, because of my sister?"

"No, Tessa. Because of your mother."

Twenty-One

ON THE BUS FROM GLASNEVIN to my office, I sit with my hands in my lap, ignoring the roads flashing past the windows, staring straight ahead at a safety poster that says IF YOU SEE SOMETHING, SAY SOMETHING.

My mam likes Rod Stewart. She fancies Michael Caine and your man off *Holby City*. She votes Soc Dem. She likes prosecco and margaritas, and her eyes swim when she laughs. She gives a standing ovation at most concerts and at every single musical, even the worst ones. She will often send me a picture of, say, a wooden cutting board or a pair of sandals, with absolutely no explanation. She distrusts therapy, open-water swimming, and all triathletes. She works as a dog-walker, and when people ask if she makes enough to live on, which they always do, she says, "Well, I'm not troubling the *Sunday Times* rich list."

She has a glamour, like her sisters, like other women from west Belfast, that has nothing to do with clothes or money. They know how to dance, how to tell a story, how to have you wheezing with laughter. You want to be near them.

What else do I know about her? I know that her first memory is of walking up outdoor stairs at a holiday house by the beach in Bundoran, when she must have been only about two years old. She remembered the tar-paper steps burning under her feet.

But I've no idea what she thought about, during all the years she worked as a housekeeper. I don't know where her mind went in those large empty rooms while she mopped the floor or scrubbed stains from the tiles. I've no clue what she prays about at church. I don't know if she's asking for forgiveness, if that's why she goes to mass, week after week after week.

I'm an adult, but the word I hold for her in my head is mam, not her name. Her name is Catherine. My mam's name is Catherine.

MAM IS STAYING OVER at Marian's house to help with the baby while Seb's away filming. When I step inside after work, Marian is on her sofa holding Saoirse, and mam is in the kitchen rinsing the baby's bottles. "Are you here for dinner?" says mam. "I made a fish pie. Where's Finn?"

"Does Marian know? Did you tell Marian and not me?"

Mam sighs, and says, "Oh, for god's sake."

"Excuse me?" I ask, but she's already turning away from me, sliding the clean bottles onto the draining rack.

"Tessa?" Marian calls through the open doorway, and I move into the front room with mam following me. "Is Finn here?"

"No, he's on a playdate at Caroline's."

"At six o'clock? What's going on?" says Marian, tucking her chin to check Saoirse, asleep at her shoulder, in a small green suit patterned with rabbits.

"Mam was in the IRA."

Marian laughs. "Sure."

Carefully, mam says, "No, I was never in the IRA."

"Obviously," says Marian, adjusting the muslin cloth under Saoirse.

"Not officially," says mam, and slowly Marian lifts her head. "But when I was a teenager, I did lend them a hand."

The room rings with silence. Marian is watching mam with an amused, patient expression, like she's waiting for the end of a joke.

"Why can I not just have a normal family?" I say.

"You don't mean that, Tessa," says mam.

"Of course I do. I wish we had another sibling so I wouldn't be the only adult in this room who was never a terrorist."

Marian stares into the middle distance, not hearing me. "Lend them a hand?" she asks mam, her voice deadly. "How did you lend them a hand?"

"The lads had trouble at the security checkpoints, so some of us helped. The soldiers never thought to look inside our shoes, they were too busy searching the lads."

"Stop calling them that," I hiss. "Stop making them sound harmless."

"I never said they were harmless," says mam. "But they were my friends, back then."

"Good," I say. "Grand. Your friends ordered us to be killed for informing."

"No, they didn't," says mam. "That was the younger generation coming up. They're different."

The air in the room has hardened. I remember playing dress-up in mam's closet, trying on a silver lamé skirt, a sailor-collar dress, a pair of velvet platform heels. I picture mam, years before, balancing on those heels, drinking a Babycham at the Odeon or the Mint, then walking on them past an army roadblock, nodding at the soldiers.

"What was inside?" I ask, my voice faint.

"Messages," she says. "Or fake papers, for anyone skipping town."

"Did our father know?" asks Marian.

"That's not why he left, Marian."

"But he knew?" she asks, and mam nods. Our father lives with his second wife and teenage sons in Twickenham, outside London. For our entire lives, he has allowed us to take mam's side against him, and he never told us her secret, which would mean more if he didn't act like he couldn't be bothered with any of us.

"You let me apologize to you," says Marian. "For joining the IRA. You stood there and let me apologize over and over."

"For your own sake," says mam. "You needed to apologize. Hearing about me wouldn't have helped."

"But you could have saved me from all of it, you could have stopped me from joining in the first place."

"I thought I had. As far as I knew, you were a paramedic all those years. I never told you because I didn't want you two thinking you came from a republican family. You know what that does, it's a self-fulfilling prophecy," says mam. "Things were different for us. You weren't even meant to tell your children if you'd been married before, or had a miscarriage. I thought I was doing the right thing for you girls."

"Get out," says Marian.

"I'll take the washing down first," says mam, and Marian snorts.

"Is this a joke?" she says.

"Does it make you feel any better?" I ask once mam has stepped outside, and Marian looks at me like I'm mad. "Can you forgive yourself now? Maybe that's why you joined. It was in your blood."

"You don't inherit terrorism," she snaps. "It's not hay fever."

We did inherit mam's hay fever, though. Her eyes, her features. When Marian starts to cry, it's mam's mouth she's covering under her hand.

During my pregnancy, I read that a female fetus develops eggs in utero, at around four months. So thirty-six years ago, when mam was pregnant with me, the egg that would become Finn was already inside my body, inside hers, like a set of nesting dolls.

And sixty-one years ago, when my granny was pregnant with mam, inside mam was the egg that became me. My first cell was there, in Belfast, inside mam, inside my granny, in 1968.

The Troubles were beginning in 1968. Maybe Royce was right, who knows what we've inherited.

Before leaving, I find mam on the back patio taking down the clean washing. "Are you happy, Tessa?" she says and sighs. "Was that what you wanted to happen? You should have let me tell Marian."

"I thought she already knew, I thought the two of you had been keeping it a secret from me," I say. "But you're right. I'm sorry."

Mam folds a striped bedsheet. I wait. "It's your turn now, mam."

"You'll not be getting an apology from me."

I roll my eyes toward the sky. "Oh, for god's sake. Don't make this worse."

"I was seventeen years old, Tessa. It was before you were even born."

"Do you not regret joining?"

"No, I regret quitting," she says, and the hairs stand on my arms. "I never should have left. If everyone like me had stayed, we would have won, we would have ended the thing, and you girls would have been saved from all of this."

"You should have told us."

"You never asked, Tessa. And you never asked your sister, either.

You're so stubborn, you just go around assuming other people think the same way as you do, or else they're wrong."

I rear back. "So Marian lying to me was my fault?"

"I didn't say that. But you decide who you think people are, and ignore anything that doesn't fit."

"Was our father in the IRA?" I ask. I've never considered that possibility before, not once. He left Belfast when I was two and Marian was an infant. Maybe he'd gone on the run.

Mam lets out a laugh. "Your father could never keep his mouth shut. When he was in school, he was sent out of the classroom every single day for talking. Those lads wouldn't have touched him with a barge pole."

"So when he left—"

"He was just unhappy, Tessa. I'm sorry there's not more to it."

"No, that's fine." The last thing we need is to find out our father was on the IRA army council. And yet. I never used to think much about our father, but since having Finn I can sometimes feel this bewilderment tugging at me. How did he not miss us? Ten minutes after Finn falls asleep, I'm back in the doorway to check on him. If our father had left Belfast because he'd been in trouble, if he'd left to keep us safe, that I could understand.

Behind mam, the white bedsheets ripple on the line. I can hear the sounds of other families down the terrace, plates rattling in sinks, children playing. "How did you find out?" asks mam.

"Eoin Royce told me."

"Wee bastard," she mutters. "And you waited how long to ask me?"

"No, he told me today, mam. I saw him this morning," I say, and confusion slips over her face. "Eoin Royce came to see me. The IRA told me to pretend to be an informer again. They told me to meet with Eamonn, so I can turn him."

"Mother of god." She stands for a moment with her hands on her hips. "So Eamonn thinks you're working for MI5. And Eoin Royce thinks you're working for the IRA."

"Yes."

"Whose side are you actually on?" she asks.

"Finn's."

Twenty-Two

FINN SHOUTS FOR ME in the night. When I come into his room, he is bent over the bed, being sick onto his duvet. "It's okay," I say, "it's okay, it's all right," while taking off his pajamas and guiding him into the bathroom. I rinse him off in the shower, wrap him in a clean towel, and hurry downstairs to pour him a glass of water. He's half asleep, too tired to drink the water, falling into bed the second I get clean sheets over the mattress.

When he wakes again coughing, I give him water and rub his back. He's feverish, his chest and the soles of his feet like hot sand. Tomorrow he will need to stay home from playschool. I won't be able to work, or meet with Eamonn, or Royce. A pause, one day with nothing else in it.

In the morning, I try to take Finn's temperature, but he dislikes all thermometers, even the one that only hovers at the forehead. "Look, it won't touch you, okay? It's not even touching you," I say. The display shows a high fever, and I wonder how many degrees to add since he was moving.

I am stabbing open the foil on a bottle of Pedialyte when mam calls me, saying that Marian still won't speak to her. "Maybe," I say, "you should try apologizing."

We read books, watch *Bluey*, build Legos. Finn is sick another three times, always to the side or below the bowl I hold out for him. I am crouched on my knees, spraying cleaning fluid on the floor, when I realize I've not checked the burner phone today. I won't know if Royce has tried to contact me, but I can't leave Finn, I can't walk around the corner to the hiding place. Mam would come over to help me, but she'd want to talk about her past, and I'm not able for that yet.

I finish cleaning the floor, scrub my hands, and return to the sofa to read a picture book to Finn. I can hear my own voice, as if it's coming from very far away. "'And the tiger drank all the milk in the milk jug and all the tea in the teapot.'"

A pressure builds in my skull. I can't live like this, with Royce always at my back. "'And then he looked round the kitchen to see what else he could find.'" I hold my hand to Finn's forehead. He's still burning. "'He ate all the supper that was cooking in the saucepans and all the food in the fridge, and all the packets and tins in the cupboard.'"

That evening, Finn loses his voice. He tries to speak and fails, looking confused, then tries again. I look down at him, small and suddenly, abruptly mute.

"You're only hoarse from coughing," I say, "don't worry," and fix some warm chamomile tea with honey for him. Of all the things I check, his voice has never been one of them. It has never occurred to me as something to protect, the way I protect the rest of him. I hardly even understand the mechanics, the vibrations in his throat that let him speak.

I don't sleep, not really. I am waking in the night, pulling dirty sheets off the mattress, holding Finn in the shower, finding the cleaning spray. By Thursday night, I am exhausted. Dark stains spread under my eyes, and at the top of the stairs I feel myself wobble, like I'm about to pitch down the steps.

I kneel in front of the washing machine, bundling in clumps of crumpled, mucky clothes that will come out of the dryer soft and fresh. I twist the dial, thinking, When will that happen for me? I've been trying for so long, but every bit of me is as creased and stained as ever. When will I come out clean?

Twenty-Three

ON FRIDAY EVENING, Tom comes to collect Finn for the weekend. The thought of saying goodbye to him makes my chest ache. This is always the worst part, right before Tom picks him up. It's easier once Finn has actually left. At least then the clock is moving in the right direction, toward a reunion instead of a separation.

Finn starts working on a jigsaw puzzle. I look at the gaps in the puzzle, thinking, any minute now, and then Tom is ringing the bell and Finn is leaping to his feet. The remaining jigsaw pieces lie scattered on the rug, and I step over them to open the door.

After Tom tosses our son in the air a couple of times, I hand Finn a tote bag. "You can choose your favorite toys to bring for the weekend, okay?" I say, and he darts up the stairs toward his room. I ask Tom if he wants a coffee for the drive, and he says, "That'd be deadly, thanks."

In the kitchen, I take down a mug for Tom. "Do you've any plans for the weekend?" he asks.

"Not really, no," I say. "Relax, chill out a bit."

Tom looks at me, nodding slowly. "Right, well, enjoy that." I tell

Tom about Finn's flu this week and ask him to call me if the fever comes back. Tom says, "He's going to be fine, Tessa."

Finn skips into the room. "What are you talking about with dada?"

"Nothing," I chirp, because Finn doesn't need to worry about fevers, I do that for him, we both do. Tom pretends to be nonchalant, but I've seen him slide across a room to catch Finn in midair, I've seen him shove a pot of boiling water out of reach on the cooker. Tom just hides his vigilance better than I do.

"I need another bag," says Finn, before trotting back upstairs to gather more toys. Tom and I sit with a calendar, talking about different weekends. I mention my coworker's wedding in November, and Tom says, "I can't take Finn then, we're going to San Sebastián for Briony's birthday."

"That's fine, I'll ask mam or Marian to mind him."

"No. I've told you, I don't want Finn staying over at Marian's house," he says.

"She's his aunt, Tom." Even in the beginning, Tom and Marian never got on. Marian thought he was boring, and he thought she was shallow. Which she wasn't, as it happens, she was just hiding the things she cared deeply about.

"Why is she even in your life?" Tom asks.

I feel myself bristling. "She's my sister. I don't have a choice."

"Of course you do," he says, "and you choose your mad sister, always. When are you going to cop on?"

"What are you talking about?"

Tom gestures around the room. "Why are we here, Tessa? Why does my son live a hundred miles away from me? Because your sister asked you to inform, and for some reason you decided that was a good idea. You lost your home, your job, you almost died. She wrecked your life, Tessa."

"My life's grand, actually. It's fucking lovely."

Tom screws his finger into the side of his head. "I'm just asking you to think for once. She's a terrorist, Tessa," he says, and I feel something crack apart, like pack ice. "You should never have agreed to help her."

"Right, and where were you, Tom? Where were you back then? Finn was six months old, you should have been there looking after us."

Tom goes still. "Tessa, you told me to move out. You're the one who wanted to separate."

"Because you cheated on me," I say, outrage slamming through me. "I was pregnant, Tom. How did that even work? You'd come to a scan with me and then go ride someone else?"

Tom frowns. "What's going on here? We've already had this conversation a thousand times, so what are you actually angry about?"

"You didn't help me," I say. "Even if we weren't a couple anymore, I was still Finn's mother, and I was completely on my own."

Tom grips his hair in his hands. "How was I supposed to protect you? You didn't even tell me anything." He draws his hands down, cupping them over his mouth, shaking his head. "No. No, Tessa. Marian was a terrorist, and you forgave her. You could have forgiven me, too, you just didn't want to. But Marian snaps her fingers, and for some reason you come running."

"Guess what, Tom? We're divorced. You don't get to tell me what to do. You don't get a look in, okay?"

"I do if it's hurting my son."

I reel back, like he has thrown cold water on me. "You think I'm hurting him?"

"Finn was in the house when they came for you. Do you ever think about what could have happened to him? Because I do." Tom shakes his head. "I don't want Finn seeing Marian. Enough, Tessa."

"He loves her."

"Right," says Tom, pointing at me, "and when are you going to tell him? When are you going to tell him his auntie was a terrorist? Or do you want me to tell him?"

"Don't threaten me. Do you know how easy it would have been for me to get full custody?"

"Who would that have helped?" asks Tom. "Would it have helped Finn?"

"Exactly," I say, my voice rising. "That's why I didn't do it, because Finn needs his whole family, he needs as many people who love him as he can get. Marian's his family."

Tom clasps his hands together, like he's praying. "If our positions were reversed, if my brother were some IRA murderer, you wouldn't let Finn within a mile of him. You'd tear strips off me if I even suggested it."

He's right. We both know he's right.

"She's not a murderer."

"Grow up, Tessa. It's been three years, when are you going to wise up?"

"I'm—"

"Mama," shouts Finn from upstairs, and we both go quiet. Tom spreads his hands on the table, dropping his head, and I look at him for a second, then wheel out of the kitchen.

"What is it, sunshine?"

Finn is holding his elephant and his rabbit. "Can I bring both?"

"Of course," I say, kneeling near him at the top of the stairs. My heart is still pounding from the argument, and I can feel the flush on my cheeks. Tom is raging with me, without even knowing about the mess I'm involved in now. I pull Finn against me, wrapping my arms tightly around him.

When we return downstairs, Tom is waiting at the bottom of the steps, and he smiles, clapping his hands. "You ready to go?"

Neither of us looks at each other, keeping our eyes on Finn. I walk them outside and strap Finn into his car seat while Tom loads the bags in the boot. Finn reaches around the straps to give me a hug. "Did you pack bunny?" he asks.

"Of course," I say, trying to keep my voice bright. "I love you." Saying goodbye to him makes something drain from my body, leaving me lightheaded. I can't do this, I think, but then I am closing his door and stepping back onto the footpath. I can see the shape of Finn's car seat through the back windscreen, and then the car turns, and I go back inside and slam the bathroom door over and over again until it nearly falls off the hinges.

At some point while slamming the door, the anger ebbs enough for me to understand what I'm at here. Tom would be horrified if he could see me, but then, he has always been better at compartmentalizing, controlling the places his mind goes. He will be grand by now, he won't even be thinking about our argument, while I'm here breaking my own house. I slam the door one last time, though my heart's not in it anymore.

After we decided to separate, Tom and I sat for hours in a booth at the Barking Dog in Belfast, setting out our rules. We didn't even use a solicitor, we worked out the split on a piece of paper at the restaurant table, with our bank balance and mortgage up on our phones. It didn't take long, since we'd barely any money between us.

We talked about how we would be respectful. Always come into the other's house at handoff, no shoving Finn out the door between us. Always have a bit of a chat. Never make him think he can't have both of us at his school concerts, his birthdays. Tom would have Sundays to start, while Finn was nursing, and then two weekends a month, and a week during summer holidays and half-term breaks. I'd have Finn for Christmas and Tom would get New Year's, which he was delighted about, since he'd never have to attend a New Year's party again. We talked easily, sensibly. I held my hands on my stomach, feeling the baby kick. We were going to be such good parents.

Twenty-Four

"DID YOU GET HERE SAFELY?" asks Eamonn as I step inside the safe house in Stoneybatter.

"No one followed me."

I lift a hand to push the hair back from my face. I have on jeans and a soft mohair sweater, like this is a normal Sunday. In the kitchen Eamonn presses coffee into the machine. I turn to take down cups for us, starting with the least likely cabinet, so I've an excuse to open every single one. I don't know what I expect to find. A recording device, a gun. Instead I find stacks of cheap ceramic plates, bowls, glasses, and the set of plain white cups with saucers. I set two on the counter. "Milk?" I ask, and Eamonn nods. I consider the open fridge, then say, "You need some vegetables in here."

"Sorry?"

"It's too clean," I say. "It's not believable. You need some vegetables in here that are about to go off."

"My fridge at home is this clean," says Eamonn.

"Right, but you don't cook, do you? This person would cook. They've a kitchen full of cookery gear."

"I'll pass that along," says Eamonn, and we carry our cups into the front room. "What makes you think I don't cook?" he asks, and I shrug. "Do you?" I ask.

"No."

"Marian visited Niall again this weekend," I say. "He said they're working out the order for the hunger strike. They're deciding which prisoner will start first."

"How many prisoners?" asks Eamonn.

"Seven."

"Ask Marian to try to find out their names," he says, and I nod.

"How many other informers do you have?" I ask, since Eamonn might answer the question eventually. "Do you have any loyalist informers?"

He doesn't answer. I wouldn't envy them. The loyalist paramilitaries are brutal. They recently set a restaurant on fire, and then shot the guests as they ran outside. "Tell me what else you're doing to stop the conflict."

"I can't," says Eamonn, but I need to stay longer with him, I need to keep him talking. And I have time, since Finn is with Tom this weekend. Eamonn doesn't seem in any rush to leave, either. I drink my coffee while he asks me questions about the archive at our newspaper. Eamonn looks relaxed, sitting across the low table from me. "Your back's to the door," I say, and he frowns. "I'd think you'd always want to face the door."

Calmly, he says, "If someone wants to shoot me, it won't really matter which way I'm facing."

"Do you carry a gun?"

Eamonn hesitates, and I wonder if I've already gone too far, if I'm being too obvious. "Would that make you uncomfortable?" he asks.

"It's not something I generally want to be around, no."

"You never considered getting one?" he asks, and I shake my head, which is true. I've spent my whole life despising guns, I'm not thick enough to think owning one now would keep me safe. I have been looking into adopting a German shepherd, though, or a Rottweiler. Rottweilers were bred as butchers' dogs, and I don't know why that makes them seem even more frightening.

"Do you feel safe living here?" asks Eamonn.

"Yes," I lie.

"But you've extra locks on your front door."

I can feel my face turning hot. "My mind tends to go toward the worst outcome. Doesn't yours?"

"Yes." Above us, a simple pendant lamp hangs from the ceiling, and I wonder if a listening device is hidden inside it.

"Are you lonely?" I ask, after a moment. "Do you've any friends in Belfast?"

He smiles. "Yes, I've friends."

"But they don't know the truth about you."

"Neither do yours here," says Eamonn. "None of them know what happened to you and your sister. They don't even know your real name. Does that bother you?"

"Yes. I don't like lying to people."

He pushes his empty cup across the coffee table and props his elbows on his chair. "But you think I do?"

"I don't know. Why else would you choose to live like this?"

"You make it sound so deliberate," says Eamonn. "I barely knew what this job would mean when I applied. I was young." He talks easily, his gaze resting lightly on my face, but I don't know if he's telling the truth. It's what he would say if he wanted to seem ordinary, if he wanted to seem like a normal person.

His face is so familiar. His sharp nose, his dented bottom lip. I look at the welt under his eye, the small scar, and wonder if he was burned while working in the security service, or before he joined.

Eamonn shifts his weight in the chair, leaning back. Outside, rain clouds are sweeping in from the coast, stacking over the city. "Do you've any hobbies?" I ask, and he laughs. "What? It's not fair, you know everything about my life and I know nothing about yours."

"Knitting," he says.

"Catch yourself on."

Eamonn tells me that he went to a fairly rough secondary school. "I started a knitting club, and twenty other lads joined. The knitting club had a wait list," he says, which makes sense, since Eamonn has the sort of confidence that makes other people lose the absolute run of themselves.

We stay together, talking, for the next hour. "Can I've a beer?" I ask, and he nods. Eamonn follows me down the hall, and I turn away from him to reach into the fridge. The space between my shoulder blades tingles, and I have the strongest sense that he's about to reach out and put his hand on my back. "Do you want one?" I ask, and he nods. I pull the cap off, passing him the bottle. I can see my handprint on the condensation on the bottle, and then he wraps his own hand over the mark, and pours.

That evening, I take myself for a swim at the Forty Foot. From the rock, I can see the sailboat masts jostling together in Dún Laoghaire harbor. Who are all these people with sailboats, I wonder. Do they not have jobs? Or children? I reach up to tug the elastic from my hair and walk to the rock's edge. The horizon line is only three miles away. It seems farther, a huge distance, but I could run there in about half an hour.

I strip to my swimsuit, ignoring the dents left behind on my thighs from the bruises. Eamonn will be back in Belfast by now. I picture him in his flat, ordering a takeaway, turning on the news, sitting with one arm resting along the top of the sofa.

He might live in the cathedral quarter, or along the harbor, or in south Belfast. It doesn't really matter. I already know how stepping into his flat would feel. It would feel spacious and neutral, like him.

I would bet anything that his flat doesn't have curtains on the windows. That he has some specific way of making espresso, with a machine or on the stove. That he has an expensive mattress. That he has tall shelves of books, and more books stacked on tables and by the bed.

Standing on the rock, I slowly turn my head, so the dry end of my ponytail brushes back and forth over my bare back. Chills spread down my spine, toward the low scoop in my swimsuit. It's fully autumn now, I'll need a wetsuit soon. Ahead of me, the late evening sunlight slants onto the sea from between splits in the clouds. I can hear the wind whistling in the rolled masts of the sailboats, an eerie, haunting sound.

I lower myself down the rock steps into the water, feeling the cold foam rushing around my ankles, and dive under a wave, surfacing with my wet hair smoothed down my head. I tread water, facing out toward the horizon. The next wave hasn't started to break yet, and I let the swell lift me. Being in the water is gathering my attention from all the places it has scattered today. This tide is being dragged by the moon, and when I let a wave lift me, I'm actually letting the moon lift me, from far in space, feeling its power across all those thousands of miles. What is Eamonn thinking about right now, I wonder. I lick the corner of my mouth and taste salt.

Twenty-Five

I'M HAVING TROUBLE focusing at work. Outside, across Kildare Street, the long shadows of trees cross the parliament courtyard, ticking over the cobblestones like clock hands. The burner phone sits in my bag under the desk. When I finally checked the hiding place after Finn's illness, there were several furious messages on it from Royce, asking where I was. From now on, he said, I'm to carry it with me, hidden inside the lining of my bag.

At five, I collect Finn from playschool and walk to Marian's house. "Thank god," she says, when we arrive. She has on a navy pinafore, her hair tied back in a braid. "I need to get out of this house. Are you hungry?"

We walk to a quiet Japanese restaurant on Clanbrassil Street. Saoirse sits in a high chair, mashing rice in her fists. Finn finishes his tempura in about one minute, and trots over to sit on a stool at the empty bar, watching a rugby match on the television.

Finn seemed cheerful when his father dropped him off after the weekend. Tom hasn't said anything about Marian to Finn, I don't think, he hasn't overheard Tom and Briony talking about how I'm a melter, how my sister's mad. Not yet anyway, but Tom's threat of telling Finn about Marian keeps nudging at me. Tom wouldn't be delicate, he wouldn't consider how Finn might take the information.

While Finn watches the rugby, Marian and I sit together, eating sushi and drinking sake, talking about Eamonn. "I don't know how you ever fancied him," says Marian. "He looks like a banker."

I consider this, while levering my chopsticks. Not a banker, he's too angular, too precise. He looks clean, always. And convincing, fully in his body. I lift my head, aware of Marian watching me. She considers my expression, then slowly exhales and says, "No, Tessa. No."

"What?"

"You're smarter than this."

I shrug. "It's not like I'm going to do anything."

"Over the past few years," says Marian, "have you missed him?"

"No, I didn't miss him." But if I had been in a restaurant, for example, and someone had told me Eamonn was there, too, I wouldn't have been able to leave without seeing him. I would have needed to be dragged away.

"How are things with mam?" I ask, to distract her. "Are you speaking to her?"

"She hasn't even apologized," says Marian. "Can you credit it?"

"Her generation's different," I say, and Marian rolls her eyes. She says, "Do you know why she got involved?"

"No, she won't tell me. But she was seventeen, that was the year loyalists bombed the Mint. She must have been terrified."

Marian says, "Why aren't you angry with her? You were so angry with me."

"Finn's four years old. Do you want me to tell him he can't see his granny anymore?"

"You did that to me."

"For a few weeks, Marian. And Finn was too little to know the difference." I look across the restaurant to Finn, his small feet hooked under him. On the television above the bar, the match is at halftime. A news clip shows the British prime minister reading a statement outside Downing Street, praising the resilience of the country during the cost-of-living crisis. "Wagon," says Marian.

"Do you want to hear something mad? Royce said Rebecca Main's not actually a hard-liner. All that carry-on was only to get herself elected. He said she wants a peace deal."

Marian's eyes widen, and I say, "Don't hold your breath. I'm sure someone will find a way to wreck it."

Marian frowns, dredging her roll in soy sauce. "How's it going with Eamonn anyway?" she asks.

"I still can't tell if he's committed to MI5 or not."

"Your way's not working, then. It's time to blackmail him," says Marian. "Find some kompromat, threaten to tell his wife."

Cold needles prickle my skin. "Eamonn's not married."

"How the hell would you know?" says Marian.

"He's not married," I repeat. "He doesn't have children, either, I'd know. And threaten to tell her what anyway?"

"You want to sleep with him, don't you?"

"Not like that. Jesus, Marian." I chew on the end of my chopstick. "Maybe he was telling the truth about being at the farmhouse."

"Oh, god," says Marian. "You believe him now? Eamonn's lying. You only want to believe that because it makes you feel better about wanting to ride him."

"Come here to me, Marian. Am I that thick?"

"You tell me. Why do you fancy him?" she asks.

"It doesn't matter," I say, reaching for the dish of ginger slices.

"Why on earth would you trust him?" she asks. "Do you think he loves you?"

"Jesus, I haven't completely lost the plot," I say.

"Good, you were starting to worry me there. Just mind yourself around him. Okay?" Marian says, considering me. "They tell Eamonn what to say to you. You know that, right? The security service trained him for this."

I feel my nose wrinkle. "You think Eamonn practices talking to me?"

"Listening, probably," she says. "They will make him practice listening."

I think about the quality of Eamonn's attention, the dense weight of it. I'd thought that was part of his character, his personality, not a skill he'd learned. Wouldn't I know, if that was something he'd been taught? I'd see the cracks, the gaps in his patience.

"Have you ever thought about his other informers, Tessa?" Marian asks. "How do you think they feel about Eamonn? Do you think he acts this way with them, too? Or do you think it's only with you?"

I fold back the cuffs of my shirt, avoiding her eyes. I feel, childishly, on the verge of tears. "Is it Stockholm syndrome?" she asks. "Do you think fancying him will help you get out of this?"

"No." If anything, it's the opposite. I already know that fancying Eamonn makes this situation more dangerous for me.

"Do you want to be with him? Do you want to introduce him to Finn?" she asks, and I shake my head. "Of course not."

"So what do you want, Tessa?"

I don't answer. The truth is that I want to spend thirty-six hours with Eamonn in a hotel room. Those thirty-six hours feel inevitable, like something that has already happened. I look down at my hands, quiet.

"That's interesting," says Marian. "I always thought I was the self-destructive one."

. . .

ON THE BUS HOME, I hold Finn on my lap. Rain starts to fall, and I watch it sliding down the scratched Perspex windows. We pass Stephen's Green, the rain falling on the old streetlamps inside the park. I'm thirty-six years old, but maybe Marian is right, maybe something is wrong with me. I remember calling Marian from Trinity once, saying, "Do you want to hear about my new boyfriend?"

"Yeah, go on," she said.

"He's a musician."

"Ah, Tessa, no."

"No, listen, it's grand. He said he's enjoying being single, but he can imagine developing feelings for me," I said. I kept quoting him and soon both of us were in hysterics, laughing too hard to breathe. Maybe nothing has changed, maybe I've never known who's good for me.

Twenty-Six

BEFORE MY NEXT meeting with Eamonn, I leave work early and bike to the Forty Foot again. Today the waves are gray with a curled white fold, like an oyster. I watch sailboats moving out in the strong wind, keeling so far their sails nearly skim the water. On one boat, I can see a figure sitting on the hull across from the sail, balancing its weight to stop the boat from capsizing.

When I dive in, cold water presses against my forehead and the backs of my eyes. I swallow, tasting the saline drip of salt water down the back of my throat. I swim until my arms are sore, then stop, treading water, breathless. Marian once told me that there is a period of time, between high and low tide, when the water is neither coming in nor going out. For about fifteen minutes, the tide stops. It's called slack water. I need a break, I need to be in slack water, so I can work out what to do.

AT THE SAFE HOUSE in Stoneybatter, Eamonn has his head tipped back onto the sofa, the line of his throat and jaw exposed. His shirt looks soft and clean. I look out the window at the clear, washed sky.

I dreamt about Eamonn last night. In the dream, I'd found a loophole for us to be together. I was aware of myself dreaming, and told myself to remember the loophole in the morning, to not forget it. Maybe the Agnes Martin painting is the solution, maybe we're almost free.

"You need to tell me if you have any loyalist informers," I say, and Eamonn looks at me.

"Why?"

"Because I need to know the odds of you getting killed, and I can't without that piece of information."

Eamonn adjusts his shoulders on the sofa. "Do you worry about me?" he asks matter-of-factly.

"Yes."

"No one worries about me," he says.

I frown. "Do your parents not know what you do?"

"Not the specifics, but generally, yes."

"Then they must worry."

"They trust that I can look after myself."

I stare at him. "That's the craziest thing I've ever heard."

Eamonn blinks, raising his eyebrows. I wonder if I've offended him, or overstepped the mark, but he is looking at me with surprise and happiness, like I've just said the single best thing he could hear.

We finish discussing the plan for Marian's next visit with Niall. "I won't be able to come back to Dublin until after then," says Eamonn. "The fourth of October."

"That long?" I say, without thinking.

Eamonn smiles toward the ceiling, letting his eyes close. We've never kissed, we've never even touched.

"I thought I saw you once, walking down the Malone Road. I was driving and almost smashed the car," Eamonn says, almost lazily, his eyes still closed. Warmth rises on my skin. I am aware of the rough lace cups of my bra, the soft fabric of my jumper, the stitching inside my jeans.

"Are you married?" I ask, my voice quiet.

A look like disappointment crosses his face. "No, Tessa. I'm not married."

At the door, I turn around to hug him goodbye. My whole body is roaring, like I'm about to jump from a high dive. I seem to have forgotten the steps. What if I raise my hands and he steps back? I'm trying to work it out when Eamonn steps forward to hug me, pressing his hands against my back. Even through the fabric of my jumper, it's like his hands have extra nerves, or activate extra nerves of my own. I'm leaning into him, my skin tingling, and then I'm stepping back and opening the door, and rushing away down the road.

AFTER WORK ON THURSDAY, a group of us walks to Toners. Mam is bringing Finn to her ballroom class tonight, to show him off to her friends, so I've time for a drink. At the bar, I unwrap my scarf while ordering a red wine. I've on autumn clothes, corduroy trousers and a black rollneck jumper.

I carry my glass of wine to the snug in the back, where the others are arguing with raised voices. The threat level for Northern Ireland has remained critical for the past two and a half weeks, which means an attack is highly likely, though no one knows when, or where. This morning, a dozen trains near Belfast were stopped and searched by police officers, though the government hasn't confirmed rumors about possible targets.

Andrew is claiming to support the IRA and the armed struggle, even though he went to Eton and Cambridge. He points his bourbon at Emer and me. "What do you think? You're both from working-class Catholic families."

"Give my head peace," mutters Emer.

"What about me?" asks Aisling. "I'm working class."

"Piss off," says Lorcan. "You grew up in Dalkey."

"I tried to defect from the Catholic Church, actually," I say, taking a sip of my wine.

"Defect?"

"Be taken off the rolls," I say. "But the church won't let me without a priest's approval."

"So you've a heathen soul, then?" Emer asks, and I smile.

"Something like that, yeah."

Oisín is coming back from the bar with drinks in both hands and a bag of crisps gripped between his teeth. "But you sympathize with the IRA, don't you?" asks Andrew, as Emer rolls her eyes.

"I've a bomb right here in my bag," says Emer. "Since you're ready to die for the cause, aren't you?"

Oisín splits open the bag of salt and vinegar crisps, and I reach over Aisling for one.

"You look rough," says Emer to Lorcan. "Were you on the lash last night?"

Lorcan nods. "Appalling hangover. I've had the fear on me all day."

"Let me tell you something," Andrew interrupts in his loud, boarding-school voice. "After the Good Friday Agreement, more people died by suicide in Northern Ireland than died during the whole of the Troubles."

"That can't be right," says Lorcan.

"No, in fairness, he's not wrong," says Oisín through a mouthful of crisps. "The suicide rate is triple England's."

"And the IRA's fixing that, is it?" asks Emer.

"What about freedom?" says Andrew. I set my drink down too hard, sending arches of red wine splashing down the glass.

"Have you ever seen footage of a kneecapping?" asks Emer. "Some of those lads can't walk afterward. None of them will ever run again. I've a different understanding of freedom to the IRA."

After my second drink, I step outside of Toners, untangling the white cords of my earphones, and listen to Joy Division while walking home. I catch myself wanting to ask Eamonn if he knows this song, and think, You need to have a word with yourself.

Twenty-Seven

ON FRIDAY EVENING, mam comes over to see Finn and complain about Marian. Before she arrives, I smash garlic for a dressing, tossing the salad leaves in a large wooden bowl with my hands, wiping the oil from them onto a dish towel. I cut bread into cubes, scatter them in a large pan, and place a roasting chicken on top, then cover the pan with white wine and butter. As the pan roasts, the bread cubes turn crispy and golden, and the whole kitchen starts to smell like garlic and herbs. Marian and I used to argue about cooking, in our twenties. "I find it relaxing," I said.

"No one actually finds cooking relaxing," said Marian. "That's just something women say, because they think they should."

"Right," I said, "and you're a radical because you order Deliveroo every night?" Marian dropped the argument then, which is not something she does, generally speaking. Mam was right. There were clues, all the time.

When mam arrives, I pour her a Bailey's from the bottle I keep for her. "Thanks, love," she says. "When was your last haircut?"

"Jesus, mam."

"Are you trying to grow it longer or something?" she asks, and I sigh. Finn is kicking a ball on the back patio, and I poke my head outside, telling him to stop aiming at our windows. "Do you have a spray for this?" asks mam, running her hand over the kitchen surfaces.

"No."

"You should."

"Okay," I say, thinking, Pillow me. "I need to tell you something, mam. Do you remember when the Dunlops put in a swimming pool?"

Her employers installed a heated single-lane swimming pool under their house, with slate tiles that made the water look like warm black ink. Every day, mam scrubbed the tiles around the pool, and they never once invited her to try it.

"I swam in their pool once," I say. "I did four lengths, in my bra and knickers."

"You never did."

It was a frigid day in January, but the pool was warm, with thick steam floating above it. I stripped off my clothes, dropping them on the tiles, and lowered myself into the heated water.

I wanted to get back at the Dunlops for how they treated mam. All the days she worked sick instead of missing pay, all the nights they made her stay late. The Dunlops were always pleasant to me, but I could see the script running in their minds. Here I am, they thought, being nice to my cleaner's daughter. They ended up firing mam without any notice or severance, even though she'd worked for them for fourteen years. I hope Royce does steal their painting. They don't deserve to own it.

"I could have lost my job," says mam.

"You're right, I'm sorry," I say. After a pause, I say, "Do you see what I did there, mam? That was an apology."

"Give me strength," mam mutters, and I understand that she will never apologize to me or Marian.

When we first moved here, mam joined a support group for Dublin widows. Marian pointed out that mam was not, in fact, a widow, and she said, "There's no word for what I am."

AT PICKUP ON MONDAY, Finn says, "Mama, did you know there was a fire drill today? It was actually during snack time. We put on our shoes but *no* coats and *no* bags."

"Were you nervous?"

"No, but Owen was. He kept asking, Is there a real fire, is there a real fire?" says Finn, and I picture all the children lining up outside their playschool, while fire alarms ring through the empty rooms. I wonder if any of the teachers were also worried about a real fire.

We're out of milk, I remember, and I shepherd Finn through the supermarket, holding his hand. In the chilled aisle, I reach in for the milk, cold air curling around my back, and when I turn around, Finn has disappeared. The fridge door starts to swing shut as I walk toward the back of the shop, craning up the next aisle, and the next, until I find Finn standing in front of the chocolate bars. "Don't run off again," I say, and he nods, gripping a Kinder hippo. "Yes, fine, after dinner," I say. Last week, Finn made a holy show of me in here over wanting to buy a mop. "But we already own a mop," I said, like he'd see reason.

At the checkout, I am rummaging in my wallet, talking to the woman at the till, when Finn slips away for the second time. I find him at the newspaper carousel, staring at a photograph of a terraced house in west Belfast, bombed by the UVF. The front of the house is stoved in, like someone punched it, and wires and cladding trail down its open walls. "Was it an accident?" asks Finn.

"Sort of," I say. I don't want to lie to him, but I also don't know how to explain a bombing to a four-year-old. I put my hand around Finn's shoulders, and he leans against me. At dinner, Finn says, "Is our house going to fall down?"

"What? No."

"But that other one did," he says, frowning. I've been waiting for this conversation, I realize, for years. I rip paper from a notepad and draw two islands next to each other, a large one and a smaller one. "This big one is Britain, and the smaller one is Ireland. For a long time, Britain controlled all of Ireland, but now it only controls this part, here," I say, drawing a dotted line around the northeast corner of Ireland. "And some people want the British to leave, and some want them to stay."

"Are they fighting?" he asks.

"Yes, they're fighting," I say. I don't say: they're bombing hotels, shooting into crowds, burning down buildings. Murdering informers.

"The soldiers are trying to hurt each other? Are they driving in cars or out on the ground?" he asks, which I attempt to answer. On the map, I draw a star for Belfast, and an oval below it for Strang-ford Lough. "We used to live here," I say, drawing a dot along the lough shore for Greyabbey. "Do you remember it?"

"No."

"Well, you were very small."

I hold the tip of my pen to the dot, and it's like the map floods, turns dimensional. I can see the lough and the brent geese flying over the water, and our house, and the sheep moving in the pasture be-hind it. "Was it dangerous?" asks Finn, not quite managing the word.

"No, not there," I say, which is mostly true. I will have to tell him the full story one day, but not tonight, not for years.

At bedtime, we climb the stairs, leaving my map on the kitchen table under the lamp. From the stairs, I watch a draft catch the paper and shove it across the table, an invisible hand sliding it across the surface, then stopping, bringing it to rest at a different angle. It makes no sense, I think. The conflict is simple enough for a four-year-old to understand. So why won't it end?

Twenty-Eight

MARIAN ASKED ME to mind Saoirse this morning while she hikes at Glendalough. Damp clouds are hanging over Dublin. South of the city, the Wicklow Mountains will be shrouded in fog, but the bad weather hasn't put her off.

When we reach the Liberties, I let myself into Marian's house, and Finn races to the basket of toys in the corner of the front room. "Don't take the baby's pacifiers again," I call over my shoulder while moving toward the kitchen, where Marian is eating a piece of toast, wearing a cream-colored fisherman's jumper and jeans.

She hands me the front carrier to strap around my shoulders, then gently lowers Saoirse into the harness, and I bounce a little to keep the baby asleep, cradling her head. Finn wanders into the kitchen, holding, for reasons of his own, a hairbrush and a remote control.

Marian dashes upstairs to change, clattering back down the steps in gray tracksuit bottoms and a yellow fleece. "What's your route?" I ask, while she sits on the bottom stair to lace her hiking boots. "Up from Glendalough to the top of Camaderry," she says.

"What's the elevation?" I ask. "Are you up for that?"

"Two thousand feet," says Marian, without answering the second question. Not being able to walk or run after her cesarean drove her mad. She doesn't like to admit that her body is still recovering. "There's one bottle in the fridge already, and more milk in the freezer if you need it. I'll be back at two," she says. "Am I forgetting something?"

"We'll be grand," I say. Marian hugs me goodbye, dropping a kiss on the baby's head and rugby-tackling Finn before swinging out the door. After she leaves, we walk up the road to the playground behind St. Patrick's, and Saoirse sleeps in the carrier on my chest while Finn climbs on the structure.

When Saoirse wakes, I undo the carrier straps and lift her under the arms so her face is level with mine. "Hello," I say, and she pats her warm hand against my cheek, then turns her head across the playground, making small sounds. She's looking for Marian. "Your mammy's on a walk, but she'll be home soon," I say, before giving her a bottle.

Marian will have reached Glendalough by now. She will be leaving her car behind the hotel and starting down the path past the ruined monastery. She will be missing Saoirse, feeling unsettled at being alone for the first time in weeks. When she reaches the first slope, the broad upland moors and peat bogs will start to work through her veins. She loves the mountains, we both do. And she has been restless with Seb back on Inishmore for reshoots, careering between nappies and night feeds, worn out from worrying about our situation.

When a chill sets in at the playground, we return to the warm rooms of Marian's house. I fry bacon sandwiches for Finn and myself, and feed Saoirse a jar of fruit purée. After lunch, I set Saoirse in her crib for her afternoon nap, then lie down on the sofa with Finn.

He stopped napping months ago, but tearing around the playground has worn him out. I rub his back, humming, and after a few minutes he drops into sleep.

I wake first, easing myself from the sofa, tucking a wall of pillows around my son before tiptoeing into the hall. I check on Saoirse upstairs, then carry the baby monitor back downstairs with me, gripping it in my hand. I make tea and begin clearing the kitchen, washing bottles, scrubbing the spilled puddles of strawberry jam. On the counter, static rushes from the baby monitor.

The microwave display must be paused on a timer. I hit the clock button, but the same numbers reappear: 4:16. That can't be the time. Did we sleep for three hours? I hit the clock button again, feeling a flare of alarm. Tonight will be impossible, Finn will never go to bed after a three-hour nap.

Upstairs Saoirse is still asleep, her cheek and mouth rounded against the crib mattress. I lower my hand to her back, feeling the little electrical pulses in her arms and legs, her slow, regular breathing. I'm leaning over the crib rail when fear shoves into me. Marian is late. She is over two hours late.

I call my sister, standing in the dim hallway, and listen to her phone ring. She doesn't answer, and something in my chest gives way, a bridge collapsing.

Before calling Marian again, I move into the kitchen, like being in a different room will help somehow. From here, I can see small, smudged prints on her back window, from my son pressing his hands to the glass.

"Have you heard from Marian?" I ask mam, when she answers her phone.

"Your sister won't speak to me," says mam, and starts off on some story about our aunt Bridget.

"Mam," I say, cutting her off. "She was meant to be back at two."

"Well, then she must be enjoying having some time on her own for once."

"Listen, Saoirse just woke up, I should get her."

In her crib, Saoirse is wailing, red-faced. I hold her in one arm while rummaging in the freezer for a sachet of pumped milk. Marian always writes the dates on the plastic. This one says 25 September. She pumped this milk four days ago. She assembled the parts, switched on the machine, adjusted the speed. I am warming the milk under the tap when the thought occurs to me that Marian might already be dead. Her baby might be about to drink milk from a mother who is no longer alive.

I shake the thought away, focusing on the frozen milk melting to liquid. Once I get the cap on the bottle, Saoirse pushes it away. She doesn't want milk, she doesn't want to be swaddled, she only wants her mam.

Finn staggers into the kitchen, hot and irritable from napping for so long, and I rock Saoirse while trying to comfort both of them. I give my son a glass of water, and the baby finally calms down enough to accept a bottle. She takes a few deep pulls, her chin quivering, her face blotchy from crying. When she finishes, I lower the baby into her bouncer and jiggle a rattle for her, then type out an email to Seb, since I can't ring his mobile. He doesn't have reception on Inishmore. I try Marian again and again, then I hang up and send Eamonn our emergency signal. My phone rings a few seconds later, and Eamonn says, "What's happened?"

"Marian's missing. She went hiking in Glendalough this morning, and she hasn't come home," I say.

"You need to call emergency services," says Eamonn. "They'll organize a search."

"What if someone took her?" I ask, through a high, shining fear.

"We'll be running our own search, too," he says. "But you need a rescue team on the mountain. Chances are Marian fell, or went off the path. You have no reason to believe otherwise, right? No one from the North knows where you are."

I can feel the blood draining from my head, then a sudden swerve of nausea, like I'm going to pass out. Eamonn doesn't know about Eoin Royce. He doesn't know the danger we've been in, all this time.

The room seems to spin under me. I need to tell Eamonn the truth. But then MI5 might not search for her. They might decide Marian's not worth their time once they find out that she and I have been cooperating with the IRA, that I've been lying to Eamonn.

"No," I say finally, and on the other end of the line, I can't tell if Eamonn believes me.

"We'll talk to our other sources. Find out if any of them has heard anything about Marian," he says, and I close my eyes. Eamonn might find out the truth anyway, if he starts talking to other informers about us. This is it, the dam's about to break, I can feel it.

"We'll find her," says Eamonn. We've never spoken on the phone before. His voice sounds warm and urgent, concerned for me. He's going to hate me, I think, when he finds out the truth. "Try not to worry."

After we hang up, I dig in my bag for the burner phone and call Royce. "Where's Marian?" I ask.

"What're you talking about?" says Royce. I can't hear any sounds behind him, no traffic, no other voices. He sounds sealed, like he's underground.

"Is Marian with you right now?" I ask. My mind seems to be skipping, with a sensation like déjà vu. Royce might have followed Marian onto the mountain, with a knife, or a rock.

"This isn't a good time," says Royce.

"Where's my sister?" I ask. I'd be screaming if the children weren't nearby.

"Calm down."

"I have a photograph of my handler," I say, which isn't true. "I took a picture of him at our last meeting."

"Send it to me," says Royce.

"Not until you tell me where Marian is."

"I've no clue where your sister is."

"I don't believe you. What do you want? Do you want me to bring my handler to you?" I ask, not sure what I'm offering, or how to protect Eamonn if he says yes.

"Is he ready?" asks Royce, and I want to crack my head against the wall. "You said he wasn't ready yet. We don't want to blow our chance."

"Who was that?" I ask, my body icing over at the sound of a woman's voice in the background. "Whose voice was that, just now?"

Royce lets out a long sigh, and I press my hand to my mouth. "Here, say hello to this melter," says Royce to someone else, and a moment later a woman's voice says, "Hiya."

It's not Marian. Relief washes through me, and I fold in half over the kitchen counter. "Who's this?" I ask.

"Daphne," she says. "I'm his girlfriend." He has a girlfriend? I think, while saying, "Is there a woman with you, Daphne?"

"No," she says, sounding puzzled. Royce takes the phone back, and says, "What's gotten up your nose today?"

"Marian's late. She went for a hike at Glendalough, and she's late. Could the UVF have taken her? Could they have found out where she's living?"

"God knows," he says.

"I'm going to call the mountain search team."

"Like fuck you are," says Royce. "They'll make you talk to the cops."

"She's alone in the mountains," I say. "She could die."

"That's not my problem, is it?"

I think for a moment, then say, "Of course it's your problem. If she dies in the mountains, the police will investigate. They know she was an informer once, they'll assume someone else was involved. It will come back to you. You need Marian to be found as much as anyone."

"Fine," says Royce. "Don't tell them a thing about me. Not a thing, do you understand?"

As he lets out a curse, I end the call and dial emergency services on my regular phone. "Which service do you require?" says the operator, and I don't know how to answer. All of them, I think.

"My sister went for a hike in the Wicklow Mountains this morning, and she's missing."

The operator asks for both of our names, and I recite them off. "Hold the line, I'm transferring you to the Gardaí."

"Can you connect me to mountain rescue instead?"

"Not directly, no," says the operator. "The guards will decide whether to task mountain rescue. I'll transfer you now."

The line goes quiet, then a man's voice says, "You've reached Kevin Street Garda Station. I understand that you're concerned about your sister's whereabouts. When did you last see her?" he asks, and despite everything, a part of me is convinced that this can't really be happening.

"At her house this morning. She left for Glendalough at about eight."

"What was she wearing?"

"Gray tracksuit bottoms and a yellow fleece, and hiking boots."

"Was she planning to meet anyone in Glendalough?"

"No," I say, though I hadn't thought to ask her.

"Is your sister an experienced hiker?"

"Yes," I answer gratefully, like Marian's experience is proof that she must be fine. "She's done overnight hikes on her own."

"And when was she meant to return?" he asks.

"By two this afternoon."

"Oh," he says, sounding relieved. "She's only a couple of hours behind, then."

"She has a six-month-old baby," I say. "Her baby's still nursing, she wouldn't come home two hours late. And she's not answering her phone."

"Does she have any medical conditions? Any heart trouble? Asthma, seizures, anything along those lines? Does she require insulin?"

"No."

"Do you have any particular reason to be concerned for her safety?" He waits for me to answer. I hesitate, but I can't waste any more time. Marian might be in trouble now, she might be in danger now.

"She was an informer in Belfast."

After a pause, the officer says, "Can you give me a physical description of your sister?" I have trouble finding the words. All of my usual descriptions of Marian are relative, I realize: she's slightly shorter than me, her face is slightly rounder.

"She's five foot six, she has brown hair and hazel eyes."

"I'm going to stay on the line with you," says the officer, "but I'd like for you to send us a recent picture of your sister." He reads off a number, and I take it down on the back of a crumpled supermarket receipt. I scroll through my camera roll, my hands shaking, and find a picture of Marian at Hogans, holding a pint.

"Right, that photograph came through, thanks," he says. I give him our real names, and our former addresses in Belfast, despite every instinct. "Are you able to make your way to the garda station on Kevin Street?" he asks. "Or do you need an escort?"

"Sorry?"

"Are you concerned for your own safety?" he asks, and I blink in the quiet room. I can see the window above the sink, its lock slid back. I drop the phone, taking off down the hall.

Finn is pushing a train on the carpet, his chin propped on his knee. The relief is instant, like pouring boiling water into snow. I hurry the children outside, murmuring to Saoirse as I strap her into the pram, helping Finn with his shoes.

I turn down my sister's road toward Bride Street. Heat flashes through me, and my stomach churns. Marian's fine, she's fine, she's fine. She's sitting up on the mountain with a sprained knee. Tonight she'll be at home with a cup of tea in one hand and the baby in her other arm, saying, "What a palaver." We are balanced on a razor's edge. Everything is fine, or nothing.

Bride Street is busy with weekend crowds, and I push the pram through them, clutching my son's hand, my heart pounding. I ring mam while waiting to cross Arnott Street. As soon as she answers, I want to start crying. I have the urge to ask her to come and get me, like I'm homesick. "Listen, can you meet me at the Kevin Street garda station? I need you to mind the children while I speak with the guards."

"Tessa—"

"Please come as fast as you can." Mam lives in Inchicore, one of the inner suburbs. The drive into town will take her thirty minutes, with traffic.

I push the pram across the lobby of the garda station, its rows of glass offices rising high above me. The poured concrete floors make the building look more like a gallery than a garda station. A young man watches me from behind the reception desk. I give him my name, and he rings up to one of the offices. At my side Finn has his head tipped back, staring up toward the distant ceiling.

While we wait, I search for Camaderry on a map. The ovals showing its elevation grow smaller and smaller toward the peak. Marian is there, in one of those loops. I pinch my thumb and finger together, bringing more of the map onto the screen.

Glendalough appears below the mountain, the upper and lower lakes. I hesitate, holding the lakes in place, then slide my fingers closer so more land appears on the screen, more villages, roads scrawling between them. I slide out until Arklow and Clonegall appear, and the motorways, the M7, the M8, the M9, slicing across the island, and feel defeated by the amount of green space on the map, the acres and acres of open land. I snap my phone off, and the black glass of the screen looks like the darkest thing in the world.

Twenty-Nine

A UNIFORMED GARDA brings us into the lift and presses the button for the fifth floor. Normally Finn would roar about pressing the button himself, but he stays quiet, intimidated by the uniformed man standing silently beside us, and I gently squeeze his hand as the lift starts to rise. Chills sweep down my arms. My clothes, a striped navy jumper and jeans, weekend clothes, feel too cheerful, too casual, especially when the lift doors open to a detective waiting for us in a tailored black suit.

"Hello," he says. "Detective Inspector Byrne." I have to drop Finn's hand to shake the detective's, and my son protests, clinging to my leg. The detective is taller than me, with blond hair combed back from his head and skin fair enough to show reddish shave marks on his jaw. He stops outside an interview room. "Garda Maguire will mind the children."

"No, they're staying with me," I say, wheeling the pram through the doorway before the detective can argue, and moving one of the chairs over to the window for Finn. I crouch in front of him, whispering, "Do you want to watch a show on my phone?" He nods.

"Yes, good man." I slip my headphones over his ears and play *Octonauts* for him. Saoirse is happy enough in her pram for now, angled toward me, staring up at the unfamiliar ceiling tiles.

The detective gives the sergeant a look over my head, then closes the door and sits down across the table from me. When he thanks me for coming in, his voice has a strange quality to it, like he's pitching it for a much larger room. Something about the rise and fall of the words makes me think he's had voice training, and I wonder if he has to speak at press conferences or if he wants to be the chief commissioner one day. The coaching wasn't for interviews like this, surely. I want to ask him to speak more softly, to keep the baby calm.

"The Wicklow Mountain Rescue Team is on its way to Glendalough to look for your sister. To better assist them, I'd like to get a sense from you of what's been going on with Marian recently," he says, and nerves prickle through my body. Listening to him, I make a bargain with myself to tell the detective about Royce in one hour, if Marian is still missing. Telling the gardaí might only put us in worse danger, but there are no good options here. "How's your sister's health?"

"Good. She's barely sleeping, though. She had a baby six months ago," I say. The detective doesn't seem to consider sleep deprivation a risk factor, which means he has never been up every two hours with an infant. The other week, I watched Marian sing Saoirse a lullaby, so exhausted she was leaning over the crib, her forehead resting on her arm, her eyes closed.

"And Marian's nursing," I say, but the detective's face stays blank. "She didn't bring a pump with her. She'll be in pain, going this long without nursing. She might get a fever or mastitis. Something's wrong, she'd never be this late on purpose."

He nods, without seeming to absorb the information. "We haven't had a frost yet, luckily. With the damp, though, she'll be at risk of hypothermia," he says, and I stare at him.

"But the rescue team will find her soon, right? Since they know her route."

"Camaderry includes complicated terrain," he says. "You've rough ground, cliffs. These searches aren't always straightforward, even if the team knows the hiker's planned route. The average search-and-rescue in Wicklow lasts fourteen hours."

I hear the air leave my body. Marian will have run out of water by then, she will be in pain, she will be cold. The mountains will grow dark in a couple of hours, and she will be alone then in the darkness.

"How would you describe your sister's state of mind recently?" asks the detective. "Has she taken well to motherhood?"

"Yes. She's crazy about her daughter."

"Any postnatal depression?" he asks, and I pause before answering. Marian would hate for me to tell him any of this, but the detective has already caught me hesitating. "It's nothing to be ashamed of," he says. "It's normal."

"I know it's normal," I say.

"So Marian has been depressed?"

"No, not anymore. She had trouble at first, but anyone would have done. Her daughter was born eight weeks early, after a placental abruption. She spent her first thirty-eight days in a neonatal intensive care unit," I say. Marian was beside herself, out of her head. She was convinced the abruption was her fault, that already she'd failed to protect her baby. "That was in the spring, though. She's grand now."

The detective scratches the razor burn on his jaw. He looks like the sort of man you see in the expensive restaurants on Dawson Street, or smoking a cigar outside the Horseshoe Bar.

"Has Marian ever talked about harming herself?" he asks, and I glance at Finn, but he's absorbed in his show. Past his small shape, I can see construction cranes out the window, and the dark ink spots of crows turning in the air.

"No. She'd never leave her family, she's not a danger to herself."

"Everyone can be a danger to themselves, unfortunately," he says. "I understand these questions can be difficult, but I need you to answer them honestly. The rescue team searches for someone differently if they've been despondent. They check certain areas of the mountain first."

"Marian hasn't been despondent."

"Would she tell you?"

"Yes."

The detective's eyes are a very bright blue, aquamarine. He considers me, and I wonder what he sees. A tired, ordinary woman in her thirties, dark eyes, dark hair that could use a cut.

"Is Marian working currently?" he asks.

"She's an air-ambulance paramedic," I say with pride. "They're based out of the hospital in Tallaght."

"Is she in debt?"

"No," I say, stung. I'd expected another question about Marian's work. "She's not exactly minting it, but she's fine."

"And her home life? Any trouble in her marriage?" asks the detective.

"They adore each other."

"So no arguments recently?"

"I never said that. Seb shaved his beard over the sink the other day. You should have seen Marian, absolutely raging."

The detective leans back against his chair, and I say, "Marian didn't hurt herself, I swear."

"Has Marian been acting differently recently?" asks the detective. "It could be something small. A change in her routine. A new friend, a new hobby."

"Marian works and has a baby. When's she finding the time for a hobby?"

"Well, she goes hiking, that's a hobby."

"You think walking's a hobby?" I ask, and the detective smiles, like he has nothing but patience for me. He won't lose his temper, not yet anyway.

"There's also a chance," says the detective, "a very slight chance, that someone else is involved. We're checking the registry of known offenders in the area."

The phrase confuses me, that the police already know about certain men, men who should never be left alone with a woman. Why are they living here? I want to ask. If you knew about a man my sister should never come across alone on a hiking path, why is he here?

"Given what you told us about Marian being an informer, we are also investigating the possibility of paramilitary involvement."

Sensation rushes up my legs, like I'm leaning over a high balcony. If I tell the detective about Royce, the police will arrest him, and the IRA will punish us. Royce probably isn't involved anyway. He hadn't sounded like he was lying to me on the phone, but I could be wrong. Or it could be someone else from the IRA besides Royce, someone with a vendetta against her. It could be Niall, directing others from inside prison.

If the IRA or the loyalists are involved, I will need a force to match theirs, I will need an army, too. Patrol cars, dogs, an armed unit. It might already be too late, an IRA executioner might have already shot Marian and left her bleeding into the mountain.

"Over the past few days, has Marian seemed uneasy, or frightened?"

I hesitate, then say, "I don't know." Maybe something happened, maybe Royce went to see her. I remember Marian's hands shaking as she screwed the cap on a bottle, the shadows under her eyes. Would I have been able to tell the difference between exhaustion and fear? Same pounding heart, same dry mouth, unsteady nerves. With Finn at that age, the fatigue made me feel hunted.

By now, the mountain rescue team will be climbing the moor above Glendalough, the searchers spread out across the heather. They will be shouting her name. The rescue helicopter will be beating through the air above them, searching the cliffs and the rough land. Marian might have fallen. She might be lying on the rocky ground, but she'll hear the searchers soon and shout back to them.

The baby starts to fuss, and I lift her from the pram, holding her against me. I can feel her bobbing her head above my shoulder. She still has on the strawberry-print romper Marian dressed her in this morning, and I spread my hand across her back, feeling the soft weave of the fabric.

"How did Marian become an informer?" asks the detective. "She's a paramedic, how did she have any access to paramilitary information?"

"Marian was in the IRA."

The detective's blue eyes sharpen. It takes me a moment to understand the change in his expression, in the atmosphere in the room. At first I think he's angry, before realizing that he is excited and trying to disguise it. He had been bored before, running through

190

the motions, feeling sorry for himself for having to work on a Saturday on the disappearance of some sad woman who couldn't cope with having a baby and was probably off crying her eyes out somewhere up a mountain, wasting everyone's time.

The detective does not look bored anymore. He leans forward over the table. "For how long?"

"Seven years."

"Which brigade?"

"Belfast."

"What was her role?" he asks, and I say, "Does it matter?"

"Of course it matters. If the IRA is involved in her disappearance, we need to know about Marian's background," he says.

"Her unit did mostly fundraising and industrial sabotage. They bombed power stations." Marian would spend eight hours at a farmhouse on the River Bann, assembling a charge of Semtex or gelignite and a detonator.

I look away from the detective, out the window, sliding my hand along my neck, under my collar, trying to loosen the fabric from my skin. I say, "They always called in a warning first. No one was ever hurt."

"Is that what she told you?" he says. "Can I ask you something, Tessa? Do you trust her?"

Thirty

I SIT FACING the detective in the interview room, with an elastic knotted in my hair. It's Saturday evening. I should be at Marian's house, cooking dinner, telling her she's peeling the potatoes wrong.

"Would you consider yourself a good judge of character, Tessa?" asks the detective, and from his tone of voice, I realize how little this man likes me. I'm about to answer when Finn appears at my side. "Mama," he says. "Mama, I'm hungry."

"Sorry, do you've anything here? Biscuits or something?" I ask the detective.

"No, that's not a service we provide," he says crisply.

"Right, okay. Where's your vending machine?"

"We don't have any in this building. I told you we could have someone else mind the children. You didn't want that, remember?" he says, and I can tell that he knows I'm lying about something. He's trying to put pressure on me.

"Mama, I'm hungry," says Finn, tugging at the hem of my jumper. Saoirse's nappy is wet, too, I can feel the damp weight of it sagging under her clothes, but I've nothing to change her. Shame wells through me.

"I'll go down to the road, then," I say.

"We're not done yet," says the detective, and under the table I clench my hands into fists.

"I'm sorry, sweetheart," I whisper to Finn. "Your granny will be here very soon, okay? You've to wait just a little longer." I stand up with the baby on my hip, and shepherd Finn back to his chair. "Can I put on another show for you?"

I sit back across from the detective and lift my chin, waiting for him to speak. He sets his pen upright on the table, like he's lining up a domino. "Did Marian have a history of violence?" he asks. "Did she get into fights at school?"

"No," I say, rubbing my eyes. "She's a normal person."

"Normal people don't join the IRA," he says.

"What about the police?" I ask quietly.

"Excuse me?" he says.

"Do normal people join the police?" I ask.

He smiles, and his teeth are straight and white, like veneers. "Do you hate the police, Tessa? I know that's common, where you come from."

"You don't know anything about where I'm from."

When we were children, loyalist gunmen shot into a house on the next road, killing our friend's father. For a year, Marian crawled to the bathroom on her hands and knees at night so she wouldn't be shot through the window.

"Were you ever approached to join the IRA, Tessa?" he asks.

"No."

"You grew up in a republican area, though," he says. Half the gable walls in Andersonstown have murals of gunmen painted on them. Men in ski masks holding rifles, or pointing them at the road. Every day, Marian and I walked to school with the giant faces of masked gunmen towering over us, watched by their eyes. Above us, rainwater slid down the painted faces of the gunmen, over their open mouths, dripping from their hands.

The truth is, I barely noticed them. The Troubles were over anyway. Those murals were a relic, more boring than mass. Their earnestness and seriousness embarrassed me. Those men did not, to my mind, look like good craic. Most of them were dead anyway, shot by loyalists or soldiers, or by one another in internal feuds. They were in the IRA plot at the cemetery, and I was up here, with the living, walking past them with music playing in my headphones. I noticed the lads playing football in the park, the sequined dresses in the charity-shop windows, the posters in the record shop. Over the years the murals faded, the pigment settling on the plaster, turning them stippled, like a bruise.

I sit Saoirse up on my lap, letting her play with my necklace. "Your sister never tried to recruit you?" asks the detective, while the baby tugs sharply on my necklace, making the chain dig into the back of my neck.

"No." Saoirse clutches my pendant in her fist, and I can feel the chain biting deeper into my neck. The clasp will snap soon if she doesn't stop. "Marian wouldn't have bothered trying to recruit me. I knew the IRA wasn't going to unite Ireland. It was only history repeating itself."

The detective stretches his legs under the table, pushing his hands into the pockets of his suit. "But you're from a republican family," he says, and the chain snaps at my neck, the two strands of the necklace breaking into the air. Saoirse coos in surprise, and I look down at the broken gold strands, remembering, distantly, that I like this necklace, bought last year from the market in Temple Bar.

"Marian didn't even tell me she had become involved with the IRA. I only found out after she became an informer."

"Who recruited your sister?" he asks, but before I can answer, a sergeant knocks on the door. "Your mother's in reception," she says, and I bolt from my chair, tucking Saoirse into the pram, crossing the room to take Finn's hand. "My show's not over," says Finn crossly.

"It's all right, come on now, you can finish it later." I lift Finn into my arms, maneuvering the pram down the corridor with my free hand. As the lift starts to drop, I close my eyes, burying my face against Finn's hair, kissing the side of his head. I want the ride to last forever, but then the lift is stopping, the doors opening.

As soon as I see mam, exhaustion crashes through me. My body seems to think I can rest now while she takes over. Mam is busy at once, fussing over the children, asking Finn if he's thirsty, if he wants to come over to her house. She bends over the pram, undoing the straps to pick up Saoirse. "Her nappy's soaked through," says mam.

"I know, I forgot the changing bag."

"Come on, pet," says mam, clucking her tongue. "Let's get you dry."

I look at the set of her shoulders, and realize that mam's angry with me. She's fuming. She thinks that if I hadn't rung the police, if I'd stayed at the house and acted as if everything were fine, then Marian would have turned up by now.

I want to argue with her, but there's no time. I crouch down to say goodbye to Finn. "Are you doing my bedtime?" he asks, and I look into his clear eyes, forcing myself to smile. "I don't know yet, sweetheart. It will be either me or granny, okay?"

Mam says, "Do you know Marian once came home from a hike three days late? She was walking in the Cairngorms and decided to take a longer route."

"She didn't have a baby then, mam."

"Exactly," says mam. "She's worn out. She probably laid down for a little rest, and she's sleeping through all of this." Mam is speaking very clearly, out of superstition, like some force is listening, and then she is saying goodbye, moving toward the doors, asking Finn if he wants a pizza for his dinner. I watch them step out onto the road, and the automatic doors slide shut behind them, leaving me alone in the lobby. I tilt my head back, looking up at the modern chandelier hanging from the ceiling high above me, a perfect halo of white light. When I finally look away, miniature versions of the halo float across my field of vision.

I follow the sergeant back into the lift. "It's an act, isn't it?" I ask her. "The detective. He's not really like this, is he?"

The sergeant clears her throat, and my stomach drops. The detective isn't playing anything up in the interview room. He's not pretending to be cold, or contemptuous. I follow the sergeant down the corridor, my arms weightless at my sides without the children. "Sorry, can I use the toilet first?" I ask, and she waits for me outside.

Above the sinks, I can see my reflection in the mirror. My pale face, dark eyes. My sister and I, we look so similar. I rinse my hands, brushing them down my jeans, and return to the interview room. The detective has moved Finn's empty chair back to its place at the table. Without letting him see, I place my hand on the chair, like it might hold some of my son's warmth.

"The mountain rescue team has just reached the eastern col. They're about a third of the way to the summit," says the detective, and I start to ask him a question, but my voice has gone.

Granite boulders are scattered across the mountain slopes. My sister might be behind one of them, she might be injured, she might be bleeding, she might be hiding from someone.

"Thank you," I manage to tell the detective. He raises his fingers from the table and nods without looking at me. "How did Marian's unit raise funds?" he asks.

"They robbed cashpoints and taxi offices, and they sold counterfeit perfume." The perfume brought in more than the robberies, apparently. Marian told me the nose was some lad from Ardoyne. I pictured women in expensive houses around the North, spraying French perfume on their necks, breathing in the scent, none of them knowing it had actually been made in a tower block in Belfast.

"And they sold counterfeit wine," I say. Once a week, Marian met a waiter from the restaurant at the Mirabelle Hotel and bought empty bottles of wine from him, flash bottles that had been ordered and drunk at the restaurant that week by property developers and bankers. Château Margaux, Château d'Yquem, Côte de Nuits. Marian blended other, cheaper wines with port, poured the mixture into the empty bottles, resealed the corks, and packed them into crates, padding the bottles with strands of brown raffia. Someone from the north Antrim brigade posed as a private wine distributor, selling rare vintages from Europe. None of the customers ever complained. They all thought they were drinking old-world burgundy, not wine mixed in Marian's kitchen.

Because of those years, Marian knows an inordinate amount about wine. A Pomerol vineyard, she told me, is worth half a million euro per acre. Nebbiolo is named for the fog, the nebbia, that hovers around the vineyards in its part of Italy. And I remember her telling me that eight hundred years ago, a mountain in the Alps collapsed, and a wine is still made from the vines that grew from the rubble. Château l'Abysse, House of the Abyss.

"And did your sister enjoy that?" asks the detective. "Did she like playing Robin Hood?"

"Yes. The poverty rate in Northern Ireland is worse than in the republic or England. Marian thought they were building a socialist republic."

The IRA was fighting a decolonization campaign, and other decolonization campaigns had ended. The British had left Cyprus, India, Kenya. The partition of Ireland was only about a hundred years old. It wouldn't last forever. Every day, Marian thought this is it, this will be the week the British announce their withdrawal.

"Then why did she become an informer?" he asks.

"She stopped believing an armed campaign would work. She wanted a peace deal," I say.

The detective starts asking more questions about Seb, and I describe him and his work. He says, "Not to be rude, but why would someone like him be with someone like her?"

"You'd need to ask him."

"Can you think of anyone in particular who might hold a grudge against your sister?" he asks.

I look at him, confused. "How many active members are in the IRA at the moment? Five thousand? So, any of them."

The number would be higher than that, actually. Most of the community hates touts. Mam once told me about a girl from her school who smiled at a British soldier on the Andersonstown Road. No one talked to her for the rest of the year, and that girl was lucky. Other girls, the ones who let a soldier buy them a drink, or take them to a dance, were sent to kangaroo courts. Some of them were held down while their hair was shaved. One was tarred and feathered, and left tied to a lamppost as a warning to other girls. Those were lesser offenses than ours. What Marian and I did, giving information to the British, some of our neighbors would consider the worst possible offense. They'd have an easier time forgiving murder.

"Did anyone within the IRA suffer particular damage as a result of Marian's informing?" asks the detective. "Were any IRA members convicted on her information? Were any of them killed by state forces because of her?"

"No, I don't think so."

"Is there anyone outside the IRA who might hold a grudge against her? Anyone who would want to see her suffer? A victim, or a bereaved family member? Maybe someone wants her to understand what they went through," he says.

"I don't know."

"Has anything happened recently to upset Marian? Anything in the news?" he asks.

"The news is always bad," I say.

The detective crosses his arms over his chest. "How did you end up in Dublin, Tessa?"

"The Belfast police set us up in safe houses in Dalkey for the first year. Neither of us could afford a house there after the year was up, and we both work in Dublin."

"You could have gone anywhere, though. Why didn't you move abroad?"

"This is my home. Neither of us wanted to emigrate." I call my son by Irish endearments, *mo leanbh*, my child, *mo ghrá*, my love, phrases that once vibrated in my great-grandmothers' throats. "And I couldn't take my son away from his father. Moving here was bad enough, and he can still visit twice a month."

"He visits twice a month?" the detective asks, frowning. "We'll need his name and contact details," he says, and I wonder what Tom is doing right now, on a Saturday evening in September, while I sit talking about him in a garda station. "Is your son's father in the IRA?" the detective asks, and I laugh. He says, "Can you answer the question, please?"

"No, Tom's not in the IRA. He's an architect."

"Why are you divorced?"

"We grew apart," I say simply. I don't plan on sharing the details with him.

"He might have given your location to the IRA, if they put pressure on him," says the detective, and I shake my head.

"No, Tom would never do that. We've always stayed on good terms for Finn's sake," I say, which is mostly true, except for our last argument.

"The mountain rescue team saw your sister's car, by the way," says the detective. "They found it parked behind the hotel in Glendalough."

The hotel is an old stone building, with a pub and an open fire. We stop there sometimes for a glass of wine after a hike. Marian might not have even made it onto the mountain, someone might have found her inside the hotel or in the car park. "Did anyone see her?" I ask.

The detective says officers are reviewing footage from the hotel's CCTV, but I don't want to think about surveillance tapes. I don't want to think about Marian being caught by a security camera, a woman walking across a car park alone, before disappearing. No crime has occurred here. Just an accident, a fall.

"Have you set up any checkpoints?" I ask.

"On every road leaving Glendalough, and on the N11."

If Marian was taken on the mountain, I don't know where the IRA will bring her, if they will try to bring her north across the border. I check my watch. Ten more minutes, then I'll have to tell the detective the truth. It's nearly six o'clock. Marian will be in pain now, her breasts stiff with milk, leaking through her shirt. She must be trying to express it by hand. I remember that sore ache as the milk hardens into discs.

The detective says, "Is the IRA planning an attack in Dublin?"

"How would I know?" I ask. The sergeant will interrupt us again soon, she will knock on the door and say that they've found Marian, she's grand, not a scratch on her, they're bringing her down the mountain now.

"Does Marian have an office or flat on O'Connell Street?" asks the detective.

"No. I gave you her address, she lives in the Liberties."

"But does she have access to any buildings on O'Connell Street?" he asks, and I shake my head. "Does she have sniper training?"

"Sorry?"

"Is she in a sleeper cell?" he asks.

"Marian left the IRA. They tried to kill us for informing."

"But they didn't. You're alive, aren't you?" he asks, and waits, like he's expecting me to answer. Yes, I'm alive, I think, in this body, with windburn on my cheeks, and stretch marks on my hips, and hard ducts left in my breasts from nursing. "So why did the IRA let you go?"

"They didn't. We fought our way out."

"Maybe, or maybe all of that was staged. It was theater," he says.

"Staged for whose benefit?" I ask.

"I don't know yet. But you're both embedded in Dublin now," he says, and the back of my skull tightens. He looks down at his watch. "Your sister went missing at, what, two o'clock this afternoon. At seven this evening, the English prince will appear with the Taoiseach at the unveiling of a new statue on O'Connell Street."

"And, sorry, you think Marian is planning to do what, exactly?"

"Will you unlock your phone for me?" asks the detective. I key in the passcode and hand it to him, watching him swipe through my messages, taking his time. Finally he sets the phone down, then drops back into his chair, thinking, with his thumb hooked under his jaw. "Is Marian finding it difficult?"

"Is she finding what difficult?"

"Being a mother," he says. "It's very different from what she did before."

"That's true for everyone."

The detective tips his head at me. "Do you find it difficult, Tessa?" he asks. This man has never brushed someone else's teeth, I'm convinced. He will never understand. I'm exhausted, and I'd do it every day for the rest of my life, I'd do it for a million years.

We face each other across a table in an interview room in the south inner city, and a few miles away officers are climbing the stairwells of buildings along O'Connell Street, knocking on flats, shouting for doors to be opened, breaking down the locked ones.

At the same time, rescue officers in red uniforms are climbing over the mountain. They must be halfway to the summit now, climbing in a long, ragged, uneven line, their dogs coursing ahead of them through the tall heather, the rescue helicopter banking in the sky overhead.

"Marian isn't on O'Connell Street. You found her car in Glendalough."

"Someone may have picked her up in Glendalough. That may have been the meeting point," he says.

"You can't actually be worried about an assassination attempt. If you were, you'd have called in a credible threat and the prince's appearance would be canceled."

"Are you absolutely certain we shouldn't be worried?" asks the detective, and I look down at my hands in my lap, turning over my palms, like I'm searching for marks. I remember, hours ago, holding the chains of the playground swing while Finn climbed down, glancing back and seeing the empty swing swaying as we walked away.

"Marian would never go back to the IRA," I say, finally.

Parents weren't allowed to stay overnight at the NICU, and every night at handover, the nurses had to almost physically force Marian off the ward. She begged them to let her sleep in a chair, or on the floor under the incubator, she pleaded and pleaded with them. It was my job to drive her and Seb home from the hospital, and Marian always spent the trip keening for her baby. I remember my sister slumped in the back of my car, crying soundlessly, and she will be feeling that now, wherever she is, she will be frantic for her daughter.

"Marian would never do anything that would take her away from Saoirse."

"But she left her baby with you this morning. Why didn't Marian want to spend her day off with her baby?"

I hear a sort of laugh leave my throat. "Are you joking me?"

Outside, crows drop through the gray air. I look out at the vast chambered city, all the bedroom and office windows, the construction cranes suspended above them. Marian might be here, she might have come back to Dublin, if Royce forced her.

"Marian spent seven years at war," says the detective. "That doesn't just go away. I mean, clearly it doesn't. She works as an air-ambulance paramedic."

"What's wrong with her job?"

"Why isn't Marian working for a regular ambulance service? Why is she going up in a helicopter every shift?" he says. "She must need the adrenaline. Your body gets used to war, you know. On a cellular level. Those years will have changed her. Do you really think she's happy shut up inside a house with a baby? She must be bored out of her mind."

While he's talking, I start crying. My face is wet suddenly, and I can taste salt in my mouth, between my teeth. I don't know why this is the most upsetting thing he has said. The thought that my sister has been unhappy, that she preferred her old life.

"Marian stayed in the IRA for seven years. She must have liked something about it," he says. "You studied history, Tessa. You tell me what happens to soldiers when they stop fighting a war."

I sit with tears sliding down my face and throat soaking into the collar of my jumper.

"Marian's life had meaning before. She was fighting for Irish freedom, and she cared enough about the cause to risk her own life. What's in her days now? The supermarket shop? Standing around a playground? She must be going out of her skull. Why else would she want to spend her day off hurling herself up a mountain? Does she even like hiking? She must want to escape, all the time," he says. "What about yourself?"

"Do I want to escape?" I ask quietly, tears slipping into my mouth.

"No, Tessa," the detective says, smiling, like I've proved his point. "Do you like hiking?"

There's a knock on the door, and the sergeant steps inside. She stands for a moment looking between our faces, his smirking, mine sticky with tears. She says, "They found her."

Thirty-One

ALL THE ENERGY DRAINS from my body. "Where did they find her?" asks the detective, and I listen with my chest rising and falling. Everything seems to be happening very slowly. The detective is sliding his hand along the edge of the table, waiting for the sergeant to answer. He reaches the edge and lets his hand drop into the air.

"On the mountain," says the sergeant, looking confused. "The search team spotted her on the western col, below the ridgeline. She'd fallen."

"Is she all right?" I hear myself ask.

"She broke her ankle, but she's conscious, she's talking to them," says the sergeant, and I hunch forward, gasping, my hair falling in front of my face. Marian's safe. Suddenly we've been restored to the rest of the day, the week, the rest of our lives.

"Well, that is happy news," says the detective. He looks disappointed, and I resist the urge to reach over the table and slap him.

The sergeant says, "They're bringing her to the hospital in Wicklow town."

"Was she alone?" asks the detective, and the sergeant nods. I shove back my chair and start toward the corridor. When I step into the lift, the detective reaches out to grip the doors, to stop them from closing, and I look back at him from inside its gleaming metal walls. "Ask her for yourself," he says. "Ask if she has been bored."

He steps back, standing with his hands in his suit pockets and the lights gleaming on his blond hair as the lift doors close and we start to drop through the building. In the lobby, the halo lamp glows white, and I can see the shapes of figures moving on the upper floors, behind the glass.

After ringing mam and messaging Seb, I head off down Bride Street, aware of the garda station rising at my back, with its rippling levels of windows. From under the clouds, the setting sun is casting a bronze light over the roads and the faces of the people walking past me. Joy bursts through me, making me break into a run. Someone in the crowd outside Flannery's drops a pint as I run past, and at the sound of breaking glass, everyone outside the pub cheers.

I laugh, running faster, pelting down Camden Street. Bicyclists veer through the traffic, checking over their shoulders, standing up from their seats. The restaurants and takeaways are in the thick of the dinner rush, the Saturday night air smelling like spices and fryer oil, like diesel exhaust and other women's perfume. When I reach the canal, I catch my breath on the bridge, looking downstream at the crowds on the banks, bundled in jackets, drinking tins and cheap bottles of wine. The water flows past them toward the lock, painted orange with the sunset.

AT HOME, I set a holdall on my bed and begin folding clothes into it to bring Marian in the hospital, socks and pajamas and a loose jumper, and add two new novels. Marian doesn't normally read magazines, but I pack a few food glossies anyway. She can look through them and choose what she wants me to cook for her while she's recovering. While Saoirse was in the hospital, I stayed up for hours after Finn went to bed at night, cooking dinners to bring Marian and Seb, and I'll do the same now to help with the shock, to help her sleep.

I'm ravenous myself, I realize, and stand at the kitchen counter wolfing down a bowl of leftover spaghetti with tomato oil. I wash my bowl and set it on the drying rack, then hurry out to the car, slinging the holdall into the back seat. I set the satnav for the hospital in Wicklow, and a blue line unravels across the map, leading me across the southside to the N11.

Seb will be on the ferry to the mainland by now. He'd been on location all day, filming in a cove on Inishmore, and didn't see my messages until five o'clock. I picture him pacing up and down the ferry deck, or leaning his weight against the prow, like he can make the boat go faster. Inishmore is thirty miles offshore. The slow crossing must be driving him mad, but at least there's not a gale, at least he's not stuck on the island. Once he reaches the coast, he will hire a rental car, and start the long drive east toward Wicklow.

When I reach the hospital, the red letters of the emergency department are glowing in the darkness. A few people sit coughing in the lobby, and a man with a homemade bandage wrapped around his fist stares into the middle distance. Two paramedics in yellow hi-vis jackets are speaking to the man behind the desk, then they leave and I step forward. "I'm here to visit my sister. She was admitted earlier tonight."

"What's her name?" asks the man, and I catch myself just in time. Marian will have been admitted to the hospital under her new name.

He prints off a visitor's pass. "Thanks," I say, fixing the sticker to my shirt and walking onto the ward, past the stretchers and monitors in the corridor, and a group of nurses chatting at their station. When I step into her room, Marian is having blood drawn and arguing with her nurse. "Will you talk some sense into her?" the nurse says to me.

"What's going on?"

"They won't let me see Saoirse," says Marian, as her blood lifts into a plastic vial.

"This is an emergency department," says the nurse. "One visitor at a time, no children."

"She's a baby, though," says Marian. "She'd only be on my lap."

"That's even worse," says the nurse. "You need to rest. If you'd been in a car accident, would you want your baby brought to you?"

"Yes," says Marian stubbornly.

The nurse sighs. "You can see her tomorrow morning, when you're in the step-down unit. You'll be able for it then."

"I'm fine now, though," says Marian. "I'm grand."

"That'll be the adrenaline," says the nurse, capping the last vial and throwing out the sharp. She presses a bandage inside Marian's elbow, then strips off her gloves.

"She's right. You've no business minding a baby right now," I say, and Marian scowls at me.

"Right, love," says the nurse. "I'll be back soon to bring you for your X-rays."

After the nurse leaves, I lean down to hug Marian. Her hair smells different, like cold air and peat smoke. "Saoirse's probably asleep by now, do you really want mam waking her up to bring her to a hospital?"

Marian presses her lips together. "You don't understand. I thought I might never see her again."

"Oh, Marian. What happened?"

"I slipped on the ridgeway," she says, and I wince, looking at the deep scratches on her arm and down the side of her cheek. At the end of the hospital bed, her left ankle is raised in a sling, hidden under a cold pack. Marian's face and throat are dry, and her mouth is chapped. A drip is running clear fluids into her arm for the dehydration.

"I fell down the slope," she says. "It hurt too much to crawl. I must have passed out at some point, which was good, in a way."

I notice two bottles of pumped milk on the swing table, and Marian says, "Fourteen ounces, and I've to throw them away, can you credit it? The amount of morphine they've given me would get Saoirse absolutely trolleyed."

"Ah, that's desperate," I say, reaching over to take her hand. "Do you want to sleep?"

Marian shakes her head. The whites of her eyes look very bright. "I'm so lucky, Tessa," she says, and I nod, wondering if that's the adrenaline or the morphine. Marian's in shock, clearly. Soon she's going to cop on that she has weeks and weeks of recovery ahead of her. "Have you talked to mam?" I ask, and she nods.

"I was scared of dying before we'd made up," she says, and I breathe out.

"Thank christ, the two of you not talking was exhausting for me. Do you know how many messages she was sending me a day?" I say. "Thousands. Where's Seb now?"

"Driving. He was just leaving Galway when we talked, so he'll be here by nine, if he doesn't have a heart attack." Marian squeezes her eyes shut. "I'm so sorry, Tessa."

"Don't apologize."

"It was my own fault. I was going too fast on the ridge."

The nurse raps on the door. "Off we go," she says, kicking down the latch on the hospital bed and wheeling Marian out for X-rays. I blink as they go past me. In her mint-green hospital gown, Marian looks like she's about to go give birth.

While they're out, I find a vending machine and buy a Wispa for Marian and a Twirl for myself. When she's wheeled back into the room, I hand her the Wispa and she tears the foil open with her teeth.

"Are you bored at home?" I ask.

"What, with parenting?" asks Marian through a mouthful of chocolate. "Sure, a bit. Sometimes minding a baby is like watching a sunset. It's gorgeous and boring at the same time."

"Do you ever miss being in the IRA?"

"Jesus, no. The IRA was much more boring than parenting," she says, taking another bite of chocolate. "Being sat in a car for hours and hours doing surveillance. Or being stuck in a safe house in the back of beyond for a week. Why are you asking?"

"Eamonn told me to call emergency services, to report you missing. A detective interviewed me."

Marian frowns. "And he asked if I'm bored?"

I hesitate. "He asked if you're in an IRA sleeper cell."

Marian laughs. "Hang on, sorry, are you serious?"

"He wanted to know if you have sniper training."

"Oh, god," says Marian, lifting her hand to her mouth. "What have you done? What did you tell him, Tessa?"

"Nothing. I said you'd left the IRA."

"But you shouldn't have said anything, you shouldn't have talked to the cops at all. Do you know how easy it would be for them to take Saoirse away from me?"

"Of course they can't take her away. You have immunity from prosecution."

"In the North," she says sharply. "Not here. This is a different jurisdiction. Tessa, what did you say?"

"Nothing." I can feel the scratch at the back of my neck, from the baby tugging on my necklace earlier. Marian makes me go through every one of the detective's questions, every one of my answers. I remember one of his questions, and wince. "He asked if you had postnatal depression."

Marian's whole body stiffens. "What did you say?"

"I said you'd a bit of a hard time at first, when Saoirse was in the NICU," I say, and Marian's face drops. "I was only trying to help them find you."

"Are you out of your actual mind?"

"Should I have lied to him?" I say, and hurt washes over Marian's face. She says, "Did you think I'd harmed myself? Did you think I'd leave Seb and Saoirse?"

"Of course not."

"But you told the police I'm having trouble coping."

"I never said that."

"You think I'm struggling. You think I'm not a perfect mother, like you."

I laugh. "Are you joking me? I feel like a failure every single day," I say, and Marian turns away, too angry to look at me.

"You don't even know how to apologize to me," she says. "You're so used to being the right one, you've forgotten how."

"That's not fair, that's not how I think about us."

Marian says, "You don't need to win every argument, Tessa. Just say you're sorry."

"I was trying to do the right thing."

"You still don't think I'm normal," says Marian. "You don't think I'm a normal person."

I frown. "Because you've been having a hard time recently? I don't think depression is wildly uncommon, in fairness."

"I'm not depressed," she says through gritted teeth. "I'm tired. Do you think I'm a bad mother?"

"Marian."

"Seamus said I should never have children. He said I'm not the mothering type," she says, and anger surges through me.

"And you believed him?" I say. "What's a mothering type anyway?"

"Seamus was right, though. I love Saoirse so much, but I'm not good at this, am I? Why aren't I good at it?"

"She spent a month in intensive care, Marian. You're still recovering, but you're brilliant with Saoirse. You must know that."

"I just want to do this year over again. I've been so worried with her being early, and then Royce. I've missed everything."

"It's only been a few months, Marian. You're going to be her mam for the rest of her life. Maybe you two will have a really amazing few months when she's eight years old," I say, and Marian shakes her head. "Saoirse is grand, Marian. Don't worry about her. Mam didn't exactly have a smooth time of it either, when we were little."

"What do you mean? Mam's a battleship. I've never heard her complain once."

"We were both tiny when dad left. She was a wreck."

"Was she? She never told me," says Marian. "Anyway, is that meant to be reassuring? I mean, given the state of us now."

"Ah, sure, look, no one's perfect."

Marian snorts, and I watch her look down, smoothing the foil from the chocolate bar on her lap. "Did you tell the detective about Royce?"

"No. And I didn't tell him you've been visiting Niall in prison. What if he finds out?"

"We'll ask Eamonn to call him off," she says.

"Want to hear something?" I say. "Royce has a girlfriend."

"No chance, mate," says Marian.

"He has a partner and I don't, can you explain that to me?"

We carry on talking about Royce, and Eamonn, and the detective. At some point, Marian starts crying, and I climb onto the hospital bed to sit beside her, our shoulders touching. Beside me, Marian falls asleep, her body worn down from the pain. I sit next to her, hearing the rustle of her hospital gown, the click of the IV drip.

When the nurse comes in, she says, "Oh, good, she needs to rest," and I nod, feeling guilty for making Marian agitated earlier. Eventually I start nodding off, feeling oddly peaceful. There's nothing to do right now, no tasks for us to complete. All of this mess will still be here in the morning.

I'm nearly asleep when a new sound makes its way toward me. Marian's teeth are chattering. I stand from the bed, opening the cupboard for another blanket, and smooth it over her.

Her teeth don't stop chattering, though. I'm about to buy her a tea from the canteen when her legs start to shake, and I stumble out into the corridor. Marian's nurse is at the station, and when she sees the look on my face she comes hurrying into the room. She wakes my sister, and Marian looks down at her shivering body, puzzled. Another nurse appears and takes her temperature. "You have a fever," says the first nurse as she twists open a new vial and fastens it to the

213

drip. "I'm giving you intravenous antibiotics now. You might have an infection from those scrapes."

Just then, Seb appears in the doorway, and his face sinks when he sees the nurses working around Marian. "Seb," she says, through chattering teeth.

The nurse whips her head around. "One visitor," she says, and I step out to the corridor and stand with my forehead against the wall, breathing against the paint.

I can see a pond outside, and under the moon its black surface looks like watered silk. I stand watching the water until Seb finally appears, shaking his head, trying to smooth down his unruly hair.

"The antibiotics are working," he says, breathing out. His eyes are red-rimmed and swollen. "Her fever's already down. God almighty, what a day." Seb buys a Galaxy from the machine and bolts it down in two bites, then buys another, and an Aero bar for Marian. I look past him at the row of red exit signs hanging below the ceiling, one after the other, tabbed away into the distance. "I thought she'd been killed."

"Seb—"

"I have to find her doctor," he says, and I duck back into Marian's room.

"Are you okay?" I ask, and Marian nods. "I meant to ask you earlier. Why were you going too fast on the ridgeway?"

"I thought someone was following me," says Marian. "It was stupid, but there was a man farther down the slope, and he made me nervous."

"Why?"

"He wasn't dressed for a hike. He was wearing jeans."

"Did you recognize him?"

"No, it must have been nothing. I was lying there with my ankle broken. If he'd wanted to hurt me, he had his chance," she says. I start to ask Marian another question, but then Seb is coming back into the room with a doctor and the nurse. "Oh, for god's sake," says the nurse when she sees me. "One visitor."

Thirty-Two

UNDER THE RED EMERGENCY SIGN, I stand breathing in the damp night air. Across the car park, an ambulance drives slowly out toward the main road with its sirens off.

I follow the narrow road toward the M11. My car's headlights illuminate a space under the dark trees, sending a fast tunnel down the road. Beside me, the side mirror suddenly brightens with the reflection of another car's headlights. We are alone, somewhere between Wicklow town and the motorway, and the other driver seems to be accelerating, closing the distance between us. I speed up, too, racing down the winding country road, but soon the other driver is just behind me, close enough for his headlights to bleach the interior of my car.

I reach my hand out to push down the automatic locks. If the driver rams me off the road, I can either sit inside my locked car or take off running into the darkness. I can't see any houses along the road. My pulse beats in my throat, but then the other car is turning, its headlights rotating, and I continue straight, the distance growing between us. It was only someone speeding, nothing to do with me.

. . .

MAM LIVES IN a cul-de-sac of pebbledashed houses in Inchicore. She has a row of seashells on the windowsill and a driftwood sign on the front door that says FÁILTE. Marian and I always tease her about that sign, and the WINE O'CLOCK one in her kitchen, but tonight, standing in the dark on her front step, I'm glad at the sight of it.

When I let myself into her house, mam is scrubbing her kitchen surfaces in a pair of yellow rubber gloves. She drops the gloves in the sink and gives me a tight hug. "If you hadn't rung the guards, Marian would still be up there."

"It's all right, mam. She'll be fine," I say. Over her shoulder, the kitchen is scrubbed to a shine. Mam must have been cleaning since putting the children to bed. She can never sit still when she's worried.

I watch her scoop formula into a bottle for Saoirse's night feed. "Ah, sorry, I forgot to tell you there was pumped milk in Marian's freezer."

"Honestly," says mam, "the carry-on you girls have over milk. Do you know what I was reared on? Condensed milk and golden syrup."

She takes down a bottle of Bailey's and two glasses. "Do you've nothing stronger?" I ask, pulling a face. I want a brandy, something to relax my nerves enough for me to sleep. Mam shakes her head, and we carry our glasses into the front room. I move some of her thousand throw pillows aside before dropping onto the sofa. I take a sip of Bailey's, and it tastes cold and sharp, like spiked eggnog. I lean my head back against the sofa, hugging a throw pillow to my chest.

"Marian's going to hate being laid up in bed," says mam. "And how on earth will she look after Saoirse?"

"Seb will do it."

"He's on a shoot," says mam. "He'll lose the job if he doesn't go back, and they need the money." Of course they need the money, everyone's budgets have been tightened recently, and yet Marian still sent cash to Niall in prison.

"The detective was a prick," I say, twisting the tassels on the pillow.

"Can't say I'm surprised," says mam. Two of her brothers were battered by cops at Musgrave in the eighties, just for being in the wrong place at the wrong time.

"He put a lot into interviewing me today. He won't want all that time to have been wasted."

Mam frowns. "But it wasn't wasted. They found Marian."

"That's not what he wants," I say, taking a long swallow of my drink. "He wants to uncover an IRA sleeper cell."

Mam laughs. "Well, he needs to cop on, then."

"I'm worried about him. What if he doesn't let it go? What if he keeps after Marian?" I picture the detective after our interview ended, looking at our chairs, switching off the lights. He won't leave it there. I know he won't.

"He'll not find anything," says mam. "You worry too much."

"There's no such thing," I snap. "Not for us. There aren't enough hours in the day for all the worrying I should be doing."

Mam's face softens. She starts to speak, and I stand from the sofa. If mam tells me, one more time, to speak to a priest or come with her to mass, I'm going to lose my head. She thinks going to church will stop me worrying all the time, which is ironic, since the church is why we're here. The churches. "Night, mam. Thanks for minding Finn."

Saoirse is asleep in a travel crib in mam's room, and Finn is in the smaller back room. I touch his forehead, and he feels warm. His body always seems to heat by a couple of degrees while he's sleeping. In the darkness I look at his small face, his snub nose and the arch of his eyebrows, his closed dark lashes. I climb in beside Finn, my body tucked around his, the warm soles of his feet resting on my knees, relieved to be with him, in this house, with mam downstairs waiting on *Fair City* to start, with the sloped roof above us and the other small houses curving around the cul-de-sac.

Darkness will have settled over the mountains by now. The ruined chapel and round tower in Glendalough will be dark, and the bare slopes of the mountain rising above them. Marian could still be there, unconscious, her body crumpled against a boulder. Ringing the gardaí today saved her life.

I'm aware of something tugging at me, something I'm missing. There was something from earlier I'd meant to think about when I had time, but my body is already sinking into the mattress and I can't remember what it was.

AT HOME THE NEXT MORNING, I squeeze my car into a spot on Northbrook Road. I lift Finn out of his car seat, and hold him close for a second before spinning around and lowering him to the footpath. We round the corner onto Dartmouth Terrace, and it occurs to me that the detective knows my address. He might have driven here after his shift last night. He might have sat in his car on the road, staring up at my house, but that's a mad thought. Surely he must have better things to do. Mam's right, I do need to have a word with myself.

The detective wouldn't have seen much, even if he had come here. I usually draw the front curtains before we go out, although I hate when other people do. I like being able to glance into strangers' houses, especially during the holidays, when decorations twinkle in some of the front rooms.

Inside, I turn off the security alarm and open the curtains while Finn scatters his train set onto the floor. I watch him scoot around the carpet, finding pieces, fitting them together. The sun catches in his hair, on the tip of his nose, and on the round curve of his cheek.

While he plays, I make a spanakopita to bring Marian in the hospital. I separate the phyllo sheets and brush oil onto them with my fingers, then blend the spinach and cream, grate the cheese. I work quickly, glad to have my hands busy. While the spanakopita cooks in the oven, the kitchen starts to smell rich and golden, like a place where no one is ever anything but safe.

On the drive to the hospital, I glance from the road to Finn in the rear mirror. Before we left, I set a thermos of water and a fruit pouch in the cups of the car seat, and in the mirror I watch Finn drink the fruit purée with a look of concentration. "Here," he says, straining forward to hand me the empty pouch.

"I can't take it right now, I'm driving."

"Here, mama."

"Put it in the cup for now," I say, and he sighs.

AT THE HOSPITAL, Marian, Seb, and mam are ravenous. They fall on the spanakopita like wolves, savaging the entire pan inside of ten minutes. "Was that meant to last me the week?" asks Marian, licking crumbs from her fingers.

"I'll make something else," I say. "What do you fancy?"

"Chicken Marbella? And your polenta one," she says, clapping her hands over Saoirse's. The six of us barely fit in her room in the step-down unit.

"Has your fever come back?" I ask.

"No, thank christ for antibiotics."

"A hundred years ago," says mam, "she'd be dead."

"Jesus, mam."

"In fairness," says Seb, "she would probably have already died from the flu or something."

Seb tells her that he ordered a satellite messenger for her next hike, and an avalanche beacon. "Ireland doesn't have avalanches," says Marian.

"Not yet," says Seb darkly.

"You need to go home," says Marian, and Seb shakes his head. "You'll be up with Saoirse tonight."

"I'm fine," he says. Early tomorrow, Seb has to travel back to the Aran Islands for the reshoots. The two of them were arguing over it when I came in. Seb said, "Don't you want me to stay?" and Marian said, "Of course I want you to stay, but I also want to pay our mortgage. If word gets out that you up and left in the middle of a shoot, no one will hire you on the next job."

Mam and Seb bring the children down to the canteen for tea, leaving Marian and me alone in the room. She says, "Can you research the detective? Find out what other cases he has worked on."

"Why?"

"So we know what he wants."

"Do you want me to run surveillance on him, too?" I ask, and Marian's head rears back. "You're thinking like an IRA member."

"At least I'm thinking. What about yourself? What are you even doing? You've made no progress with Eamonn. I could have finished this weeks ago," she says, her eyes glittering. I'm about to answer when Seb and mam crowd back into the room with the children, balancing paper cups of tea. "Finn, time to go," I say, not looking at Marian.

Mam turns between the two of us, looking at my clouded face, Marian's arms folded over her chest, and says, "Are you girls rowing?" Neither of us answers, and she mutters, "Give my head peace."

Mam walks me outside, both of us holding Finn's hands as we cross the car park. After buckling him into his seat, mam stands beside me. "I popped up to Belfast this morning," she says.

"What? When?"

"Before visiting hours," she says, like the drive across the border and back was nothing. "I saw Sheila."

"You went to see Eoin Royce's mother? Are you out of your mind?" I ask, and mam tuts. "What were you thinking, mam? You're going to get us killed."

"Oh, I trust Sheila. We're old friends."

"You shouldn't have gotten involved," I say.

Mam reaches into her bag and takes out a stack of handwritten letters. She says, "Will you not be wanting these, then?"

AFTER LEAVING WICKLOW, I take back roads instead of the motorway, like it's a dig at Marian, like she will somehow know that I'm in no humor to hurry home and make her a tray of chicken Marbella. Asking me to research the detective, like we're in an active-service unit, and she is divvying up the jobs for an operation.

I won't research the detective when I get home. I won't start reading through his press statements, I won't work out when he joined the Gardaí, which of his cases went to court, or which school he attended, though I know that he might be researching me. And I won't read through the handwritten letters mam has given me, not yet. It's Sunday afternoon. After Finn's bedtime, I'm going to watch television and do laundry, and tomorrow I'm going to walk into work like this weekend never happened.

At home with Finn, I think finally something simple, something good, and being alone with him is like pouring molten gold into all the day's cracks.

During dinner, Finn looks at me over his plate. "I don't want this," he says. "I want plain rice."

"It is plain rice," I say. "Risotto is basically plain rice."

Finn jumps down and shoves his chair over to the cabinet, reaching for a biscuit. "No," I say. "Not until after dinner." He kicks the cabinet, wailing, and I mutter, "Jesus christ, can I never get a break?"

Finn looks at me, startled, and guilt floods through me, because it's not his job to be good for me, to make up for anything for me. "Sorry. Sorry, sunshine, I'm tired. And we both need to eat our dinner. Do you want some parmesan on yours?"

"I want to grate it myself," he says. He gives the cabinet a final kick, which I decide, for both our sakes, not to see, and sits down at the table. After precisely three bites of risotto, Finn is happy again, babbling away to me, swinging his legs under the table, like the tantrum never happened, and I understand why mam still asks Marian and me if we're hungry anytime we're in bad form.

Finn has been overwrought all evening, I realize. Earlier, when his scissors wouldn't open, he started sobbing, almost doing himself a violence. "Were you worried about Aunt Marian yesterday?" I ask him at bedtime.

"Granny said she could have frozen to death," he blurts out, and I'm amazed it took me so long to cop on.

"She's fine now, *mo leanbh*, she's safe." He asks if he will freeze, and I say, "No, no. You're in your warm bed, in your safe house."

The phrase catches in my mouth, and I lift a hand to my face, trying to hide the tears springing to my eyes. How has this happened? What have I done wrong? Because I've been raising my son in hiding, in what is, for all intents and purposes, a safe house. With a security alarm, with double-paned windows, with extra locks on the doors.

"What is it, mama?" he asks.

"I just meant that you've nothing to worry about, okay? You're safe."

Thirty-Three

AT THE OFFICE, I scan my badge, then hook the lanyard over my neck, hurrying across the building. I work through assignments at my desk, editing and correcting, restoring order. My face feels dry and composed. I sit trimming a story, in a dark jumper and cigarette trousers, listening to keys tapping around me, while outside rain lashes the taxis and buses on Kildare Street.

I start editing a piece from the news desk on a shooting in north Belfast last night. A Catholic solicitor was shot in retaliation for the kidnapping of a Protestant judge, who was taken in retaliation for the shooting of a Catholic teacher, who was shot in retaliation for the murder of two unarmed Protestants, and it goes back, on and on and on. The victims are like a strand of paper dolls, each one holding hands with the one before.

The article is brief, matter-of-fact. "As part of their inquiries, police are examining a car left on waste ground in the Protestant neighborhood of Sandy Row in south Belfast." The Protestant neighborhood. How little has changed, how doomed we sound. I highlight the phrase and delete it before sending the piece on.

At ten, I duck out in the rain to buy a cappuccino and an almond croissant from a shop on Baggot Street. Crossing Merrion Square, I taste rain on the plastic lid of my coffee cup. Once I'm back in the office, the reporter comes to my desk. "Why did you change my copy?" he asks.

"Because you can't call a neighborhood Catholic or Protestant."

"But it is a Protestant area," he says, his voice raised. He is one of the most senior reporters on the news desk. He could, possibly, have me fired. Around us, the other desks have gone quiet as people start to listen.

"That's not the point. Saying the car was found in a Protestant neighborhood is like blaming an entire community for the shooting. How can you not see that? You're encouraging reprisals."

"I'm reporting the facts. Change it back."

"No," I say. This is, apparently, the hill I will die on. The reporter looks around for support, but no one meets his eyes. Finally he points at me and says to Joanna, "I don't want her touching my copy ever again. Give it to someone else."

"Ah, no, Simon," says Joanna with a bright smile. "You know we're all a team."

The reporter walks away, muttering. An hour later, Oisín leans over my desk and says, "They're using your version. It's already online."

"Good," I say, though that one edit won't make any difference. A reprisal is coming, everyone knows that.

During our lunch break, Emer, Oisín, and I walk to St. Andrew's Church to donate blood after hearing an appeal on the news. The blood donations will be sent to Belfast, a convoy of lorries loaded with blood driving north over the border. Hospitals made the appeal for donations, because their supplies are already low, and the North is bracing for a reprisal after the last shooting, this wave of revenge always poised to crash over the province. My donation won't be used right away. It will have to be cleaned first. Washed, however you wash blood.

At St. Andrew's, the nurse has trouble finding a vein. She frowns, pushing against my arm, rubbing hard at my elbow. She tries to draw blood from my left arm, but nothing comes into the vial. It remains clear, while we both frown at it. "You don't have any blood," she says.

"Yes I do," I say, stupidly.

"Your veins are constricted. I think you're dehydrated," she says. "I can't do it."

"Please," I say. "Please try, please, you have to."

When I start to cry, the nurse says, "Ah, listen, you're okay." She hands me a bottle of juice. "Drink this. I'll come back to you, all right?" And I sit drinking the bottle of juice, with a tourniquet around my arm and silent tears flooding down my face. The nurse motions me back after a few minutes. She twists open a needle, and we watch red blood lifting up the coil.

Emer and Oisín are waiting for me outside the church. Oisín says, "The victim's husband was on the news. He was asking for no reprisals."

"There are going to be reprisals," says Emer, her voice dull.

"I know."

The blood draw leaves a bruise on my arm, and the bruise deepens on my walk back to the office, gathering color, darkening like a thunder cloud.

WE ARE CALLED in for a conference at four. Joanna is going over our assignments when I catch a blur of movement on the other side of the glass conference wall. Across the table, the others are all watching the figure moving toward the door, and my body tenses. I turn in time to see the detective opening the door and raising his badge, holding it up long enough for everyone in the room to get a good look at it. He turns to me. "Can I've a word?"

Humiliation flares across my face. I stand, knocking my hip hard against the conference table. "Sorry," I say to Joanna, and she hides her surprise fast enough to say, "No bother at all, we're finishing up anyway."

The detective steps into the empty conference room next door. He thinks I'm lying to him, he thinks I have information he wants, and he has decided to start our next interview on different terms. Following him into the conference room, I can see others watching us down the open-plan office, and the reporter leaning back in his chair with his brows raised. "Let's go outside," I say.

"Why?" says the detective, sitting down, smoothing his suit. "We're already here."

I'm facing him, trying to decide what to do next, when Emer pushes through the door and takes a seat across from the detective. He looks at her, his mouth curling. "We need to speak privately," he says.

"No, I'm afraid not," says Emer. "I'm her solicitor."

"She doesn't need a solicitor," says the detective. "She's not speaking to me under caution."

"Oh," says Emer, turning to me, "in that case, do you want to be interviewed at this particular time?"

I shake my head. I'm not ready for it, not before talking with Eamonn. The detective will tear me apart.

"Okay," says Emer. She finds a sticky note and bends over it with a pen. "Here's my number. If you want me to bring her over to the station for a chat, give me a buzz."

I follow Emer out of the room, with the detective watching us. She turns down a corridor and opens the fire door onto the external staircase. The two of us stand on the fire escape, under the gray clouds, while I gulp down air. I look at Emer's small, catlike face, her sharp pointed nose. "How did you know to do that?" I ask, and Emer shrugs.

"Coming into your office, with that face on him. I didn't like it," she says. "And I've a civil liberties degree, so I actually know what the cops are and aren't allowed to do, which they assume most people won't."

I nod, adrenaline thumping in my veins. The detective was about to wreck me. "He's going to hate me for this."

"In fairness," says Emer, "he didn't look like your biggest fan to begin with."

"No, I suppose not."

"You don't need to tell me," says Emer.

"I can't," I say, and then realize, with a bright burst in my skull, that I don't need to worry about Emer dobbing me in to the IRA. The IRA already knows exactly where I am, I don't need to hide anymore. My mind is pinwheeling, bursting into colors. I have no reason to lie. That's one silver lining. I want to laugh out loud, or burst into tears. "He wants to arrest me."

"Truly," says Emer. "I'm not asking, you don't need to say anything."

"He thinks I'm in the IRA."

Her eyes startle. "Why?"

"Because my sister was," I say quickly, and the release is like cutting myself out of a net.

"But why now?" she asks, her legal mind shifting ahead. "What made him come here today?"

"My sister went missing on a hike this weekend. I went to the gardaí for help, and now he thinks he's closing in on a sleeper cell."

"And you're certain he's wrong?" asks Emer.

"My sister became an informer, before we left Northern Ireland. We both did."

"Funny," says Emer. "You never talk about your home life. I thought you were having an affair with someone in the office."

I snort. "Chance would be a fine thing."

"Does he have any evidence against you?" she asks, and I shake my head. I almost tell her about the bungalow. My fingerprints on the wall and the radiator, the card table. And I remember coughing, my blood disappearing into the black fabric of the Range Rover. Normally the IRA burns a car out after an operation, but they'd hate to with one that expensive. They might try to get away with just cleaning it.

Emer looks at me, and she knows I'm holding something back. "Well, think about it," she says. "If you think of anything he might have against you, tell me."

Slowly, feeling my way along the edges, I say, "There are some things I'm not allowed to talk about yet."

Royce looking at me, saying, If you call the police, if you tell anyone, we will kill your family. Eamonn saying, Can you meet me?

"I understand," says Emer. "But whatever it is, you'll be wanting to get ahead of him. My bet is he already has someone going through your phone records and emails."

"But I haven't been arrested," I say, and Emer shrugs. She says, "If they find something, they'll arrest you, get a warrant, and then say they found whatever it is afterward."

Something prickles through me, but I shove it aside. "Well, look, I don't envy the cop who has to read through our work group chats. The ones about Secret Santa alone, can you imagine?"

"Financials, too," says Emer.

"Then he'll know how often I'm in my overdraft," I say, but the prickling feeling has grown worse.

"What about your sister?" asks Emer.

"Joint account with her husband," I say. Marian would never have been stupid enough to wire money to Niall in prison from her account. She said the payments were anonymous. All the cops will find are a lot of Tesco and Dublin Bus receipts. Though Marian does spend an absolute fortune on skin-care products. Sometimes I feel like we're running a sort of accidental experiment, with her using expensive serums and me using off-brand lotion, and in ten years we'll see if her routine has worked. By which point my own face might be too wrecked to fix, but there you have it.

Emer is looking at me like she's about to snap her fingers in my face. "Do you think the detective has sent people into my house?" I ask, and the prickling feeling bursts down my arms and back. Not in my house, not where I give Finn a bath, cook his dinner, read him stories.

"I doubt it," says Emer. "It would be hard to get a search team in and out without leaving any trace. If they were caught searching without a warrant, their whole case would be ruined."

"Good."

"Listen," says Emer, "something has him convinced the two of you are worth his time. If I were you, I'd want to find out what it is before he drops it in my lap."

"I'll think about it, I promise. Thank you, Emer."

"Anytime. Zakura for lunch tomorrow?" she asks, and I nod, feeling childish for thinking she wasn't really my mate because she has never gone to the toilets with me in a pub.

I motion down at her athletic sandals. "Were slippers too formal, no?"

. . .

No one else in the office mentions the detective's visit. I catch them sneaking glances toward me at first, but they stop soon enough, distracted by their own work, their own daydreams. Somewhere, a cop is reading transcripts of my phone messages. I picture a man, younger than me, paging through the messages in Kevin Street Garda Station.

I swipe open my phone and scroll through my messages, choosing a few at random, to see what the officer might be reading. They're almost painfully dull, all of them. A fair few desperate messages to mam, begging her to mind Finn when his playschool is closed. Group chats with other parents, arranging playdates on the weekends. A work chat, full of low-level gossip. Good luck to the cop reading month after month of this clabber.

I click back onto a story for our financial pages, and I'm editing a passage about lender rates when the hairs rise on my arms. I have to wait for nearly an hour until Emer finally leaves her desk and starts toward the canteen, and I can follow her into the hall.

"Sorry—"

"What's wrong?" she asks.

"My phone records," I say, holding up my mobile. "Do you mean this phone, that I've now? Or the one I had in Belfast?"

"Oh," says Emer. "Both, probably."

"Even if I haven't used the number in three years?"

"Depends on your server," she says, "but odds are they'll find that data, too. Are you okay? Want to come get a coffee?"

"No, I'm all right. Thanks," I say. Emer waits for a second, then heads toward the canteen, and I lock myself in the women's toilets, digging my hands into my hair.

All of my messages are harmless now, but what about before, in my twenties, when I took my privacy for granted, when I never thought that anyone else would ever be reading through my conversations? What was I saying back then?

Already I can think of two conversations. When the cop finds them, he will sit up in his chair, take a screenshot of them, send them up to the detective. I sit with my knuckles pressed to my mouth, staring at the toilet door.

The first conversation was a group chat with my friends, one summer when I was home from Trinity. We'd been to a protest that night in Ballymurphy. The protest's organizers were all future IRA leaders, but we didn't know that at the time, we thought we were protesting the housing board and income inequality. One of the protesters got hold of a loudhailer, and read off part of a Black Panthers speech from the sixties. "This is a hold-up. We've come for what's ours," he said, and the crowd roared. We were all buzzing afterward, messaging back and forth about the protest. I wrote, "That was deadly."

And the other conversation was a few years later, soon after the conflict kicked off again. I sent Marian a picture of the Dark Hedges, in north Antrim. I'd never been before. You wouldn't want to, with the buses crowding the lane, but the tourists had stopped coming because of the conflict. In the picture I took that day, all you can see is the long tunnel of twisted, ancient thorn trees. I sent the picture to Marian, and wrote, "Dark Hedges, and not another soul in sight."

Marian wrote back, "Never say the IRA is good for nothing."

"Fair play to the lads," I wrote. "Something had to be done about the tourists."

Thirty-Four

WHEN EAMONN OPENS THE DOOR, my whole body becomes so relaxed I feel almost tired. "Hi," he says, "hey," and he is smiling, holding his hand to the top of his head. I smile back at him, then he steps inside, looking at me, walking backward down the hall. He forgot to ask me the usual question. Did you get here safely? It occurs to me that I did not, in fact, look around myself on the road, that I was distracted, thinking about seeing him again.

"Coffee?" he asks, and I nod, locking the front door behind me.

While he makes the coffee, I tell him about Marian's rescue on Camaderry. Describing it to him makes me almost giddy with relief, and he listens while leaning back against the counter. We finish our coffees and bottles of mineral water.

Halfway down the hall, I stop at the bottom of the staircase, resting my hand on the banister. "Do you ever sleep here?" I ask, then stop, blushing. I hadn't realized how it would come out sounding.

"Sometimes." Eamonn is standing a few feet away from me. The light in the house is like platinum, titanium. Under my clothes, I can feel the silk straps of my bra running over my shoulders, the bands of my stockings. Eamonn clears his throat. "Do you want to see the upstairs?"

I nod, and he turns at the banister post, passing within inches of me, and starts up the stairs. I follow him, my stockings brushing against each other. I've waited so long for this, I've been so patient. Now that it's here, I feel calm. Our situation isn't complicated, after all, not anymore.

Eamonn shows me the office upstairs, and the bathroom, and the main bedroom. I step into the room, my heart pounding, my pulse blooming, and turn to face him. The inside of my mouth flushes with heat. He reaches out to hold my arms, and sensation surges to the surface of my body. He presses me back against the wall, lifting my skirt above the tops of my stockings.

We undress each other, our clothes falling to the floor, and he leans me back onto the bed, the sunlight through the window flooding our bodies. I raise my head to kiss him, and his mouth tastes like my mouth, like we match.

On the bus home, I roll my bottom lip inside my mouth, like he's still kissing me.

"Can you stay over tonight?" he'd asked, and I shook my head. "How long do we have?" We lay together afterward, his body pressed against mine. Five minutes, and then I was searching for my clothes, walking toward the bus stop, with his aftershave rubbed on my skin. My arm still aches from giving blood, and what's happening to me, what is happening to me?

Thirty-Five

THE DETECTIVE RINGS ME at work in the morning. "I need a word, Tessa. Bring your solicitor if you like," he says, and something about his tone has me pulling on my coat without asking Emer to come with me. I know, somehow, that bringing her won't help me. My hand reaches to switch off my monitor, and I slide my notebook into my bag.

Across Kildare Street, the elms in the parliament courtyard are rustling against the overcast sky, the security hut lit with watery fluorescent light. I walk down Molesworth Street and across the city center toward the garda station. The roads feel damp underfoot. A buried river runs under Dublin, and today it's like I can feel it flowing under the pavement, a dark, old current.

Inside the garda station, I stop with the halo light suspended far above my head. For the past few days, I've been waiting for the detective to call me back here. I've known that he has me on a lead, ready to reel me in whenever he wants.

The detective sits down across from me in the interview room and asks the sergeant for tea, which she brings to us in thin plastic cups. The detective didn't offer me tea or water during the first interview, and I wonder what has changed. The razor burn on his jaw has grown worse since Monday. Some of the bumps are tipped with spots of dried blood. He knows those bumps are there, but he'll shave over them again tomorrow morning. He won't let the rash heal, too fixated on how he wants to look.

The detective taps one of the two folders in front of him. "Your phone transcripts," he says. "I've to say, they make for disturbing reading."

"Right, I'm sure they do," I say. I can't tell if this is the same interview room we were in last weekend or a new one. Hundreds of people have sat in this chair before me. Suspects, witnesses, victims. Answering questions, describing events, giving accounts of themselves. You'd think all those words would leave some mark, but the room feels new. I could be the first person ever to enter it.

The detective lifts a page between his thumb and finger, and starts to read. "'I hope his dogs savage him. I hope they tear the face off him.'"

"Sorry? I never wrote that. Those are someone else's messages," I say. I still have on my work clothes, the dark top and cigarette trousers, small gold hoop earrings, the *Irish Observer* badge on a lanyard around my neck.

"Are you sure? Would you swear to it?" he asks in his loud voice, like he's speaking to someone else, standing some distance behind me.

"Are you trying to fit me up?" I ask.

The detective raises his eyebrows. "Mind yourself. That's quite an accusation." He lowers his face and continues to read. "At two fifteen p.m., Clodagh O'Malley wrote: 'Ian Crowley was just acquitted.' At two eighteen p.m., you wrote back: 'I hope his dogs savage him. I hope they tear the face off him.'"

"When was that?" I ask, finally, and the detective tells me the date.

"That was ages ago," I say. "I was, what, twenty-three years old?"

"What else were you doing at that age, Tessa?"

"Nothing. That was a text message, that's it."

"Ian Crowley owned pit bulls, isn't that right?" asks the detective, and I shake my head.

"They were just messages. I worked with Clodagh. She was a reporter at the BBC, she was covering Ian Crowley's trial."

"Are you in the IRA, Tessa?"

"That case had nothing to do with the conflict, you know that yourself. Ian Crowley attacked women in Belfast."

"Was Crowley Catholic or Protestant?"

"He was a psychopath. His religion is beside the point."

"It's never beside the point, not where you're from," says the detective. "'I hope his dogs savage him. I hope they tear the face off him.'"

"I was upset. I shouldn't have said that."

"I'll tell you something, you shouldn't have lied about saying it. You just sat there, looked me in the eyes, and lied."

"Do you remember every message you've ever sent?" I say. "That was a private conversation. What's the crime here? Inciting violence? Clodagh was a reporter at the BBC, do you think I was actually encouraging her to set that man's dogs on him?"

"I think it's an interesting fantasy," he says.

"Fantasy?" I ask. "Jesus, you can't be serious."

"What would you call it, then?" asks the detective. "Crowley was punished, wasn't he? Mob justice, just like you wanted."

Six months after his acquittal, Crowley was found dead in his house after a gas leak, which might have been an accident, or someone might have tampered with his cooker.

"You lied to me, Tessa. You're a liar."

"That didn't sound like something I'd say, it didn't sound like me."

"Are you sure about that?" he says. "Maybe it sounds exactly like you." I look at the detective's face, the blue eyes, the flat cheekbones, and it's like I've known him for years and years.

"I spoke with your ex-husband," says the detective. Bastard, I think. Tom didn't tell me. "He seems like a good man. Devoted father."

"Sorry, what does that have to do with you?" I ask.

"Custody arrangements aren't permanent, you know. They can change."

"Tom's not about to start a custody battle. He would never do that to Finn."

"Like I said, he's a good man. He'll do what's best for his son."

"Is this why you wanted to become a cop? So you could threaten to take children away from their mothers?" I ask. He's holding something back, but I can't tell what, if it's disdain for me, or doubt. "Why am I even here? Am I a suspect in a criminal investigation? No? Am I a witness in a criminal investigation?"

"You tell me," says the detective. I look at the blond gleam in his hair, the red rash on his jaw from shaving, the heavy fabric of his suit. "Why was your sister hospitalized four years ago, Tessa?"

"She wasn't."

"Marian was in hospital having her stomach pumped. Someone found her and dumped her outside the Mater Hospital in west Belfast. She was unconscious," he says. His voice, the volume of his voice, sends the words straight through me. And the worst part is, I know, instantly, that he's not lying. "She'd tried to kill herself."

I struggle to get my voice back, fighting something under me. "Why? Why would she do that?" I say, and the words sound wet and desperate leaving my throat.

"Well, according to your first interview, Marian has no history of depression or self-harm," he says, "and then one day she up and took an overdose. So if I'd to guess, I'd say she was trying to punish herself. Something happened that made her think she didn't deserve to live anymore. And if you ask me, she was probably right."

He tells me the date in April when she was admitted to hospital. "Can you think of anything significant around then? Did anything happen to distress her?"

"I don't remember," I say. Different moments with my sister, different conversations, twist through my mind, but I can't place them in order.

"Come on, Tessa," says the detective, drawing out my name like an exasperated teacher. "Are you even trying?"

"My son was four months old, that April," I say, passing a hand over my eyes. "Sorry, I know that's not important, I'm just trying to think."

"Would you like me to give you a hint?" he says, the words clicking together like marbles, and I suddenly understand. The atmosphere in the room changes. I can see dust motes spinning between us, the whole room turning with them. The detective watches me, leaning forward in his seat, like I'm about to leap from my chair. He says, "Where was Marian at the time of the Victoria Square bombing?"

"In Belfast," I say, and the weight is dragging me down with it. "I told you she was a paramedic. She was off duty that day, but she ran to help."

"And you never thought to ask Marian why she was at the scene?" asks the detective, and I shake my head. I don't seem to be breathing properly anymore, it's like the atmosphere has thinned, like the room has lost its oxygen. "What did Marian tell you about that day?" he asks.

"She came to my house afterward," I say. "She was in shock. I gave her some brandy."

Marian's jeans were stiff with blood. She'd been kneeling on the wet floor of the shopping center, giving first aid to the victims. I remember the stunned look on her face, how I kept having to repeat myself because she seemed to be having trouble hearing me. I poured her a brandy and we sat together at my kitchen table.

"I need you to try very hard to remember exactly what Marian said."

"She said, When is it going to end?"

"But Marian was a paramedic," says the detective, faking a puzzled expression. "She'd spent years as a paramedic by that point, during the conflict. She'd been called out to plenty of similar scenes before."

"So it should have been easy for her?" I ask, but I'm not arguing with him. All the fight has gone out of me, and I don't actually know the answer, if most paramedics find their work easier or harder as the years go by. Harder, I'd guess. "Marian said Victoria Square was an accident. The IRA had planned to set off the device at night, when the shopping center was empty."

"So Marian had never planned to hurt anyone," says the detective.

"No, hang on, I never said that. Marian wasn't involved."

"Do you know how many people died in the Victoria Square bombing, Tessa? Twelve," he says, "and upward of fifty suffered injuries, a fair number of them life altering."

I grip my hands on the chair to stop myself shuddering. "Victoria Square was attacked on the twelfth of April," he says. "Your sister tried to kill herself two days later."

He opens the second folder and begins laying out photographs until they fill the table. They're images from surveillance cameras. Black-and-white stills, of Marian.

Pressure rises behind my forehead, tightening over my skull. I can feel the weight of the small gold hoops in my ears. Often at the end of the day, I take the earrings off, dropping the two rings into my palm. "You're going to lose those," says Marian every single time, because she's my sister.

The surveillance images are all from different roads, different street corners, in Belfast. Marian is in each one, a younger version of her, her hair longer, dressed in jeans and a dark top. "Read the date," says the detective, and my eyes move to the white numbers printed at the top of each image. They're all from the day of the Victoria Square bombing.

"I already knew Marian was in the city center that day," I say.

"For three hours?" he says. "Marian was walking in circles. She didn't go into a single shop, she didn't meet anyone, she didn't buy anything to eat. Marian spent the three hours before the attack circling around Victoria Square." I slide one of the images closer to me, studying her face, like I will be able to tell the truth from her expression. "When Marian came to your house in Greyabbey, you gave her some brandy."

"Yes."

"What did you do with her clothes, Tessa?"

My heart drops. After a long time, I say, "I washed them."

"Why?"

"Because they were covered in blood."

The detective stares at me. "You destroyed evidence."

"No, it wasn't like that. My sister came to my house in dirty clothes and I gave her clean ones, that's all," I say. "Marian was a paramedic, sometimes she got blood on her uniform, or her shoes."

"Did the stains come out?" he asks, and I shake my head. "So then what did you do?"

"I threw them away," I whisper.

"Including her shoes?"

"Yes."

"You obstructed a criminal investigation, Tessa. An IRA bomber came to your house, in bloodstained clothes, and you disposed of them for her."

"I put them in with my rubbish, they went out in the regular bin. I wasn't hiding anything."

"I want you to go home now, Tessa. And I want you to think very carefully if there's anything left that you need to tell me."

"That's all?" I ask, confused. "I can go?"

"Why?" asks the detective, stretching his neck to the side, making his vertebrae crack. "Do you want to stay longer?"

Thirty-Six

I TUCK MY JACKET around myself at the school gates, waiting to collect my son.

"Finn's not here," says his teacher, and I blink at her. I can feel the pins pressed to my skull, holding the hair back from my face, how they cross into an X.

"Oh, right. Sorry. Where is he?"

"His father picked him up."

"No, his father's in Belfast," I say, and the teacher frowns. She starts to say something, but I'm already stepping back from the play-school gate, stumbling through the crowd of other parents, their own children drawing toward them like magnets. All around me, small children are shrugging on their rucksacks, waving bright drawings. Through the open door, I can see the empty hook where Finn hung up his bag and raincoat this morning, and the cubby with his blanket for rest time.

I move toward the playground, scanning the climbing struc-ture, ready to spot Finn winding down the slide. A part of me is de-tached, almost bemused. This has happened before, many times. Finn has vanished in supermarkets, on footpaths, in crowded restaurants, always running a few paces ahead of me, always curious about something just out of sight. I stand on the edge of the playground, watching all these small hearts, and where is mine? Where is my son?

I ring Tom while circling the playground. "Where are you?" I ask, barely hearing my own voice.

"What?" he says.

"Where are you?" I ask again. "Are you in Dublin?"

"Are you okay, Tessa?"

"Just tell me."

"It's Friday," Tom says slowly, and I've to stop myself from screaming at him to answer the question. "It's half term, remember? Finn has off school this week. I'm bringing him to Ardara," he says, and I sink down onto the playground bench. I thought someone had taken him, I thought the playschool had handed my son over to Eoin Royce.

"I didn't say goodbye to Finn this morning, I forgot to tell him the plan."

"Well, we're in Drumree already, I'm not turning around," Tom says, and I rub my forehead.

"Sorry," I say. "I don't know what's the matter with me."

Tom sighs. "Here, I'll put you on speaker."

I say hello to Finn, and he calls hello back at me. He chats to me about his school day, then Tom interrupts. "Look, I need the phone for directions."

"Sorry. Thanks, Tom. Have fun with your granny and grandda, okay, Finn? I love you."

When I finally stand up, the blood drains from my head, and for a moment I'm on the verge of blacking out. Eventually the lightheadedness fades enough for me to walk to my street and climb into my car, and drive to the Liberties.

Marian opens her door, in woolen socks and a pair of loose denim overalls, with crutches under her arms, and something about my expression makes her reach for my hand. She says, "Are you okay?"

"Yeah, I'm fine," I say. I can barely bring myself to look at her. "Want to come for a swim?"

Part Three

SISTERS

Thirty-Seven

MARIAN FROWNS AT ME. "I can't swim right now, Tessa. I'm with the baby."

"But mam's here, too, isn't she? She can mind Saoirse."

Marian reaches back to fix her hair, thinking it over. "The cold water would be good for my ankle. Maybe I should."

"Grand. Go get your swimming things."

I drive us through the afternoon traffic to the Forty Foot. Over the sea, the sky is gunmetal gray, and the water looks thick and cold, unforgiving. No one else is here, and the air smells damp and brackish with seaweed. On the rock, Marian sets down her crutches. She unbuttons her overalls and unstraps the boot around her foot, and I look at the dent on her shin and her pale, swollen ankle. "It's colder than I thought," she says, and with my back to her, I say, "It's fine once you're in."

Marian tugs her shirt over her head, and I can see strands of hair standing from her head with static electricity, like Finn's does when I take off one of his jumpers. Below us, the waves foam against the rock. The whole promontory feels like it has come loose from the shore and is moving out into open water, buffeted by the currents.

I shove my jeans down my legs, watching chills rise on my bare thighs. Cold seeps into my feet from the damp stone. Below us, a rope of black seaweed is tangled on the rock, each wave trying and failing to rip it loose. Marian frowns at the deep water, and I look at the chipped red polish on her toes. She's flexing her calf muscles, an unconscious reflex against the chill, making her Achilles tendons strain.

I come to stand beside her where the rock has a blunt edge, like a high dive. Below us, the water lifts and sucks away from the rock. I look out, and there's no sun, nothing to stop me staring all the way out to the horizon, where the sea is even darker, like charcoal. "Should we just go and get a coffee?" asks Marian.

"No, we can jump in at the same time. Ready?" I ask, and she nods. "One. Two. Three."

Marian leaps from the rock, kicking her feet in the air, and I watch her crash through the surface, the sea turning her limbs pale and blurry, distorted. The ring of foam she made when she jumped starts to come apart, strands of it carried on the backs of the waves.

Marian surfaces, yelping, and turns back to me. She lets some salt water spill into her open mouth and then blows it back out, and I want to start crying because that's something I do in the sea, too, like we're both trying to turn into selkies.

"What're you doing? Hurry up," Marian calls, laughing, windmilling her arms under the surface to keep herself upright in the waves.

I stand on the rock, looking down at my sister in the water, at her wet hair, the waves slipping over her shoulders. "I'm not coming in."

Marian stares at me for a moment, and then she lets her head sink under the surface, like she doesn't want to hear what I'm about to say. Below the surface, she won't be able to hear anything except the pebbles on the sea floor rattling as the waves surge, and if she opens her eyes she'll only see the grainy, dusty water, and the shadowy base of the rock ahead of her.

After a few seconds, Marian surfaces, blinking the water from her eyes. She treads water, bobbing in the waves, and I stand at the very edge of the rock. The tide is moving her, almost imperceptibly, further out from shore.

"Why did you try to kill yourself?" I ask. Marian's movements slow, letting the waves shift her.

"I didn't think I deserved to live anymore," she says.

"Did you bomb Victoria Square?"

"No."

"Stop lying to me, Marian," I say. "Just stop. I know you spent three hours circling it." Another rope of seaweed is drifting in the current, tangling below her legs, and Marian jerks away as it brushes against her foot.

"I wasn't circling Victoria Square. You remember what's across the road from it," she says. "I was circling the police station. I was going to turn myself in."

"Why?"

"Because I killed someone."

Thirty-Eight

WAVES ARE BREAKING AGAINST the rock. If I focus, I can feel microscopic droplets from the spume popping against my bare skin. The water is cold enough to already be turning my sister's mouth purple. She could swim over and haul herself out, but I know she won't, not until I say so.

"I killed someone," she says again, and the words reach me at the same time as a wave bursts onto the rock, exploding into foam. "He was twenty-four years old."

"Why?" I ask. I'm having trouble balancing on the promontory's edge, like the waves are making it rock, about to pitch me into the water.

"Seamus told me to build a bomb for the power station in Camlough," she says. "It would be like all the other ones, we'd call in a warning first. I'd worked the night before, I'd done a twelve-hour shift in the ambulance. I asked Seamus to let me sleep for a few hours first, but he said they needed the device right away. He told me to use gelignite instead of Semtex, and I did something wrong," she says.

Her voice is the same volume as the waves, I can't tell if I'm actually hearing her speak or reading her lips, but it doesn't matter. It's like she's telling me something I already know, something I've known for years.

"Conor was in another IRA unit in south Armagh. He was driving the bomb to Camlough, and it went off in his car."

I don't remember hearing about it at the time, but those deaths have always been the least reported ones in the conflict. The fuck ups. No one seems to care when the IRA or UVF inadvertently kills one of its own. The tabloids call them own goals.

Marian doesn't call his death an accident. If she did, I'd lose the plot. Those deaths aren't accidents, that word doesn't come close.

"I talked to Conor's parents. I told them I was going to turn myself in, and they told me not to. They told me to become an informer."

"That's not the reason you told me. Jesus, I never even questioned you. You must have thought I was so stupid."

"I'm sorry, Tessa," she says. Marian's eyes are bloodshot, irritated from the salt water. While we've been talking, she hasn't been protecting them from the waves, blinking in time.

"Were his family angry? Were they hard on you?"

"Yes."

"Good," I say. Marian's teeth are chattering now from the cold. "Why didn't you tell me?"

"Because you're my sister," she says. "And I knew if I told you, you wouldn't love me anymore."

I take a step back. My feet don't leave any sort of mark on the rock, like I was never here. I pull my jeans back on, and my hoodie, with my hands shaking. "Do you have money for the bus?" I ask.

"Tessa—"

"Find your own way home," I say, turning away, with Marian still in the water, floating in the gray waves below the rock.

Thirty-Nine

At the safe house in Stoneybatter, Eamonn unzips my hoodie, reaching his hands beneath it, around my waist. He pauses. "Why do you've a swimsuit on?"

"I'll tell you later," I say. "Can we go upstairs?"

I can't tell if the next hour we spend in bed is taking me apart or putting me back together. We drowse together afterward, before rolling onto the pillows and falling into conversation. I mention something from a book I've been reading, then ask, "Are you reading anything at the moment?"

"*David Copperfield.*"

"You're reading Dickens?"

Eamonn nods. "But I was on George Eliot before, and I liked her better."

"How do you mean? You read all of her books?"

"She only wrote seven novels," he says.

"Had you read them at school?" I ask, and he says, "No. It wasn't that sort of school."

"What sort of school was it?" I ask, and Eamonn searches for the right word. "Chaotic."

"Violent?"

"Yes."

"Did you get into fights?" I ask.

"Ah, no. The students weren't the problem, really. They were predictable. We'd tournaments behind the portacabins, for fighting. That part wasn't so bad. The teachers were worse," he says. "I saw our religion teacher on the street a few years ago. I almost shoved him in front of a bus."

Eamonn rubs the bridge of his nose. "The teachers hated us, they thought we were animals. They'd laugh if they ever saw me reading a book like that."

"I'm sorry, Eamonn. That's disgraceful."

He shrugs his shoulders against the pillow, patting his hand on his chest. "It's all right. Are you hungry?"

I watch him, in only a pair of boxers, find his phone and call for a takeaway. "Hi there, can I order a few things to pick up? Grand, thanks," he says, and his voice doesn't change on the line. He doesn't have different voices for different occasions, like some people do. He's serious, straightforward. If Eamonn worked in a restaurant and a hundred euro went missing from the till, you'd never suspect him of taking it. And if we were together—if we were together, I'd never worry about him cheating on me.

Eamonn leans over the bed to kiss me. "The takeaway's right around the corner, I'll be back soon," he says, and it's only when he returns with our food that I realize I could have spent the time while he was out searching the safe house. The thought appalls me now.

Eamonn unpacks the bags while I take down our plates. I like the way he eats, with relish, popping a piece of naan in his mouth, swallowing a cold beer. After wolfing down our food, we move to the front room, and Eamonn pours both of us a whiskey. I sit facing him, my feet drawn in on the sofa, and he runs his hand up and down my legs. He says, "Why the dry swimsuit? Did you get there and realize it's mad to swim in this weather?"

"Marian killed someone," I say. I tell Eamonn what happened, and he exhales slowly. Softly, he says, "That man knew the risks when he got in the car with a device."

"He was twenty-four years old."

"Marian wasn't much older," says Eamonn.

Grief lodges in my throat. "Do you know something, I never once asked her the question. I never asked Marian if she'd killed anyone. I didn't think I could live with it, if she had."

"Would you really rather not know?" asks Eamonn, drinking his whiskey.

"Maybe." Through the window, I can see the orange streetlamps glowing on the road. "Do you have siblings?"

Eamonn pauses, then says, "Two."

"What are they like? Are you close with them?"

"You know I can't answer that."

"Tell me anything. Tell me one thing."

He thinks for a moment, then says, "My younger brother used to sing all the time, whatever else he was doing."

We sit together in silence. I take another sip of whiskey, feeling it warm my chest. I already know the two of us won't sleep tonight. We move between the sofa, the bed, and the kitchen, talking, opening more drinks, dressing and undressing. We can't stop reaching for each other, like we're magnetized. I like the way Eamonn leans against the wall while we talk, the way he crosses his arms over his chest. Time has slowed down, finally. Two a.m. into three a.m. into four a.m.

At some point, near dawn, I am filling up water glasses for us at the tap. Eamonn leans back against the counter, gripping the edges in his hands.

"I missed you," he says. I stand in front of him, my hands full with our water glasses, and a thousand unspoken things pass between us.

"I missed you, too."

EAMONN HAS TO RETURN to Belfast early in the morning, and I spend the rest of Saturday wandering alone through Dublin. I visit the Hugh Lane Gallery, and it's like Eamonn is beside me, looking at the paintings. I stand in front of a Francis Bacon portrait, with one foot crossed in front of the other, leaning off-balance, as though Eamonn is about to come and put his arm around my shoulders.

At home, I call Tom, and Finn carries the phone around his grandparents' house in Ardara, showing me the bottom edges of curtains and cupboards while we chat. Later on, I'm washing up after dinner when I hear a knock at the door. I've been expecting her. Without speaking, I let my sister into the house and pour us both a brandy. "Were you hoping I'd drown yesterday?" says Marian.

"That's not funny," I say, swallowing my drink and refilling the glass. "Does Seb know?" I ask, and Marian nods. She starts to explain, and I say, "It's all right, I understand why you'd tell him and not me. I'm harder on you than he is, aren't I?"

Marian turns toward the window without answering. Outside, a train passes behind the house, and its windows send squares of light running over the back patio.

"Where's Conor buried?" I ask.

"Milltown," she says, and from her voice I know she has been to visit his grave, many times.

"Had you met him?" I ask, and she nods. She says, "A couple of times."

"What was he like?"

The corners of her mouth tug back as she fights off tears. "He was lovely."

I close my eyes. She says, "Can I show you a picture of him?"

No, I think, no, I can't bear that, but I nod, and then she is leaning toward me, cradling her phone in her hands. On the screen is a picture of a young man with fair hair, laughing, his head thrown back. He looks mischievous, the sort of lad mam would call a cheeky chappy. I look at him, and an ache sears into my ribs, like a cramp from running too fast.

"I think about him every day," she says. "I'm still trying to figure out what he'd want. If he'd want me to go to prison."

If Marian had turned herself in that day, she would still be in prison. Saoirse wouldn't exist. Our lives would have jumped onto a completely different track.

"Can you forgive me, Tessa?"

I don't know what to say. Conor's face is still looking up at us from the screen, between her cupped hands. "I don't think forgiving you is up to me. I wish it were," I say. "You never told me you were suicidal, Marian."

"I wasn't," she says, turning toward me with a bare expression on her face, like a room scoured by wind.

"You took an overdose. You needed to have your stomach pumped."

"I wanted to punish myself," she says. "If I'd actually wanted to die, it wouldn't have been a punishment, would it? I wanted to live."

"How on earth could you have thought that would fix anything?" I ask. "Was it close?"

"Yes." She tells me that Seamus found her unconscious in her flat, and he dumped her outside the Mater Hospital. He didn't go inside with her, in case he'd be recognized and arrested.

Seamus didn't tell me or our mam that Marian was in hospital, teetering between life and death. She was alone with the hospital staff, having her stomach pumped. I was a few miles away, oblivious, and the thought makes me just as furious with myself as her.

"You should have told me," I say. "I would have helped."

We sit together drinking our brandy, and I can see the long chain reaction, going back and back in time, that ended in Conor's death, and all the ways it might have been stopped. If mam hadn't joined the IRA, if Marian hadn't joined, if I'd found out earlier. I look across the table at Marian. "You need to tell mam."

Forty

ON MY WAY TO STONEYBATTER, I put in earphones and listen to the Undertones with the volume turned all the way up, humming along to the words. *I want to hold her, want to hold her tight, get teenage kicks right through the night.* I'm walking through the northside, nearly running, and then Eamonn is reaching for me before I'm even through the door.

Afterward, I stand in the kitchen in my shirt and knickers, while Eamonn, dressed in only his boxers, makes us toast. "Sorry there's nothing better," he says.

"That's fine," I say, "this is better than the canteen at work. We're not like your lot. We don't have baked potatoes in our vending machines."

"Sorry?" says Eamonn, and the sensation is brisk and sudden, a swift fall. I lift my wrist to my mouth, pretending to swallow. "I read that the MI5 office has baked potatoes in its vending machines."

He looks at me, his face blank, then says, "Oh, right. Never tried one."

I nod, keeping the smile on my face while my skin turns cold. I am aware of the shape of the room, the polished seat of the kitchen stool under my bare thighs. Eamonn is about four feet away from me, by the fridge. I take in his broad shoulders and bare back, the scar under his eyes. Something is cascading through my chest. Eamonn had no clue about the vending machines. But that's nothing, isn't it? I could ignore it. I could pretend not to know what it means. My body is trying to make the decision for me, telling my mind to shut up, to stop it. All I want is to walk across this room and put my hands on Eamonn's warm back, have him turn around to face me.

Instead I lift my plate, to have something to do with my hands, and set it in the sink, then move down the hall, searching for my skirt, pulling it up around my waist, trying to do up the buttons with my hands shaking. "I've to run, we have a staff meeting at four."

"See you tomorrow?" Eamonn asks, and I nod. I make it to the door somehow, waving goodbye to Eamonn from the front step. I turn down Stoneybatter Road toward the river, and lean over the bridge, gasping for air.

When I reach her house, Marian is doing the washing-up in her kitchen. I fill her kettle and drop a tea bag into a chipped mug. "You were right," I say.

"What?" she says, and I watch steam billowing from the kettle, the spout starting to whistle.

"Eamonn is a liar."

"Glad you've come to your senses," she says. "What happened? Is his accent fake? He's actually English, isn't he?"

I lean my elbows on the counter, gripping my hair in my hands. "How did Eamonn recruit you, Marian?"

"He showed up at the ambulance station in Bridge End one night. I was on my own, walking back to my car, and he stopped me. He asked me how I'd feel about peace."

"Then what?"

"We met at the reservoir, and he asked me to become an informer."

"Did Eamonn ever introduce you to anyone else from MI5?"

Marian frowns. "No, why would he?"

"Did he ever show you any proof of who he was?"

"What, like a business card? Of course not. He was in Belfast undercover. We went over everything, though. He told me the RIPA guidelines and the code of practice."

I close my eyes. "All of that's online, Marian. It's in the public domain, anyone can read it."

"I don't understand."

"Eamonn's not in MI5."

Marian's mouth gapes, but she doesn't speak. "He's not really a handler," I say. "He's been pretending."

"Oh, god," she says, covering her mouth in her hands, and I watch her mind speeding. We were never informers, we were never working for MI5.

I lift my face toward her skylight. For a long time, neither of us speaks. "How do you know?" asks Marian. "How do you know Eamonn's not in the security service?"

"Baked potatoes."

"Sorry?"

"The MI5 office has baked potatoes in its vending machines. I read about it in an interview, but Eamonn had no idea. He's never been inside their building."

"Maybe they stopped selling them," says Marian. "Maybe they changed the machines."

"No, he tried to cover it up," I say. "He tried to cover up the fact that he'd no clue what I was talking about. He's not an MI5 agent."

"Then who is he?" she asks.

There is only one possible answer. Eamonn's not MI5, he's not IRA, he's not police. There's one other option, one other army in the conflict, but I don't want it to be them.

AT HOME, I pull on a jumper and draw the curtains. I take my hair down, holding the pins in my mouth, and fasten them again. I lean against the counter, drinking a cup of tea, then sit down and start to work.

Marian and I have divided a map of Northern Ireland into a grid. She is taking half the squares and I am taking the other half. For each grid, we are searching through school newsletters, team pictures, snaps from holiday fairs, prize days, parades. We know that Eamonn is about forty years old, that he is from Northern Ireland, that he has changed his name. That he's not in MI5, which means no one has scrubbed his likeness from the internet. There will be an image of him, somewhere. Eventually we will find him.

Hours later, I push my chair back and take the pins out of my hair. My body feels drained from the hours of concentration. Four of the grids are crossed out, six remaining.

I wash my face, scrubbing my makeup off with a rough cloth. I had sex with Eamonn this afternoon, he held my face while kissing me. I look at the smears of eyeliner and lipstick on the flannel, then hurl it into the hamper.

I lie in bed, and it's like the walls have come down around me. I have that feeling of walking home late at night, that fearful impatience, that hurry to put your key in the lock, except I'm already inside, and there isn't another door to close, there isn't another lock to turn, to make me safe. I thought Eamonn might be able to help me, but I'm alone, no one's coming with a solution, an exfiltration.

And I've always been alone, since this started. There has never been a team in London, monitoring the situation, assessing the risk, like Eamonn promised me. Eamonn wasn't filing written reports about our meetings, or following any legal guidelines. No one from MI5 was tasked with saving us if our covers were blown.

The worst part, the part I can barely bring myself to think about, is that we were never resisting the IRA, or protecting the peace process. Eamonn isn't in the government, so who is he? Who were we working for?

I know nothing about Eamonn, nothing. He let me form an image of his personality—neutral, calm, warm—because that's what I wanted. I wanted a place to step inside and forget everything, all my responsibilities, all my threats.

I CALL IN sick to work in the morning, telling Joanna I've the flu and might be out for a few days, and Marian finds someone to cover her air-ambulance shift. We sit at my kitchen table, working through our grid of the North. I try to remember tricks from the investigative journalists at the BBC, how they'd find a former convict living under a new name. Marian scrolls through an encrypted folder that Seamus made years and years ago, with images of loyalists and paramilitaries from East Belfast. His adversaries.

While we click through the photographs, searching the faces, I try to tell Marian everything I remember from my conversations with Eamonn, but it's a pitiful amount. He doesn't cook, he's reading Dickens, he started a knitting club at his school.

"Did you sleep with him?" she asks. I don't answer, and Marian frowns at her screen. Thinking about sleeping with Eamonn now is like waking up after a night of getting absolutely trolleyed. You know that person was yourself, slamming vodka, throwing herself around a dance floor, hitching up her skirt to piss between two parked cars, but you can't really believe it now that you're here, sober, in your right mind again. And you can't believe, either, how happy you were.

"Why do you think you liked him?" asks Marian. Because I'm stupid, I think. Because I'm naive, because I'm greedy. "You liked Eamonn because you knew he'd never get in your road," says Marian. "He was never going to ask to move in with you, he was never going to ask to meet Finn. You don't want that right now. Maybe one day, but not now."

I don't know if Marian's right. There are too many other things crowding my mind to even consider it at the moment. "Royce sent me a message this morning," I say. "He wants me to meet him at the bungalow in Wicklow tomorrow night. He said the Gravediggers will be too crowded. Is it a trap?"

"He doesn't need a trap. If he wants to kill you, he'll send someone to your house," she says. "Sorry. That was meant to be reassuring."

"For god's sake, Marian."

"Listen, I'll come, too, I'll wait outside."

"How will you know if something goes wrong?" I ask.

"We'll be fine," she says. "I bugged that place weeks ago."

"What am I supposed to tell Royce?" I ask.

"I don't know yet," says Marian. "But we need a new plan." The IRA thinks I am working on bringing an MI5 agent to them, they think I've something to offer. If they find out that Eamonn isn't in the security service, they will kill me.

I look over Marian's shoulder at the images in Seamus's folder. "Why did he collect all of these? Was he looking for targets?"

"He said it was self-defense," says Marian. "He wanted to be able to recognize anyone who walked into a pub in Belfast."

"What, in case they'd come to kill him?"

"Yeah, basically."

"Did he actually memorize all of these faces? There must be thousands," I say, and Marian says, "Well, he had enough time. Seamus only slept four hours a night."

At some point in the afternoon, Marian stands to stretch. She lifts my book, a battered copy of *Diarmuid and Grainne*, from the sofa and flicks through it. "What is this? Never heard of it," she says.

"We did it at school, Marian."

"Did we?" she says, lying back on the sofa with the book held in front of her, skimming the first few pages. "Oh, right. The Irish Romeo and Juliet."

I frown. "Not really."

"It's a love story, isn't it?"

"No, it's about consequences."

"Isn't that the same thing?" she says. "Does it have a happy ending?"

"Ah, no. No, it doesn't."

Marian pulls her head off the sofa to look at me. "Are you joking me? What happens?"

"Diarmuid dies."

"But this is an old legend, right? Maybe the wrong version was written down."

"Maybe."

"What about the baby?" she asks. "Grainne is pregnant, isn't she?"

"Yes. Ruchladh, that's the baby's name."

"What happens to him?"

"He's grand. She calls him her bonny boy." We fall silent, then Marian says, "Nothing has changed, has it?"

"No."

. . .

LATE THAT NIGHT, I am dragging out the bins when my phone sounds. I fish it from the pocket of my cardigan, standing on the road with the bins upright behind me. Marian has sent me a photograph from Seamus's folder. A group of lads in white uniforms with blue trim, a banner hanging on the wall behind them. East Belfast 16. I recognize the uniforms, and the brass instruments in their hands. It's a Protestant marching band. I stare up the empty road, at the row of streetlamps, the dry leaves on the pavement, then slowly move my gaze over the rows of young faces until my heart skips. Standing on the dark road, I look down at Eamonn's face. He is a loyalist.

Forty-One

WE DRIVE OUT TO WICKLOW separately, and Marian parks beside some hedgerows to wait for me. We spent hours last night talking, until we'd made a plan. Behind the bungalow, the electric pylons are humming. I can nearly feel the electricity crackling through their wires. Above the pylons are dark clouds, damp stains against the black sky. When I step inside the bungalow, Royce is at the card table, shoveling down a military ready meal. "Which battalion to-night?" I ask.

"Austrian infantry. Beef bourguignon and white chocolate tart. It's not their finest work, if we're being honest," he says. "Want some?"

"No, you're all right."

Royce says, "Oh, we're looking into lifting that painting, by your one."

"Agnes Martin," I say, and he nods. "What will you do with it?"

"Use it to bargain down one of the lads' sentences," says Royce.

"My handler's ready," I say. "When do you want to meet him?"

"What changed?" asks Royce.

"He needs money. I think he'll work with you, for enough cash," I say, none of which is true. "He's in debt."

"Drugs?" asks Royce. "Gambling?"

"Fantasy," I say, and Royce raises his eyebrows. "Handlers don't get paid much, they're only on a civil servant's salary. But he joined for the lifestyle, he wants to look the part. He has an expensive watch, expensive car, expensive mortgage. It's how he thinks of himself. He'll leak some secrets before giving that up."

"What a tosser," says Royce. He scrapes up some beef, almost black from the wine sauce. "I'm wondering, Tessa," he says. "How did you get him to tell you about his money troubles?"

I shrug. "He trusts me. And I'm a good listener."

"Don't flatter yourself. He's just lonely," says Royce, though I bet Eamonn has plenty of friends, at home in east Belfast, I bet that's part of his problem, that he's drowning in them. That's how para-militaries work, isn't it.

Royce says, "Did you fuck him?"

Heat rushes up the back of my neck. "No."

"I don't believe you," says Royce, lifting his fork. "I knew you'd ride him. Why do you think I chose you for this? Because I could tell one thing about you, Tessa. You were lonely."

I don't want to start crying in front of him, but the back of my throat is already softening with tears. Behind Royce's shape, the lace curtains cover the windows. They look so delicate, their pattern cut with holes, but I still can't see the view outside, they're enough to block it out entirely.

"We would have asked Marian instead of you," says Royce. "But she's happily married, isn't she?"

"Fuck you," I whisper.

"Why are you angry at me?" says Royce. "You're the one who rode him. That was your shout, not mine. You could have kept your dignity, you know. Does he know you're our whore? No? Well, look, he's about to find out. Here, do you want this white chocolate?" asks Royce, and I'm shaking my head when he lurches over the table. My head jerks away from him, but it's too late. He punches me in the mouth, and blood bursts between my teeth.

I'm leaning forward, spitting up blood, when he takes my hair in his fist and wrenches my head back. "Why was a cop at the Grave-diggers?" he asks.

"What?"

"A cop was there asking questions," he says. The detective must have somehow tracked me to the pub.

"I didn't tell anyone about you, I swear. Nothing about you. That detective thinks I'm in the IRA."

"You stupid bitch," says Royce.

Marian should be here, she told me she'd bugged this room, she should be running in for me, but all I can hear is a ringing, like I'm hearing the electric pylons through the walls. The white chocolate is in front of me, a smooth layer of fondant untouched by my blood. I sit at the table, shaking hard enough to make my chair rattle against the floor.

I need to get a message to Marian. I need to tell her that Finn can never, ever know about this, he can never know his mam was murdered by the IRA. If he finds out, it will warp his entire life, it will make him scared and furious, it will make him think he should seek revenge. I'd rather anything else, I'd rather Tom and Briony raise him like she's his mother and I never existed.

"Don't tell Finn," I say.

"What're you talking about?" says Royce.

"I'm not talking to you," I say. Royce looks at me, then laughs. "No one's listening to you, Tessa. No one's coming to help you."

My mind goes white as Royce rings someone on his phone.

"We're going to need a cleaner," he says. "Not yet, though, give me an hour."

I can hear myself keening. Royce draws his chair up beside mine and presses a gun to my head. It's only a handgun, but it feels very long somehow, like a stick extending all the way to Royce's shoulder. "Did you tell the cops about me?" he asks. He is growing impatient, the gun barrel pressing harder against my skull.

"No." I breathe out. I think, Finn.

Royce releases the gun from my head slightly, strands of hair slipping under the barrel. "No," I say again. "I told no one."

At that moment light burns into the bungalow, through the holes in the lace curtains. It's Marian. She is outside on the dark drive, shining her headlights straight into this room.

Royce stands and moves to check the window. I picture the property from above, the dark countryside, the mountains, the car's headlights pouring onto the bungalow. I can feel myself coming apart, dispersing through the room, and then every bit of me slams back into my body. I hear my voice say, "Sit down."

Royce snorts, shaking his head. The headlights are pointing into the room, catching on the bones in his face. I lift my hands, watching them move in the headlights, and fold them on the table. Again, I say, "Sit down."

Royce looks at me like I'm out of my mind. We can hear the engine switch off outside, the creak of a car door opening, someone stepping onto the gravel. He won't be able to see Marian's face. She's standing behind the beam of the headlights, in the deep country darkness.

"That's him, isn't it?" says Royce. "You told the cop to come here." He points the gun at me, and I look past its barrel at his face.

"If you do that," I say, "you'll be shot, too."

"I'm not scared to die," he says.

"No, you're not scared to die a hero," I say. "But that's not what will happen. You'll die a tout."

He laughs. "Wise up."

I start to recite the words off. I know them by heart. "'Dear mam, I know I've let you down but I'm trying to make it better. I'm talking with the peelers about what I can do to help.'"

Royce stares at me. I say, "Sit the fuck down."

He lowers himself onto a chair. The headlights show a column of dust turning in the bungalow. We are both sitting in the middle of it, the dust spinning around us.

"You wrote to your mam after you were arrested," I say. "You told her you'd offered to inform."

Royce shrugs. "I was just telling her what she wanted to hear. I never meant it."

"Who's going to believe that?" I say, turning my hand, like I'm considering my nails. "The thing is," I say to Royce, with my sister's headlights flooding toward me across the room, "you're the one who has been abducted here. Not me."

Royce searches my face. In this light, his eyes look nearly colorless.

"The cops refused your offer. They wouldn't touch you," I say. "It wasn't worth it to them. They didn't want you to be released without charge, not after what you'd tried. Your mam gave all of your letters to my mam." I am aware of Royce listening, of the light bristling through the holes in the lace curtains. "If you shoot me, everyone will find out about you. And who's going to defend you anyway? I know what they call you in the IRA. They call you the Undertaker. Do you think that's a compliment?"

Royce's face drops. For a moment, I can see the young boy,

lifting his face for my mam to rub sun cream on it, smiling shyly when she complimented him on his manners, wanting to be liked.

"If those letters are released, everyone will make fun of you. Is that what you want?"

Finally Royce lowers his gun. He lifts the white chocolate and bites hard into it. When he finishes chewing, he says, "Get out."

I can feel the headlights arcing over my arms and neck and hair as I stand from the chair, planes of light slicing over my skin. He could still shoot me, I think, trying to keep my balance. But Royce is motionless at the table. I tug on the latch and then I am stumbling over the doorstep, and the night sky is bursting above me.

I run down the beam of the headlights and climb into the car, and feel it accelerating, fast, down the drive, the gravel spraying under its tires, and turning onto the laneway. I am hyperventilating now, huge dry sobs racking my chest. Marian says, "It's all right, it's over now, you're safe."

Forty-Two

I SPEND THE NIGHT sleeping on my sister's sofa. In the morning, I make a cup of coffee and drink it outside in her back garden while talking on the phone with Finn in Donegal. "I've been practicing my numbers, since we're going to learn a lot of numbers in kindergarten," he says.

"That's a good plan," I say, and listen to him practice.

"Seventy. Seventy-one, seventy-two. What comes after one hundred?" he asks. "Is that the end?"

"No, sweetheart," I say. "That's not the end."

Something happens, as I listen to Finn count. My chest starts to prickle and tingle, the energy building in my veins. I can hear the determination in his voice, the purpose. This is important to him, he is taking it seriously. He wants to be prepared for everything he has to learn.

Enough, I think after we hang up. I won't play by their rules anymore. I've had enough.

THE TRIP ONLY TAKES ME two and a half hours. By eleven, I am standing on the Newtownards Road in east Belfast, across from a computer repair shop. Past the plate-glass windows, I can see figures inside the shop. When I open the door, a bell rings, and the two men behind the counter look up.

Eamonn blinks when he sees me. He has on a blue polo shirt, embossed with the shop's logo. I try to speak and can't, then cough to clear my throat. "My screen's cracked," I say, while Eamonn stares at me over the counter with a dazed expression. "Let's have a look," says the other man, reaching out his hand, then Eamonn snaps to. "I'll take care of it, Stephen," he says.

I follow Eamonn past the rows of shelving to a back repair room and close the door. I take in the tools, the stations, Eamonn's uniform. Every day, he was working here. He was at a computer shop on the Newtownards Road, while I wondered about his whereabouts.

"You're not in MI5," I say.

Eamonn lifts his chin with the slightest nod. "UVF?" I ask, and he nods again. "Who's your commander?"

"Johnny West," he says, and my stomach feels it like a punch. West has been a UVF leader since the Troubles. Eamonn sees the look on my face and says quietly, "He's not that bad."

"Why was Marian chosen?"

"Because she was a paramedic," says Eamonn, and his voice sounds rusty, like he hasn't spoken for hours. "Johnny had a heart attack, and Marian was the first responder."

A dozen ambulances circling in Belfast, and hers was the closest. I say, "But how did he know she was in the IRA?"

"Because she was terrified. Her hands were shaking," says Eamonn. "She'd recognized Johnny, she knew that she was in a terrace house in east Belfast surrounded by UVF members. Everyone noticed. After the ambulance left, a few of the lads looked at one another, and said, What the fuck was that?"

"You were there?" I ask, and he nods. "Go to hell, Eamonn."

"I'm sorry, Tessa," he says. "I'd do anything to take it back."

"So you were told to approach her, and say you were MI5?" I ask.

"Yes."

"What's wrong with you?" I ask, and he shakes his head. "How many other times have you done this? How many other informers do you have?"

He hesitates, then says, "Four."

"Do you fuck all of them?"

"Are you actually asking me that?" says Eamonn. I wait, bracing myself for his answer, with my arms crossed over my chest. "Come here to me, Tessa. You know the answer."

"It must have been hard for you," I say finally. "To touch a Catholic."

Eamonn starts to speak, and I interrupt him. "All part of the job, though, right? Did you like pretending to be a spy?"

Eamonn rubs his forehead. "Yes, I did," he says. "At first."

"Did you really live in Hong Kong?"

"I've never been on a plane, Tessa."

My pride is begging me not to ask the next question, but I need to know the answer. "Are you married?" I ask.

"No."

"Do you have a girlfriend?"

"Sort of," he says, and I'm about to lay into him when he lifts his face toward the ceiling. "I think of you as my girlfriend."

I blink, and he says, "Of course I'm not sleeping with any of my other sources." I hesitate, searching myself to see if this information makes me feel any less stupid, or any less angry. Not really. I still feel like a mockery.

Eamonn says, "You vanished, Tessa. For three years, I didn't know where you'd gone, I didn't know if the IRA had killed you. I was out of my mind. And then in August someone used the gift card at a supermarket in Ranelagh. I spent three days standing outside the shop, waiting in case you'd come back."

I look at Eamonn's eyes, his mouth, his dark hair. If we'd grown up on the same side of Belfast, we would have been friends, I think. We might have played together as children. One of us might have asked the other out, as teenagers. We might have fallen in love.

"Why did you join the UVF?" I ask.

"The IRA bombed my parents' restaurant," he says. "They killed my younger brothers."

I lift a hand to my face, my eyes suddenly searing with tears. I look at the small welts on Eamonn's face and hands. They're burn scars. The truth was always there, right in front of me.

"I'm sorry, Eamonn. I'm so sorry about your brothers."

Eamonn doesn't move, but he looks like someone trying to stand upright in a storm, like someone being buffeted by heavy wind.

After a long time, I take the gold gift card from my wallet and set it on the table. He says, "Tessa—"

"I've been lying to you, too," I say. "The IRA forced me to start meeting with you again. They want me to turn you."

"Oh, god," he says. "Okay. I can help you."

"No, Eamonn. You can't." It's over now. This is the last time I will ever see him, I know that, both of us know that.

"I did start a knitting club," he says. "That part was real."

I close my eyes. Eamonn comes around the table, and I lean forward as his arms fold around me. We stand clutching on to each other, and he lowers his head to kiss me. Everything stops, the tide stops. Not coming in, not going out. For a second, two, three, we're in slack water.

Then I'm pulling away from him, the distance slowly growing between us, a centimeter at a time. I feel a wrench deep in my chest.

"I told a detective about you," I say, finally. On the drive up, I rang DI Fenton, an old friend from Belfast. "He wants information from you about the UVF. He'll be on the beach in Ardglass tomorrow at seven."

"I can't do that, Tessa. You can't ask me to do that," says Eamonn. "Do you want me to help the IRA win? They're murderers."

"No, I want this to end. So do you," I say. "You can be arrested for membership of a terrorist organization. Or you can meet with him and help end this. I think you'll like each other, for what that's worth. I think you'll work well together. It's your choice, Eamonn."

Forty-Three

A LITTLE BEFORE seven in the morning, I sit on my back step, wrapped in a coat, with a cup of coffee and an unlit cigarette. I bought the pack and a bottle of cheap red wine from Tesco Express last night, like I did after every breakup in my twenties. When I got them home, I realized that I didn't actually want either. I wanted a cup of herbal tea, a takeaway, and something stupid on television, which makes sense, since I'm not twenty-two anymore.

Now, though, my hands are unsteady, and I like the feel of the cigarette between my fingers, like an anchor. Above my patio, wind is sending heavy clouds surging over the sky, and the city has that particular damp scent of rain coming. I take a swallow of coffee and lean my head against the back door. Finn is still in Donegal with Tom, and I'm both desperate to hold my son and glad that he can't see me right now. I didn't sleep last night, and my eyes are sore from crying.

During the long hours of the night, I kept having two thoughts: that I love Eamonn, and that I will love someone else, one day. The second thought is too delicate to consider directly, but I believe it.

I check my watch. Nearly seven. I light the cigarette and let it smolder in my hand. DI Fenton will already be on the beach in Ardglass, waiting, with an overcoat on over his suit against the wind. The sea will be stormy behind him, rough gray waves crashing onto the sand.

The second hand keeps ticking. I watch it, breathing out slowly. Seven o'clock. Eamonn will be walking down the wooden path now, and then he will be stepping off it onto the sand, and feeling the full force of the wind off the sea, blowing straight at him over acres and acres of open water.

He's an informer now.

AFTER FINISHING MY COFFEE, I toss the cigarette end in the bin and lace up my trainers to run along the canal. Normally my body feels stiff at the start of a run, but today I barely feel a thing.

As I'm coming out of the shower after my run, Marian sends me a message. "Want to come over? x." I hesitate, worn out from not sleeping last night, considering the leftover takeaway in my fridge, and all the episodes of television I could watch, but it will be good to see my sister, to hold Saoirse.

I don't listen to music on my way to the Liberties. I don't need anything to make me more emotional, not now, not for a while yet. Outside Marian's house, I use my key to open her door and stop inside to take off my ankle boots, padding down the hall in my stockinged feet, calling, "Hiya."

I can hear Saoirse crying at the back of the house, wailing. Poor lamb. All the lights are on, I notice, even in the upstairs hall. I come into the kitchen and my whole body rears back. A man is standing by the cooker, another man is sitting at my sister's kitchen table, and Saoirse is strapped in her rocker, and sobbing.

I cross the room in two steps and crouch in front of Saoirse, undoing the straps of her rocker and lifting her into my arms.

Saoirse is panting from crying, her face splotched red, and I hold her to my chest, with a hand cradling her head. I can feel my own heart knocking wildly against hers as I murmur to her. "Where's your mammy?" I say to her, and turn to look at the men, thinking, Where's her mam, where's her mam, what the fuck have you done with her mam?

The two men watch me. I recognize them. They're the driver and the younger man who crashed into my car in Wicklow, and I should have called the police on them that night. Neither of them has a gun out, I notice. They're both wearing dark hooded shirts and ski masks rolled up above their faces.

Silence flicks through the room suddenly as Saoirse stops crying. The younger man tugs at his ears, like they're ringing from the sound of the baby crying.

"Where's Marian?" I ask, which they don't answer. They sent me the message, I realize. Marian doesn't end her messages with a kiss. "Why did you ask me to come here?"

"The baby wouldn't stop screaming," says the driver. "Someone might have called the cops, if she'd kept at it. We need you to keep her quiet."

I feel another updraft of panic. "How long have you been here?" I ask, which they don't answer. Jesus christ, I think. "We gave the baby some water," says the younger man, shrugging, and I want to hurl myself at him, to claw his eyes out.

I carry Saoirse into the hall, rushing toward the front door with her in my arms.

"Where are you going?" asks the driver, following me into the corridor.

"You don't need her here. I'm taking her outside."

"No, I can't let you do that," he says. At my side, the curtains are drawn over the front window. I should have noticed that from outside, the curtains drawn in daylight. "She's hungry," I manage to say.

"So feed her," he says, cocking his head toward the kitchen.

The front door is five paces behind me. I'll never make it in time. Slowly, I move back down the hall to the kitchen. I open the fridge and find some pumped milk and a clean bottle. A knife is on the draining rack. A small paring knife, with a wooden handle. The blade will be dull, though. Seb's away on reshoots, and Marian never sharpens her knives. I've told her she should, I've told her a dull knife is more dangerous, you're more likely to cut yourself.

I screw the cap on the bottle, trying to work out how to slide the knife into my shirt pocket without the men seeing. There are two of them, though. How can I fight them with Saoirse in my arms?

Saoirse drains the bottle greedily, her hand wrapped over mine. She must have been ravenous. I listen for any sounds from upstairs, but we're alone in the house. The younger man has a laptop open on the kitchen table. It looks like he's watching a film. I can see a narrow road rushing by, with trees alongside it.

"Where's Marian?" I ask again.

"Here," says the driver, and points at the laptop. He isn't watching a film, I realize. He's watching live footage from a dash camera. Marian is behind that camera, driving a car down a country road.

"Marian," I say, and I start to tell her Saoirse is all right now, I'm with her, when the driver interrupts me. "She can't hear you. It's just a camera feed, there isn't any sound."

I watch the screen. Right now, Marian is driving on a road between potato fields. The driver checks his watch. Into his phone, he says, "Five minutes out."

I turn toward him, horror rattling through me. "What's in the car?" I ask. He doesn't answer, and I feel my eyes roll back in my skull. My arms jerk tight around the baby, her weight stopping me from fainting. "Is there a bomb in the car?" I ask.

"Yes."

I sway on my feet. "What are you making her do?"

"We're not making her do anything," says the driver. "We gave her two options."

"What was the other option?" I ask, and the driver looks at the baby. I feel pressure crushing my lungs. "You're monsters."

I stand in my sister's kitchen, with snaps of her and her family on the fridge, with water dripping from the tap. I can feel Saoirse's hair against my hand, and smell the laundry soap on her cotton suit.

"What's the target?" I ask, but I already recognize the landscape, the shape of the hills in the distance. Marian's driving toward a border checkpoint.

"Don't worry," says the driver, and his voice seems to refract and bend as it comes toward me, to telescope around the room. "This is what she was born to do. She'll die helping the armed struggle."

"She won't do it," I say. "She'll run."

"I doubt that," says the younger man. "She's cuffed to the steering wheel."

I can't breathe, I can't think straight. Everything is happening too quickly, the tarmac rolling under her car on the monitor, the trees whipping past. I look at the younger man's hands, resting on the table, his skin scratched red around his nails.

Both men are watching the monitor, and I back away until I can take hold of the paring knife, hiding it under the cuff of my shirtsleeve.

"She's three minutes out," says the driver into his phone. He must be talking to whoever is waiting near the checkpoint, hiding with a detonator. That person is miles away, and I can't get to him. I try to hold myself steady against another surge of vertigo.

"Two minutes," he says, and another sheet of terror moves through me. She has two minutes left to live. My sister, my younger sister.

This is her view, right now, and it's beautiful. The silver light coming between the clouds onto the green fields and the thick branches.

"One minute," he says, and I start to pray. Not to god, to her, to my sister, to the life inside her. To her swimming into the caves on the north coast, diving under the arches and surfacing with the cold swell, to her dragging herself across the hospital ward to meet her newborn daughter, to her laughing at one of her husband's jokes, to her curling up on the sofa against her mam, to her slinging off her rucksack and tearing across the playing fields on her last day of school, to her rolling over in our shared bedroom and saying, "Wake up, Tessa," because it was morning and she wanted to play.

"Forty seconds."

I watch the monitor with tears soaking my face and her baby's hair. I want to hold Saoirse up, I want Marian to see her, but I know she's already seeing her anyway, that Saoirse will be the only thing she can see, golden and blooming.

"Thirty seconds."

I will never forgive myself, I know that. Seb will never forgive himself. Mam will never forgive herself. The three of us will spend the rest of our lives wondering what we could have done differently to save her.

"Twenty seconds."

Marian would hate that. She would want Saoirse to grow up

unencumbered by the past. Ours, and this island's, and I'll do my best to help her, I promise.

"Ten seconds."

The target is in view now. It's one of the larger border checkpoints between the republic and the North. A concrete watchtower, two portacabins. And I can see a handful of young men out on the road. British soldiers, in their khaki uniforms. They're going to die. Marian has been ordered to drive straight into them, in exchange for Saoirse's life. Even from this distance, I can see how young the soldiers are.

"Five seconds."

Marian is slowing down, the tarmac unraveling more slowly, then the car stops. Marian is about twenty meters from the checkpoint. "What's she doing?" asks the younger man.

On the monitor, the soldiers are coming toward her car with their rifles drawn. They must be able to see her, a woman behind the windscreen, pale and sweating. I watch the soldiers moving closer, and then something happens. They all stop suddenly. I can't tell what they've seen or heard, but then they are backing away, breaking into a run, scattering from the car.

It's Marian, I realize. She has rolled the windows down, and she is screaming at the soldiers to run.

Everyone else is clear of her car now. I can see the empty road ahead of her, the grasses and weeds blowing alongside it, the sun coming down through the splits in the clouds. I hold my breath, bracing myself for the explosion, for the blinding flash of light.

The device hasn't gone off yet. The road hasn't erupted, ripped up by a bomb. Both men are shouting now, at the screen and down the phone, and I take a step away and then I am wheeling out of the room with Saoirse in my arms, racing down the hall. I throw myself against the front door, drawing back the lock.

I can hear a swish of fabric, and the driver is behind me, grabbing on to my shoulder. I clamp my arm around Saoirse, and bring up the other hand with the paring knife, slashing hard at his face. I feel the blade tear across the bridge of his nose, then he stumbles back, cursing. I wrench the door open and hurl myself outside with Saoirse tight against me, and pelt up the center of the road. A taxi coming toward me slams on its brakes, and I veer around it without slowing, careening onto Bride Street, jostling between the people on the crowded footpath. Some of them call out, but I duck away from them. I can't stop running, not yet.

Two uniformed officers are standing outside the garda station. I can't hear myself screaming, but the officers are turning now and running toward me.

One of them is speaking into her radio, and the other is trying to check me and the baby for injuries, and I shake him off. I turn to the woman, who grabs hold of me, and I say, "Was there a bomb at the border?"

She looks at me, and I search her gray eyes. "Yes," she says, and my knees drop me to the pavement. I cradle Saoirse against me, pain howling through my chest.

The officer is kneeling down, too, and I feel her hands moving on my shoulders, keeping me from flying apart into pieces.

"There's a bomb at the border," she says. "But it didn't go off."

Forty-Four

NINE MONTHS HAVE PASSED, but nothing has gone back to normal, thank god. Everyone now knows my real name. It was in the news, that day.

I know what happened now. Marian slowed the car outside the border checkpoint. She rolled down the window and screamed at the soldiers to run, which they did, scattering away from the blast radius.

But one soldier came toward her, even as the others ordered him to get back, shouting that he'd be killed. He was a nineteen-year-old private from Glasgow, on his first tour of duty. He opened her car door and used his baton to break the handcuffs chaining Marian to the steering wheel. She stumbled out from the car, and they ran together for cover.

WHEN THE BOMB disposal crew arrived, they found that the bomb was never going to work. It was a dud. One of the wires had detached, by accident, maybe. Or someone had sabotaged the device deliberately. No one knows which is true.

But we do know that Eoin Royce has disappeared. And we know that, the day before the border attack, he had visited his mam in west Belfast. It was their first time together since his arrest. Mam asked Sheila if she'd told Royce to do anything. "No," said Sheila, bewildered. "I didn't tell him to do a thing."

"But what did you say?" asked mam.

"I told him that I forgive him."

MARIAN TALKS WITH the Scottish soldier every week. He came to Dublin and met Seb, she traveled to Glasgow and met his parents. They're friends.

Both of them are private, but they've given interviews together. They've described what each of them did that day. Those joint interviews have done more for the peace process than any number of police operations or army maneuvers. The first interview, on RTÉ's evening news, showed a photograph, taken by Seb, of the soldier holding Saoirse. It has become one of the most famous images of the conflict.

"Enough," people were saying, after what happened. "Mother of god, we've had enough of this."

And in our old neighborhood, in Andersonstown, in an IRA stronghold, a group went out at night and threw buckets of white paint over the murals of gunmen on the Falls Road. They dipped their hands in the paint, too, and pressed them over the walls, drew silly things, hearts and rainbows, painted cat whiskers on the portrait of an IRA commander. No one knew who had done it, who had been that brave, that reckless. Whoever it was could be given a kneecapping by the local IRA, or worse.

It was a group of girls, as it turns out. Students from my and Marian's old school.

Two days before New Year's, the IRA and UVF announced a joint ceasefire.

It wasn't because of what happened to Marian, exactly.

Those girls had been coming for the hard men either way.

Forty-Five

A HEAT WAVE BEGAN YESTERDAY. I'm escaping the sweltering city, driving out of Dublin to a beach in Wicklow. Mam is in the front passenger seat, and Marian is in the back, wedged between Finn's and Saoirse's car seats. The noise in the car is, frankly, unbelievable, with all of us talking at once, and even the baby making herself heard over the din as we argue about the music. "Play Stevie Nicks," says mam.

"Do you mean Fleetwood Mac?" asks Marian.

"No," says mam firmly. "I mean Stevie Nicks."

Soon the three of us are singing our hearts out as we drive into the countryside. In the rear mirror, I can see Marian lifting her hands in the air, and then pouncing them to tickle both children, making them delirious with laughter.

After Ballyvolan, I leave the motorway. I try to turn east, but the road toward the coast is closed for a water main repair, with signs sending us on a detour. Soon I am on a narrow road between wheat fields. The wheat is high beyond the road, dense and golden. I check the dot on the map, and turn through another field.

I frown at the pulsing dot on the map. There are thousands of acres of wheat in County Wicklow. This can't be the same field, I think, but then I see the crossing.

I stop, pulling the car over to the side of the road. "Sorry," I say to the others. "Sorry, I'll just be a second."

I climb out onto the road, in the full sun. I walk behind the car, leaving the others chatting past the rolled-down windows. Ahead of me, the road stretches away, flat and empty, with heat shimmering above the tarmac. A set of rubber tire tracks is burned into the road. They're from the collision last year, and I kneel down, touching my fingers to the black marks.

At the edge of the road, some of the wheat looks trampled. I search for the red drops of my blood, but this is new wheat, not last year's. In every direction, for as far as I can see, I'm surrounded by a new harvest.

Slowly I straighten, turning my head. Around me, wind courses across the field. A thousand ways to run appear and then vanish through the wheat.

I step back from the field, turning up the road to where my family is waiting for me. The sound of the crickets rises and rises, like they're singing.

This, what happened to me and to my sister, and what we did, is a story about consequences, but it's the same thing, isn't it? This is a story about love.

I climb back into the car and close the door. Mam and Marian glance at me, puzzled, but they will wait for me to explain. "Ready?" I ask.

"Ready," says Finn. He is five years old now. He knows how to write his name, how to ride a bicycle. Every day when I collect him from school, Finn is pleased to see me but not surprised, like he knows nothing can keep me away, like mothers always come back.

Acknowledgments

Thank you to Lindsey Schwoeri, my editor, and Emily Forland, my agent. We're eight years and four books in, and I can only begin to say how important you are to me.

Lindsey, my favorite part of writing might be our conversation after the first draft. I only really know what a book is about after talking with you, and seeing it through your brilliant eyes. Thank you for creating these stories alongside me.

Emily, thank you for your constant creativity and encouragement. You bring so much brightness to the writing process, from the first scrap of an idea onward.

Thank you to Michelle Weiner, for being magnificent. You are the source of several of the most exciting phone calls of my life. Thanks also to Steve Kloves, for taking on Tessa's story.

Thank you to Reese Witherspoon. I'm still pinching myself at being part of your brilliant group of book lovers. Thanks to all at Reese's Book Club and Hello Sunshine, especially Jane Lee and Gretchen Schreiber.

At Viking, thank you to Jane Cavolina, Sara DeLozier, Magdalena Deniz, Amanda Dewey, Molly Fessenden, Sabila Khan,